LARGE PRINT

Chase, Loretta
Viscount vagabond

JAN 22 1990

LP   **Chase, Loretta Lynda**
             Viscount vagabond
Ch

Viscount Vagabond

Viscount Vagabond

Loretta Chase

Thorndike Press • Thorndike, Maine

Library of Congress Cataloging in Publication Data:

Chase, Loretta Lynda, 1949-
  Viscount vagabond / Loretta Chase.
  p. cm.
  ISBN 0-89621-881-3 (alk. paper : lg. print)
  1. Large type books. I. Title.
[PS3553.H3347V57 1989]   89-37869
813'.54--dc20   JAN 2 2 1990   CIP

All the characters and events portrayed in this story
are fictitious.

Thorndike Press Large Print edition published in 1989 by
arrangement with Walker and Company.

Cover design by James B. Murray.

Viscount
Vagabond

1

Catherine Pelliston had never beheld a naked man before. She had never, in fact, observed a man in any state of undress, unless one counted the draped figures in Great-Aunt Eustacia's collection of classical statuary. Those, however, had been carved stone, not at all like the large, all-too-animate male who was breathing alcoholic fumes into the stuffy room. Even Miss Pelliston's ramshackle papa, so careless of all else when in the latter stages of inebriation, remained properly — if not neatly — attired in her presence.

The figure floundering near the door, on the other hand, had already torn off his coat and neck-cloth and flung them to the floor. At the moment, he seemed to be trying to strangle himself with his shirt.

Miss Pelliston was possessed of an enquiring mind. This must explain why, despite the extreme gravity of her present situation and the natural modesty of a gently bred woman, she gaped in fascination at the broad, muscular shoulders and equally muscular chest now exposed to her view. Her analytical mind automatically began pondering several biological puzzles. Was it usual for the masculine chest to be covered with fine, light hair? If usual, what possible purpose could such growth serve?

As she posed these questions to herself, the object of her analysis yanked his shirt over his head and tossed it into a corner.

"Gad, what a curst business," he muttered. "Makes a man wish he was a Red Indian. A few hides to throw on and off and none of these infernal buttons."

Apparently in search of the buttons, he bent to peer owlishly at the waistband of his pantaloons — and over-turned himself in the process. He fell face forward with a loud thud.

"Deuce take it!"

Not at all disconcerted, the stranger struggled clumsily to his feet again. He squinted into the flickering shadows of the room, his gaze flitting confusedly from one object to the next before finally fixing on her.

"Ah, there you are," he said, staggering with the effort to remain focused on one spot. "Give a chap a hand, will you?"

To bring her mind from abstract theory to disagreeable actuality required a moment. In that brief time the man succeeded in locating a trouser flap button and commenced a mighty struggle with it. The implications of this contest were not lost upon the stunned Miss Pelliston, who promptly found her voice.

"Help you," she repeated at a somewhat higher than normal pitch. "I should think not. In fact, I am certain it would be best for all concerned if you did not proceed further with — with your present activity. I fear, sir, you are labouring under a gross misapprehension — and no doubt strong drink as well," she finished primly.

"What the devil did y' say?"

To her relief, he stopped what he was doing to stare at her.

Relief swiftly gave way to apprehension as she realised what he was gawking at. The dreadful old harridan who'd abducted her had taken Catherine's clothes, providing in their place one tawdry, nearly transparent saffron gown with a neckline that drooped below all bounds of propriety. Her cheeks vermilion, Catherine hastily jerked the dingy coverlet up to her chin.

To her dismay, the great, drunken creature burst into laughter. His laugh was deep and resonant, and in other circumstances Catherine might have appreciated its tonal qualities. In the present case, the sound made her blood run cold. His laughter seemed to fill the entire room. *He* seemed to fill the room. He was so large and overpowering, so male — and so very drunk.

God help me, she thought. Then she recollected that Providence helped those who helped themselves.

Gathering the coverlet more tightly about her as though it were the courage she felt fast ebbing away, she spoke. "In your current state of intoxication, a great many matters are bound to strike you as inexpressibly amusing. Nonetheless, I assure you, sir, that your guffaws are hardly appropriate to the present situation. I am not a — a — what I seem to be. I am here against my will."

Many people have nervous habits which grow more pronounced in times of agitation. Miss Pelliston tended to become preachy and pedantic when she was agitated. Her papa found this characteristic so unappealing that he had been known to toss the occasional bottle or mug in her direction. Since he was usually three parts disguised in these cases, he never struck her. He didn't particularly want to strike her. He only wanted her to go away.

Catherine cringed, half expecting something to be thrown at her as soon as the words were out of her mouth. When no object came flying past, she glanced up.

The man smiled — a crooked, drunken smile

displaying a set of perfect, white teeth that made him look like a lunatic wolf — and advanced upon her. For a moment he swayed uncertainly over the bed upon which she seemed to be riveted. Then he dropped heavily onto it, raising a cloud of what she hoped was merely dust, and making the frame creak alarmingly.

"Of course you are, darling. They're always here against their will, to feed their poor starving infants or buy medicine for their aged grandmothers or some such tragedy. But enough of this game. You're here against your will and I haven't any, which puts us all square — and friendly, I hope."

He reached out to dislodge her fingers from the coverlet. She pulled back and leapt from the bed. Unfortunately, he was now sitting on a corner of the coverlet. She could retreat only a few feet unless she chose to relinquish her makeshift cloak.

"Now where did you think you'd go?" he asked, having watched this exercise with some amusement. "What's gotten into you, dashing about to make a man's poor, tired head spin? Come, sweetheart." He patted the mattress. "Let's be comfortable."

"Good grief! Don't you understand?"

"No," came the cheerful reply. "I didn't come here to understand — or to talk. You're making me impatient, and I ain't even patient to begin with. Oh, all right. I'll chase you if you like." He started to get up, changed his mind, and slumped back against the pillow in a half-recumbent position. "Only it's such a bother."

Miss Pelliston realised that getting this drunken creature to understand her predicament and provide assistance was an unpromising endeavour at best. On the other hand, she could not afford to wait for another potential rescuer. Even if she got this one to leave — which was more than likely, if he was the impatient sort — what sordid species of humanity could she expect to darken the door next?

Catherine took a deep breath and spoke. "I have been brought here against my will. I was most foully deceived and abducted."

"Ah, abduction," said the man, nodding sleepily.

"It's quite true. Shortly after I disembarked at the coaching inn, a thief made off with my reticule. Mrs. Grendle, who was nearby, appeared to take pity on me. She seemed so kindly and motherly when she offered to take me to my destination that I foolishly accepted. We stopped for tea. I remember nothing that happened after, until I woke up in this very room to find all my belongings gone and that odious woman telling me how she meant to employ me."

"Oh, yes." His eyes were closed.

"Will you help me?" Catherine asked.

"What would you have me do, sweeting mine?"

She moved a tad closer to the bed. "Just help me get out of this place. I can't do it on my own. Heaven knows I've tried, but they've kept the door locked, and you can see there are no windows. Moreover, before you came she promised unpleasant consequences if I made a fuss."

One unpleasant consequence was a burly fellow named Cholly, whom Mrs. Grendle had assured her was eager to teach Catherine her new trade if the young lady was unwilling to learn through trial and error on her own. Miss Pelliston preferred not to speak of that. Instead, she watched her visitor's face. She wondered if he'd gone to sleep, because he didn't answer or even open his eyes for the longest time.

So long a time was it that she began to wonder if she was going mad. Perhaps she'd never said a word and had only imagined herself speaking, as so often happened in nightmares. Perhaps, she thought, her heart sinking, *he* believed she was mad. A choking sob welled up in her throat. In the next instant she gasped in surprise as she found herself gazing into the bluest eyes she'd ever seen.

They were deep blue, the color of the late night summer sky, and framed with thick, dark lashes. Once more her analytical mind began running on its own as she wondered what on earth such a fine-looking young man was doing in this low place. Surely he had no need to *pay* for his sport. As she thought it, she blushed.

"Just escort you out the door, is that all?" he asked.

Catherine nodded.

"May a chap ask where you propose to go, with no clothes and, I take it, no money?"

Oh, heavens — he might actually help her! The words spilled out in a rush. "Why — why, you could lend me your coat, you see, and take me to the authorities, so we may report this dreadful business. I'm sure they will see justice done, and at least my belongings will be returned and I can go on as I'd intended — to find my, my friend, you know, with whom I was to visit."

Her sensible plan of proceeding seemed to leave him unimpressed — or perhaps was beyond his limited intellectual capacity — because he looked blank. Just as she was about to repeat the information in simpler terms, he spoke.

"You're serious, aren't you?" he asked.

"Oh, yes. Of course I am." Noting a suspicious twitch at the corner of his mouth, she drew herself up and continued with more dignity. "This is hardly a joking matter."

The piercing blue gaze travelled from the fuzzy light brown curls that formed a faery cloud about her head down to the bare toes that poked out from the frayed border of the coverlet. After another interminable silence, the man got up from the bed, yawned, stretched, and yawned again.

"Oh, very well," he said.

Mrs. Grendle was a plump woman of uncertain age and below-average stature. The inches Nature had denied her were compensated in part by an enormous mass of rigid curls, dyed apparently with shoe blacking and heaped upon her head like so many unappetizing sausages. Her lips and cheeks were carmine, and when she smiled, as she did now in her effort to understand just what her customer was proposing, the paint on her face cracked, loosening flakes of white powder which fluttered down upon her enormous, creased, and also thickly painted bosom. As she finally comprehended her client's request, the smile twisted into a ferocious scowl, showering more flakes onto the eroded white mountainside.

"Cholly!" she cried. "Jos!"

Two burly minions came running at the summons.

"Put him out," the brothel keeper commanded. "He's mad. He wants to steal one of the girls."

Cholly and Jos obediently laid their greasy hands on the client's shirtsleeves. The client looked down in a puzzled way at first one filthy paw, then the other. As his gaze rose to the faces of his assailants, his fist did also. He cracked Cholly on the nose, and Cholly staggered back. The customer then grasped Jos by the neck, lifted him off the floor, and threw him onto a large piece of obscene statuary. Jos and the statue crashed against the wall. The statue crumbled into fragments and Jos sank unconscious to the floor. Cholly, his nose bleeding, advanced once more. The stranger's fist shot out again with force enough to hurl Cholly back against a door frame. There was a sickening crack, and Cholly also sank to the floor.

Mrs. Grendle had not survived in a hard world by fighting lost causes. She studied the wreckage briefly. Like any experienced commander, she must have decided that a change of tactic was required because, when she turned to her guest, her painted face was sorrowful.

"Here's a beastly mess you've made, sir, and me a poor helpless female only trying to earn my bread. A sick mother I have as well. Now there'll be the surgeon's fees for these two, and that fine statue which my late husband brought all the way from Italy, not replaceable at any price." She shook her head, setting the sausages atremble. "And when I think of the time and money spent on this ungrateful young person, I could weep."

"Yes, yes," the tall customer agreed impatiently. "How much to cover your costs and hurt feelings?" He drew out his purse.

The purse seemed a heavy one.

"Two hundred pounds," said the bawd, her voice brisk again. "One hundred for the girl and another for expenses."

Catherine, who'd shrunk into a corner to avoid the flying bodies, now ran forward to clutch her rescuer's arm. "Oh, no. Good heavens — pay her? Reward her for what she's done? It's — it's obscene."

"Don't scold, darlin'," he answered, pushing her behind him before returning his attention to Mrs. Grendle. "Two hundred pounds is a tad steep, ma'am. That ugly piece of plaster must have driven scores of customers away. It certainly scared the

17

daylights out of me. Those chaps would be wanting an undertaker if I weren't in such a jolly mood, so there's more bother I've saved you. As to the girl —"

"A fine, healthy girl," the procuress interrupted.

The man glanced at Catherine, who flushed and clasped his coat more tightly about her.

"She doesn't look so healthy to me," he said. "She's awfully skinny — and I suspect she's bruised as well."

"If you wanted a plump armful, why didn't you say so?"

"Twenty pounds, ma'am."

"How dare you! She's cost me that much in food and drink alone. Not to mention her gown. Not to mention she hasn't earned a farthing."

"Then I expect you'll be glad to see the back of her. Thirty pounds, then."

"Two hundred."

"On the other hand," said the client as though he hadn't heard, "I could just take her away without this tiresome haggling. I 'magine you wouldn't like to bother the Watch about it."

Mrs. Grendle accepted the sum with much vivid description of her customer's want of human feeling and diverse anatomical inadequacies. He only grinned as he counted out

18

the money into her hand.

The much-tried madam's forbearance was further tested when Catherine shrilly demanded the return of two bandboxes.

It took another twenty pounds to jog Mrs. Grendle's memory on this matter, but at length all the money was paid, the boxes collected, and Catherine, having hastily thrust her naked feet into her half boots, followed her rescuer out into the night.

"Where are we going?" Catherine asked, as she hurried after her gallant knight, who was zigzagging briskly down the filthy street.

"My lodgings." He threw this over his shoulder.

She stopped short. "But the authorities — I thought we were going to report that odious woman."

"It's much too late. Authorities are always cross if you bother them in the middle of the night. Besides, you got your things, didn't you?" He stopped to glance impatiently at her. "Are you coming or not?"

"I most certainly cannot come to your lodgings. It isn't proper."

The young man stood and surveyed her for a moment. The crooked smile broke out upon his face. "Silly girl. Where else do you 'spect to go dressed in my coat and little else?"

A large tear rolled down the young lady's thin nose.

"Oh, drat," he muttered.

Another tear slid down her cheek.

He heaved a sigh. Then he strode towards her, picked her up, flung her over his shoulder, and continued on his way.

"There you are," he announced as he deposited her in a chair. "Rescued."

"Yes," Catherine answered a trifle breathlessly. "Thank you."

She looked about her. The room was very dingy, dingier than that she'd recently escaped and in a far worse state of disorder. Her rescuer was increasing the disorder as he searched for a drink. The quest apparently required a great deal of thrashing about, the flinging of innocent objects onto the floor, and the opening and crashing shut of what sounded like dozens of drawers and cabinet doors.

At last he found the bottle he sought. With more bangs, bumps, and oaths, he succeeded in opening it, and broke only one glass in the complicated process of pouring the wine. After filling another none-too-clean tumbler for Catherine, he sat down at the opposite end of the cluttered table and proceeded to stare her out of countenance while he drank.

"You seemed nearly sober only a short time

ago," Catherine finally managed to say. "I wish you would try to remain so, because I need your help."

"Had to be sober then. Business, you know. It wasn't easy, either, arguing with what looked like half a dozen old tarts at once. Those nasty black things on her head. Damme if I didn't think I'd cast up my accounts then and there."

"Which should indicate to you that you've had a sufficiency of intoxicating beverages, I would hope," Catherine retorted disapprovingly.

As soon as she spoke, she winced, expecting a volley of missiles. None came. The blue eyes only widened in befuddlement.

"How you scold, Miss — Miss — why, I'm hanged if we've even been introduced."

He jerked himself to his feet and made a sweeping bow that nearly sent him and the table crashing to the floor. At the very last instant he regained his balance.

"Curst floor won't stay put," he muttered. "Where was I? Oh, yes. Introductions. Max, you know. Max Demowery, at your service." This time he managed his bow with more grace. "And you, ma'am?"

"Catherine. Pe-Pettigrew," she stammered.

"Catherine," he repeated. "Cat. Nice. You look rather like a cat my sister once had —

leastways when it was a kitten. All fluffy and big eyes. Only the little beast's eyes were green and yours —" He leaned forward to peer intently into her face, causing Catherine's heart to thump frantically. "Hazel!" he cried in triumph. "Odd color, but no matter. It's time we went to bed."

"To — to bed?" she echoed faintly.

"Y-yes," he mimicked. "More comfortable, y' know."

She looked about her again. As far as she could ascertain, his shabby lodgings comprised two rooms. There was no bed in this one. Her face grew warm. "Well, then, good night," she said politely.

Mr. Demowery considered this briefly. "I'm foxed, darlin', so maybe I'm not hearing straight — but that sounded om'nously like a dismissal."

"You expressed intentions of retiring."

"And you ain't 'retiring' with me?"

"Good heavens, I should hope not. I should not be in your lodgings in the first place. It's most improper."

"Sweetheart, I can't decide," he began slowly, after he'd mulled over these remarks as well, "whether you're insane or horribly ungrateful. Didn't I just pay fifty quid for you?"

Her face flushed, this time with indignation.

"You have preserved me from a fate reputed to be worse than death. I asked you to do so. It's completely illogical that I should express gratitude by doing exactly what I wished to avoid in the first place."

As he stood gazing at her, his puzzled expression gave way to a rueful smile. "Very complicated reasoning, m'love. Too complicated for me." He lifted her out of the chair, and, oblivious to her startled protests or the two small fists pounding on his chest, carried her to the bedroom and dropped her onto the bed.

"I will not cooperate," she gasped.

"No, of course you won't. It's just my luck, ain't it, this night of all the rest?" He turned and left the room.

Catherine lay upon the mattress, frozen with apprehension. Less than an hour before, her main concern had been escaping a place that could have been one of Dante's Circles of Hell. Now, evidently, she'd leapt out of the pan into the flames. She'd left home for excellent reasons with a logical plan. Now she could not believe she'd been so naive, so horribly misguided. She had fled what promised to be a life of wretchedness and rushed headlong into what had speedily become the most horrid two — or three or four, she hardly knew — days of her existence.

Despite his drunkenness and apparent penchant for squalor she had believed that her benefactor was not entirely sunk to the depths of depravity. Yet, instead of taking her directly to the authorities, he'd carried her over his shoulder like a sack of corn to his lodgings and clearly expressed intentions of bedding her.

Perhaps he too meant to drug her. Mayhap even now he was preparing some foul concoction and would come back to force it down her throat. Catherine scrambled out of the bed and ran to open the window. It was stuck shut. Furthermore, there were three floors between herself and the ground and no visible means of descent.

Her panicked gaze darted about the room. She dashed to grab the basin from the washstand. Let him try, she told herself. Just let him try.

And if she did somehow miraculously succeed in overpowering a man nearly twice her size, what then? Where would she go, alone, in the middle of the night in this alien, hostile city? One crisis at a time, she counselled herself, as she crept to the door. She tried to close it quietly, but it would not shut altogether. Frustrated, she looked for a position from which she might take her attacker unawares.

At that moment she heard from the room beyond the terrifying noises by means of which primitive man once warned away the creatures skulking near his cave at night. She crept closer to the door and listened. It was true. Mr. Demowery was snoring.

For all that the sound might have in bygone days frightened away wild beasts, Miss Pelliston found it reassuring. She would wait another quarter hour to be absolutely certain he was asleep for the night. Papa was known to lose consciousness over his dinner — apparently dead to the world — then suddenly start up again minutes later, quarrelling with her as if he'd been awake the whole time.

Catherine was very weary, and the steady rhythm of that snoring made her drowsy. She looked longingly at the bed. She would lie down just for a few minutes and think what to do next. The few minutes stretched into half an hour, at the end of which Miss Pelliston too was fast asleep.

2

The sun, which had risen many hours earlier, strove in vain to penetrate the grimy window as Clarence Arthur Maximilian Demowery awoke. He was not at all surprised at the great whacking and thundering inside his head, since he had awakened in this state nearly every day of the past six months. He was very much surprised, however, to find himself sprawled face down on a tattered piece of carpet in front of the sooty fireplace. Gingerly, he turned over on his side. A pair of shabby bandboxes blocked his view.

"Now where in blazes did you come from?" he asked. Though he spoke aloud, he was startled to hear a faint moan in reply. Had he moaned? From what seemed a great distance he heard a cough. Then he remembered.

He'd gone to Granny Grendle's to enjoy one last night of nonrespectability. There he'd found a curiosity and had brought it — or her, rather — back with him. Though he was not at the moment certain why he'd done so, he was hardly surprised. As a child he'd regularly carried home curiosities of various sorts: insects, reptiles, and rodents, primarily. He wondered how his father would respond to this particular trophy. At eight and twenty, Max was too old and much too large to be spanked. Anyhow, there was no reason to enlighten his father regarding this or any other of the past six months' adventures.

A second faint moan from the bedroom dragged Mr. Demowery to his feet. Not only his head but his muscles ached, jogging his memory regarding several other details. He'd gotten into a brawl in a low brothel, after which he'd also parted with fifty pounds for the privilege of hearing a bit of muslin show her gratitude by politely denying him the favours he'd so extravagantly paid for.

He hauled his weary body to the partially open bedroom door and glared at the frail form entangled in the bedclothes. A cloud of light brown hair billowed over the pillow, veiling what seemed to be a very small face, out of which poked a straight, narrow little nose. Gad, he thought in sudden self-disgust — she's only a child.

At that moment the object of his scrutiny opened her eyes, and his heart sank. They were wide, innocent hazel eyes whose expression changed from childlike wonder to fear in the instant it took her to recall where she was.

"How old *are* you?" he asked abruptly, feeling unaccountably frightened himself and therefore more annoyed.

"One and twenty," she gasped.

"Hah!" He marched away from the door and threw himself into a chair.

Steadfastly he ignored the sounds that issued from the bedroom — the rustle of bedclothes, the splash of water, more rustling, and some thumps. He pretended not to see her creep out to grab her bandboxes and scurry back to the room again, pushing the stubborn door half-closed behind her.

When she finally emerged, he thrust past her into the bedroom and took an abnormally long time about his own washing up. Was *that* what he'd brought home? Dressed in a sober grey frock, with all that glorious hair yanked back into a vicious little knot, she seemed neither the curious baggage he'd taken her for last night nor the child he'd believed was swaddled in his bedclothes.

Yet the frock and bun matched what he recalled of her conversation. She had sounded like a schoolmistress last night, and that in combination with the personal charms he'd briefly glimpsed had appealed to his sense of humour — or maybe his sense of the absurd was more like it. Such a creature was not at all what one expected to find in an establishment such as Granny Grendle's.

Max Demowery was no wet-behind-the-ears schoolboy. He'd had considerable experience with the frail sorority in England and abroad, in the course of which he'd heard any number of pathetic tales. He'd not actually believed her story, but had taken her away because she amused him. Purchasing her from the old bawd had seemed a fitting conclusion to his six-month orgy of dissipation.

Not until the young woman had declined to reward him as he'd expected had he, drunk as he was, begun to wonder whether her tale was true. Besides, he'd never yet forced himself upon a woman.

That was as far as he'd been able to reason at the time. Today, in the clear, too-bright light of early afternoon, he found a deal more to puzzle and distress him. A common strumpet he could put back upon the streets without a second thought, assuming confidently that she must be able to survive there or she would never have reached the advanced age of one and twenty. Suppose, however, she wasn't street goods?

Suppose nothing, he told himself as he savagely scoured his face with the towel. If he had a sense of impending doom, that was because he was hungry and out of sorts. He'd give her some money and send her on her way.

He was debating whether to shave now or after breakfast when he heard the door to the hall creak. Flinging away the towel, he hurried out of the room to find the young woman attempting to close the door behind her without dropping her bandboxes.

He ought to have breathed a sigh of relief and cried good riddance, but he caught a glimpse of her face and found himself asking instead, "What the devil d'you think you're doing?"

Her guilty start caused her to drop one of her boxes. "Oh. I was leaving. That is, I should never have abused your hospitality in the first place. I mean, I should never have fallen asleep —"

"Ah, you meant to leave in the dead of night."

"Yes. No." She reached up to push back under her dowdy bonnet a wispy curl that had broken loose from its moorings.

Part of his brain was wondering why she'd made herself so deuced unattractive, while the other part watched, fascinated, as she struggled not to look frightened. Each step in the process of composing herself was evident in her face, and most especially in her large, expressive eyes.

"What I mean is, this is a very awkward situation. Moreover, I have put you out dreadfully, and therefore it seemed best to go away and leave you in peace. I'm sure you must have a great deal to do."

"You might have said good-bye first. It's usually done in the best circles."

"Oh, yes. I'm so sorry. I never meant to be rude." She picked up the bandbox. "Good-bye, then," she said. "No, that's not all. Thank you for all you've done. I will repay you — the fifty pounds, I mean. I'll send it here, shall I?"

Though Mr. Demowery didn't know what he'd expected, he was sure it wasn't this. He was also certain that, even if she were not a child, she might as well be, so frail was she and so utterly naive and so very lost — like some faery sprite that had wandered too far from its woodland home.

This fanciful notion irritated him, making him speak more harshly than he intended. "You'll do no such thing. What you will do is leave hold of those ridiculous boxes and sit yourself down and eat some breakfast."

"*Sit*," he repeated when she began backing towards the stairs. "If you won't on your own, I'll help you."

She bit her lip. "Thank you, but I'd much

rather you didn't." She reentered, dropped the bandboxes, marched to a chair, and sat down. "I've been flung about quite enough," she added in a low voice, her narrow face mutinous.

"Beg your pardon, ma'am — Miss Pettigrew, if I remember aright — but you picked an uncommon careless and impatient chap as your rescuer. Right now I'm impatient for my breakfast. It'll take a while, I'm afraid, because my landlady is the slowest, stupidest slattern alive. While I'm gone, I hope you don't get any mad notions about sneaking away. You're in the middle of St. Giles's. If you don't know what that means, I suggest you think about Cholly and Jos and imagine several hundred of their most intimate acquaintance upon the streets. That should give you a notion, though a rosy one, of the neighbourhood."

Catherine's host returned some twenty minutes later bearing a tray containing a pot of coffee and plates piled with slabs of bread, butter, and cheese.

They ate in silence for the most part, Mr. Demowery being preoccupied with assuaging his ravenous hunger, and Miss Pettigrew (née Pelliston) being unable to form any coherent sentence out of the muddle of worries besetting her. Only when he was certain no crumbs remained did Max turn his attention again to his guest.

Now that his stomach was full and his head relatively clear, he wondered anew what had come over him last night. She was not at all in his style. He was a tall, powerfully built man and preferred women who weren't in peril of breaking if he touched them. Full-bosomed Amazons were his type — lusty, willing women who didn't mind if a man's head was clouded with liquor and his manners a tad rough and tumble, so long as his purse was a large and open one.

He was amazed that, after taking one look at this stray, he had not stormed back to Granny Grendle to demand a more reasonable facsimile of a female. Miss Pettigrew appeared woefully undernourished, so much so that he'd thought her smaller than she actually was. In fact, she was so scrawny that he wondered just what had seemed so intriguing last night. This, however, troubled him less than the realisation that he'd come so close to forcing his great, clumsy person upon this young waif.

He'd never had a taste for the children who walked the streets of London by night and populated its brothels, though he knew of many fine fellows who did. Had six months' wallowing through every sort of low life in a last, desperate attempt to enjoy something like freedom finally rotted his character and corrupted his mind?

Still, he dismally reminded himself, there would be no more such excursions into London's seamier locales. If he sought feminine company in the future, he'd be obliged to do so in the accepted way. He would go through the tiresome negotiations required to set up some Fashionable Impure as his mistress. Even the assuaging of simple carnal needs would be complicated by some infernally convoluted etiquette. He refused to think about the greater complications he could expect when he acquired a wife — and the passel of heirs his father impatiently awaited.

Mr. Demowery glowered at the elf — or whatever she was — and was further annoyed at the fear that leapt into her eyes. "Oh, I ain't going to eat you," he snapped. "Already had my breakfast."

"Yes," she answered stiffly. "I'm amazed you had the stomach for it. My f — that is, some people are quite unfit for taking any sustenance after a night of overindulgence."

She winced — no, actually, she ducked. Dimly he recalled seeing that nervous movement before. He wondered if it were a tic.

"Oh, I'm so sorry. You were very kind to share your breakfast with me. Thank you."

She stood up. "I should not keep you any longer. I've put you out quite enough, I expect." After a brief hesitation, she put out her hand. "Goodbye, Mr. Demowery."

Remembering his manners, he rose to accept the proffered handshake. What a small white hand it was, he thought as his own large tanned paw swallowed it up. That realisation also annoyed him, and he was about to hurry her on her way when he glanced at her face. Her expressive hazel eyes gave the lie to the rigid composure of her countenance. Her eyes said distinctly, "I am utterly lost, utterly frantic."

Mr. Demowery's own face assumed an expression of resignation. "I don't suppose you have any idea where you're going?"

"Of course I do. My friend — the friend I had intended to visit —"

"I can't imagine what sort of friend would let an ignorant young miss find her own way from a coaching inn through a strange city, but I suppose that's none of my business. Still, I ain't ignorant, and I know that if you were foolish enough to be cozened by that old strumpet, you'll never make it to this friend of yours on your own. If you'll give me a few minutes to change into something I haven't slept in, I'll take you."

"Oh — that's very kind of you, but not at

all necessary. I can find my way in broad day-light, I'm sure."

"Not in this neighbourhood, sweetheart. Night or day is all the same to the rogues about here."

She paused. Obviously, she was weighing the perils of the squalid streets against the dangers of accepting his protection. She must have concluded that he was the lesser of two evils, because she soon managed a squeaky thanks, then began an intensive survey of the ragged corner of carpet on which she stood.

Max Demowery did not consider himself a Beau of Society. The process of shaving and changing was therefore accomplished in short order. A few fierce strokes with his brush were enough to subdue his tangle of golden hair, and with scarcely a glance into the stained mirror he strode out to rejoin his guest.

Not until they had nearly reached their destination — Miss Collingwood's Academy for Young Ladies — did the sense of impending doom return to settle upon Mr. Demowery's brow. A school?

He stole a glance at the young woman beside him. She looked like a schoolteacher, certainly, and her air and manners, not to mention her speech, bespoke education and good breeding. It was as he had feared: She was respectable and her story had been true and though all that had been evident by the time they'd left his lodgings, only now did the implications occur to him. Any respectable woman who'd spent two nights as she had just done was ruined — if, that is, anyone learned of the matter.

He halted abruptly and grabbed Miss Pettigrew's arm. "I say, you'd better not tell anyone where you've been, you know. That is," he went on, feeling vaguely ashamed as the hazel eyes searched his face, "you may not have considered the consequences."

"Good grief, do you think I've considered aught else? I shall have to tell a falsehood and pray I'm not asked for many details. I shall say I was delayed and pretend that my message to that effect must have gone astray. It must be simple," she explained, "because I'm not at all adept at lying."

This being a perfectly sensible conclusion, Mr. Demowery had no reason to be sharp with her, but he answered before he stopped to reason. "Good," he snapped. "I'm relieved you don't have any hard feelings. I did, after all, take you to my lodgings in opposition to your expressed wishes. Another woman would have exacted the penalty."

"I collect you mean she would insist that you marry her," was the thoughtful response.

"Well, that would be most unjust. In the first place, though you arrived at erroneous conclusions about my character, the evidence against me was most compelling. Second, you must have reconsidered, since I am quite — unharmed. Finally," she continued, as though she were helping him with a problem in geometry, "it is hardly in my best interests to wed a man I met in a house of ill repute, even if I had any notion how to force a man to marry me, which I assure you I have not."

"No idea at all?" he asked, curious in spite of himself.

"No, nor is it a skill I should be desirous of cultivating. An adult should not be forced into marriage as a child is forced to eat his peas. Peas are only part of a meal. Marriage is a life's work."

"I stand corrected, Miss Pettigrew," he replied gravely. "In fact, I feel I should be writing your words upon my slate one hundred times."

She coloured. "I do beg your pardon. You were most kind to consider my situation, and I ought not have lectured."

Whatever irritation he'd felt was washed away by a new set of emotions, too jumbled to be identified. He brushed away her apology with some smiling comment about being so used to lectures that he grew lonely when deprived of them.

They had reached the square in which Miss Collingwood's Academy was located.

"Shall I wait for you?" he asked, hoping she'd decline and at the same time inexplicably dismayed at the prospect of never seeing her again.

He had at least a dozen questions he wished she'd answer, such as why and how she'd come to London and where she'd come from and who or what she was, really. Yet, it was better not to know, because knowing was bound to complicate matters.

"Oh, no! That is, you've already gone so far out of your way, and there is no need. I'll be all right now." She took from him the bandboxes he'd been carrying. "Thank you again," she said. "That sounds so little, after all you've done for me, but I can't think how else —"

"Never mind. Good-bye, Miss Pettigrew."

He bowed and walked away. A minute later he stopped and turned in time to see her being admitted into the building. He grew uneasy. "Oh, damnation," he muttered, then moved down to the corner of the street and leaned against a lamppost to wait.

"Oh, dear," said Miss Collingwood. "This

is most awkward." Her fluttering, blue-veined hand flew up to fidget with the lace of her cap. "I sent your letter along to Miss Fletcher — that is, Mrs. Brown, now, of course. Did she not write you?"

Without waiting for an answer, the elderly lady continued, "No, I would expect not. I am sure she had not another thought in this world but of *him*, and what a pity that is. She was the most conscientious instructor I have had since I founded this school, and the girls doted upon her. Naturally, I was compelled to discharge him. I have never held with these odd conventions that it is always the woman's fault. Men are such wicked deceivers. If even Miss Fletcher could be overcome, what hope is there for weaker vessels, I ask you? To be sure, he was a most charming man. Ten years with us and always most correct in his behaviour, though the girls *will* become infatuated with the music master."

Catherine barely heard the headmistress. Miss Fletcher, that paragon of propriety, had run off with the music master? No wonder she hadn't answered Catherine's last letter. By the time that epistle reached the school, Miss Pelliston's former governess had already become Mrs. Brown and departed with her new husband for Ireland.

"I'm so sorry you have come out of your

way for naught," Miss Collingwood continued. "I feel responsible. I should have counselled Miss Fletcher: marry in haste, repent at leisure."

"I'm sure you did all you could," was the faint reply. "I should have waited until I heard from her . . . though it was inconceivable that she should not be here. She last wrote me but two months ago and only mentioned Mr. Brown in passing. Still, I was at fault."

Greatly at fault, Catherine's conscience reminded. She had let her hateful passions rule her and was now reaping the reward.

"No doubt," Catherine went on, pinning what she hoped was a convincing smile on her face, "Miss Fletcher's reply is at home awaiting me."

After assuring Miss Collingwood that the trip would not be a total loss, and concocting some plausible story about doing a bit more shopping (that explained the bandboxes) with the aunt who'd supposedly travelled with her and was now visiting friends, Catherine took her leave.

She made her way slowly down the street, not only because she did not know where to go, but because her conscience was plaguing her dreadfully and she must argue with it.

She would not be in this predicament if she hadn't run away from home, but she wouldn't have run away if her papa had only stopped now and then to think what he was doing. However, he never thought — not about her certainly. His cronies, his hounds, his wenching and drinking were much more important.

Papa should have arranged for her to have a Season. Even Miss Fletcher had believed he would, or she'd never have accepted the post in London three years ago. Instead, he had sent Catherine to live with Great-Aunt Eustacia. If that elderly lady had not died a year and a half later, Catherine would be there yet. She would have endured those endless monologues on religion and genealogy day after day until she dwindled into a lonely spinster like Aunt Deborah, who'd been the old lady's companion for some thirty years before Catherine came.

She had no illusions about her attractions. Her sole assets were her lineage and her father's wealth. She knew she had no chance of attracting a husband unless she entered an environment where suitable bachelors abounded. That meant the London Marriage Mart.

Yet, even after the family's mourning period, had Papa troubled himself about his daughter's Season? Of course not, she thought, staring morosely at her trudging feet. He thought only of himself. He went off to Bath and found himself a handsome young widow. Upon his return, he'd announced his own and his daughter's wedding plans simultaneously.

Lord Browdie, of all people, was to be her mate. He was more slovenly, crude, and dissolute than Papa. The man was ignorant, moody, and repulsive. Catherine had never expected a Prince Charming — she was no Incomparable herself — but to live the rest of her days with that middle-aged boor! She had borne much in the name of filial obedience, but Lord Browdie was past all enduring.

Now she knew better. Now she knew what it was to be utterly helpless, utterly without protection, and virtually without hope. She had no idea how to get home, dreadful as that homecoming would be. She had not a farthing to her name, and Mr. Demowery must be miles away by now.

3

Her eyes swam with tears, and Catherine scarcely noticed where she walked. She would have stumbled into the path of an oncoming carriage if a hand had not shot out to grab her elbow and drag her back to the curb.

"Damme if you ain't an accident waiting to happen," said a familiar voice.

Still immersed in her misery, Catherine looked up into a lean, handsome face. As she had the previous night, she caught her breath, as though the piercing blue of his eyes had stabbed her to the heart.

"You ought to be carried about in a bandbox yourself." He took her baggage from her.

"Mr. Demowery, how — what are you doing here?"

"Protecting my investment. I wasn't about to watch fifty quid trampled into a puddle. Not to mention how it mucks up the streets, don't you know?" With that, he strode swiftly away from the square, and she, seeing no alternative, followed him. They had not gone many yards before he located a hackney. Not until her luggage was stowed away and she had been hustled into the musty-smelling vehicle did Catherine venture to ask where they were going.

"That's what I'm trying to figure out," was the abstracted answer.

"Oh, no. I mean, there isn't anything to figure out. I shall have to go back now."

"Back where? Granny Grendle's?"

"Good heavens, no! I shall have to return h-home." Though her voice broke at the last, Catherine squeezed back the tears that had welled up as soon as she'd thought what she'd be returning to.

"Is it as bad as all that?"

The sympathy she heard in his voice nearly undid her. So unused was she to sympathy of any kind that it rather frightened her, in fact. "Oh, no. I've made a dreadful mistake. I see that now, and it has been a lesson to me — not to let my passions rule me, I mean," she explained, just as though he had been Miss Fletcher and had asked her to examine her conscience.

"What passions are those, Miss Pettigrew?"

"Resentment, certainly. And pride. And — oh, everything opposed to reason and good sense. If I'd stayed and done what I was told, none of these horrid things would have happened to me —"

"What were you told?" he interrupted.

Subterfuge was alien to Miss Pelliston's character. She was, as she had admitted, an inept liar. The fibs she'd told Miss Collingwood had cost Catherine agonies of guilt. Besides, she could conceive of no more unworthy return for his unexpected kindness than to lie to him.

She told him the truth, though she eliminated the more sensational elements in order to present the matter with dry objectivity. She did not enlighten him regarding her true identity, either, and named no other names. Though that was not precisely objective, she had rather keep her disgrace as private as possible.

"So you ran away because you couldn't stomach marrying the old fellow your father chose for you?"

"I never stopped to consider what I could endure, Mr. Demowery. I'm afraid I did not weigh the matter as carefully as I ought," she said, gazing earnestly into his handsome face. "I just took offence —"

"And took off." He smiled — not the crooked, drunken grin of last night but a friendly, open smile. "Yes, I see now what a passion-driven creature you are. Oh, don't go all red on me again. The colour's too bright

46

and you must think of my poor head. I ain't fully recovered, you know."

She drew herself up. "Actually, I am seldom ruled by emotion. This is the first time I can remember ever behaving so — so unsensibly."

"Sounds sensible enough to me. As you said before, people shouldn't be forced to marry. M' sister felt the same. Bolted, when m' father tried to shackle her to some rich old prig. They tried to get me to fetch her back, but I wouldn't. You wouldn't either, if you knew Cousin Agatha. That's who Louisa went to. That's what you need, Miss Pettigrew — a Cousin Agatha to terrify your papa into submission."

"Well, all I had was Miss Fletcher and she doesn't terrify anyone, and now she's gone," Catherine answered ruefully.

"What, no old dragon ladies in the family to scorch your papa's whiskers for him?"

Catherine shook her head.

"Then I think," said Mr. Demowery, turning his blue gaze to the greasy window, "you had better meet Louisa."

"Bolted?" Lord Browdie exclaimed. "Well, if that don't beat all."

He ran his thick fingers over the rough, reddish stubble on his chin. Probably should have shaved, he thought, though that seemed a deal of trouble to go to merely on Catherine's account.

Miss Deborah Pelliston left off snuffling into her black-bordered handkerchief long enough to offer a weak protest. "Oh, don't say it," she moaned. "I cannot believe Catherine would do such a thing. Surely there is a misunderstanding. She may have met with an accident or, heaven help us, foul play."

"And left a note? That don't make sense."

The glass of Madeira at his elbow did, however, make sense to his lordship. Therefore, he turned his attention to that while nodding absently at his hostess's stream of incoherent complaint.

Should have married the little shrew right off, he thought sourly. She'd be broken to harness now. Instead there was going to be a deal of bother and no one but himself to deal with it.

The whole business ought to have been simple enough. James Pelliston had decided to marry a handsome widow from Bath. The widow didn't think a house required two mistresses and had dropped a hint to her future husband. Pelliston, as usual, had confided the problem to his crony: what was to be done with Catherine?

The crony had considered the matter over a bottle of brandy. He considered the property

Catherine's great-aunt had left her and found that agreeable. He considered Catherine's appearance and decided he'd seen worse, especially now she was out of that hideous mourning. He considered that he himself had long been in need of an heir and therefore a wife, which in any other case would require a lot of tedious courtship. Catherine's like or dislike of himself he considered not a jot.

"I'll take her off your hands," he'd charitably offered.

By the time the gentlemen emptied another bottle, the dowry had been settled and an agreement reached whereby the two households would take Aunt Deborah by turns, until such time as neither could put up any longer with her whimpering and she might be packed off to quarters in nearby Bath.

The two men had toasted each other into a state of cheerful oblivion after settling matters to their satisfaction. Since that time, over two months ago, Lord Browdie had spoken to Catherine once, at her father's wedding. Their conversation had consisted of Lord Browdie's jovially informing his betrothed that she was too pale and skinny and should eat more. Like the other wedding guests, Lord Browdie then proceeded to drink himself into a stupor. He never noticed his fiancee's disappearance. He had enough trouble remembering she existed at all.

Yesterday, the engagement ring he'd ordered in a fit of magnanimity had arrived. He'd come this afternoon to present it to his affianced bride. The trouble was, she'd fled three days ago during the wedding celebration, and this sniffling, whining, moaning creature sitting on the other side of the room had been too busy having megrims and palpitations to report the matter to him immediately. By now Catherine might be anywhere, her trail so cold he doubted that even his well-trained hounds could track her down.

"Wish you'd told me right off," his lordship grumbled when there was a break in the snuffling and sobbing.

"Oh, dear, I'm sure I meant to. That is, I wasn't sure if I ought. I never missed her that night because I'd gone to bed so early with a terrible headache. Then, when I found that dreadful note next day, I had such fearful palpitations and was so ill I couldn't think at all, and with James away . . . Well, one cannot trust the servants, because they *will* talk and the scandal would kill me, I know it. So I kept to my room. But who could have imagined she would do such a shameful thing? Such a good, biddable girl she has always been."

"Never thought she had the pluck," said

Lord Browdie, half to himself. "Anyhow, where's the scandal in it?" he asked his hostess. "Ain't no fine Society hereabouts to be shocked. Just let on she's sick."

"But the servants —"

"Will keep their tongues in their heads if they know what's good for them. I'll talk to them," Lord Browdie assured her as he dragged his gangly body up from the chair.

"You are too kind. You make me quite ashamed that I did not confide this trouble to you immediately —"

"Yes, yes. Just calm yourself, ma'am. Important to behave as though nothing's happened out of the ordinary."

"But surely James must be told —"

"No sense interrupting his bridal trip. By the time he's back we'll have Cathy home safe and sound, and no one the wiser." He had no difficulty speaking with more confidence than he felt. Lord Browdie was accustomed to swagger.

Miss Deborah sighed. "It is such a relief to have a man take charge. I cannot tell you how beset I've been, not knowing where to turn or what to do. Why, I'm frightened half to death each time the post is delivered, not knowing what news it will bring — though she did say she would be perfectly safe. But will not her friends wonder when she doesn't answer their letters?"

As far as Lord Browdie knew, Catherine hadn't any friends. He pointed this out to his hostess.

In response, and with much fussing and flustering, the lady drew out a letter from her workbasket. "It's from Ireland," she explained, handing it to Lord Browdie. "I did not like to leave it lying about, because the servants —" She gasped as he tore the letter open. "Oh, my — I don't think — it is *hers*, after all."

He ignored her twittering as he scanned the fine, precise handwriting. Then he folded the letter and stuffed it into the tail pocket of his coat. "Good enough," he said. "Won't be no wild-goose chase after all. She's gone to London."

"Dear heaven!" The spinster sank back in her seat, fumbling for her smelling salts.

"Now, now, don't fuss yourself," Lord Browdie said irritably. "There's only the one place she can go, so there'll be no trouble finding her. No trouble at all."

Miss Collingwood's Academy had been squeezed into a tidy corner of a neighbourhood best described as shabbily genteel. Miss Collingwood catered to bourgeois families that did not yet aspire to the glory of housing governesses, but did wish to improve their daughters' chances of upward mobility by means of a not-too-taxing course of education. While the training would not make a butcher's daughter a lady, it might subdue the more blatant signs of her origins.

The streets the hackney coach now traversed bespoke an entirely different social level. Here were trees enclosed in tidy squares upon which the sparkling windows of elegant townhouses bent their complacent gazes. These streets were wider, cleaner, and a good deal quieter, their peace broken only by the rumble of elegant carriages and the clip-clop of high-stepping thoroughbreds. A gentleman stood at one doorway drawing on his gloves as his tiger soothed the restless, high-strung horses impatiently waiting. On the sidewalk, a neatly dressed female servant hastened along, basket in hand.

Catherine surveyed the passing vista with confusion at first, then growing anxiety as her companion replied that, yes, they had long since left the City proper and were now in Mayfair. She shrank deeper into her corner of the coach and wished there had been room in her bandboxes for an enormous poke bonnet. This was precisely the sort of neighbourhood in which one could expect to meet Papa's friends. Lord

Pelliston never came to Town, but his cronies did. How would she explain her presence here if one of them recognised her?

The hackney finally halted before a splendid townhouse of classical design and proportions. Catherine concluded that Mr. Demowery's sister must have married very well indeed, even if she had rejected the "rich old toad" her parents had initially selected for her.

So preoccupied was Miss Pelliston with her wonderings and worries that she scarcely attended to her companion's conversation with the butler. Only when she was ushered into the sumptuous drawing-room and beheld her hostess did the words belatedly register.

The butler had addressed Mr. Demowery as "my lord," and was not corrected. Now Catherine heard distinctly the sigh of exasperation her benefactor uttered when the butler announced, "Lord Rand to see you, My Lady." Miss Pelliston's face grew hot and her heart began pounding so hard that she believed it must burst from her bosom.

"Ah, Max," said the lady. "Am I the first to behold the prodigal's return?" She gave her brother a peck on the cheek before glancing enquiringly at Catherine.

"Louisa, may I present Miss Catherine Pettigrew. Miss Pettigrew, Lady Andover — m' sister, that is."

The ersatz Miss Pettigrew sank into a graceful curtsey, and wished she might sink through the floor. Her benefactor's sister was the Countess of Andover! Her benefactor himself was a nobleman. Demowery, indeed — he probably had a dozen names besides.

When Catherine rose she found Lord Rand staring at her in that puzzled way he'd done several times before. She gave him one reproachful look, then turned to his sister, who was expressing rather subdued pleasure at the acquaintance while dropping a quizzical glance at Miss Pettigrew's frock.

In her ladyship's place, Catherine would have been hard put to express any sort of pleasure at all. What must the countess be thinking? Catherine looked like a betweenstairs servant. She had carefully designed a wardrobe that would convey that impression. To dress as befitted her station would have aroused speculation and, probably, trouble during her travels. Her present costume, however, was bound to provoke another sort of speculation in these surroundings.

Still, for all that Lord Pelliston was an arrant scapegrace, his title went back to the eleventh century at least, and his daughter had been scrupulously trained. She returned the countess's greeting in her politest manner, apologised for intruding, made another curtsey then turned to leave the room.

Lord Rand's none-too-gentle grip on her elbow prevented her. "Dash it, Miss Pettigrew, don't be such a coward. It's only Louisa, you know. She won't bite you."

"Not, certainly, on such short acquaintance," Lady Andover observed. She gestured towards a chair. "Won't you be seated? I'll order some refreshment."

Miss Pettigrew murmured more gratitude and apologies along with a firm expression of her intentions to leave.

"Oh, sit down," said her benefactor. "You haven't anywhere to go, you know, and wouldn't have the first idea how to get there if you did. Besides which, Louisa's all afever to know why you're here and who you are, only she's too dashed well-bred to show it. Ain't that so, Louisa?"

"I am curious why Miss Pettigrew looked so stunned when Jeffers announced you, Max. Have you been running about under false colours all these months?"

Without waiting for a reply, she bade her brother ring for a servant. That personage appeared instantly — not at all, Catherine thought, like those at home, who pretended to be deaf, and then if they did heed a summons were prodigiously offended. This one appeared, vanished, and reappeared in minutes, a scrupulously polite and efficient wraith.

In the interim Lord Rand's sister kept up a light flow of amusing conversation, unaided by her two visitors and all about the weather. The tea arrived along with coffee for her brother, who gave one affronted look at the cup offered him and marched to a table upon which stood several decanters.

"Max," said the countess.

He stopped in the act of lifting a decanter.

"You require coffee, My Lord."

"Dash it, Louisa," he muttered, putting the bottle back. "It's well past noon."

"So it is. Still, I suspect you have some explaining to do not only to me, but to Miss Pettigrew, and you are cryptic enough when sober."

"Nothing to explain," his lordship answered as he studied the sparkling crystal containers wistfully. "I found Miss Pettigrew in a spot of trouble and hadn't time to discuss genealogy. Not that she's been very forthcoming herself."

The sister returned her attention to her oddly attired guest. "Sugar, Miss Pettigrew?"

Catherine, who'd been staring at the vagabond who'd so abruptly turned into a member of the nobility, dragged her gaze back to her hostess, and then wondered how one could have possibly ignored, even for an instant, this magnificent woman.

The Countess of Andover was as fair-haired as her brother and quite tall as well, but his lean, chiselled features found a softer counterpart in her lovely countenance. Clad in an aqua gown that seemed to have been poured upon her perfect form, Lady Andover was the most beautiful woman Catherine had ever seen. Though not *au courant* with the latest modes, Miss Pelliston was sure that the countess's gown must be the first stare of fashion, the handiwork of the finest of *couturieres*.

Nearly blinded by her hostess's brilliance, Catherine grew agonizingly conscious of her own drab appearance. A guilty conscience, which in recent hours had developed all the vicious attributes of a swarm of outraged wasps, did not improve her poise. All she could manage was a nod.

"What sort of trouble?"

Though Lady Andover's voice was kindly enough, the suspicious glance she sent in her brother's direction brought two bright spots of color to Catherine's cheeks. Luckily, Miss Pelliston was spared from replying when Lord Rand favoured his sister with an answering scowl.

"You needn't look as though it were my doing, Louisa. Leastways, to start off with it wasn't." He wrenched himself away from the tempting array of decanters and took a seat by her ladyship.

He seemed, Catherine thought, suddenly very uncomfortable, though she could not be sure she wasn't investing him with her own feelings. She, after all, was fervently wishing she might melt quietly into the Aubusson carpet and thus be relieved of having her outrageous behaviour and its gruesome consequences called to this lady's attention.

"Then what have you done, Max?"

"Oh, please," Catherine interrupted. "Mr. — his lordship has been everything that is kind, and it is all my fault, really."

"It *ain't* your fault, and I can't think what bloody idiot's filled your head with that sort of nonsense that you've got to be beggin' everyone's pardon for doing what any woman in her right mind would do. Dash it, Louisa, you'd think it was the Dark Ages still in this curst country."

"I must admit that at present your subject is rather dark to me," his sister replied. "Perhaps Miss Pettigrew can be more enlightening."

Miss Pettigrew had thus far managed to endure any number of indignities without weeping. Now, at being accused of nonsensicality, she gave way. Her chest heaved, and the tears she struggled in vain to keep back made it rather difficult to understand the shameful words she blurted out.

"Ran away?" Lady Andover repeated, after her brother had translated. "I don't understand. Surely Miss Pettigrew is not an apprentice."

"Of course not. What are you thinking, Louisa?"

"If she is not a runaway apprentice, why does she weep? I shall have to consult Edgar, of course, but as I understand, it is runaway apprentices who are subject to legal action. It may be a fine or imprisonment —"

"She ran away from home because her father's making her marry some old dotard." Lord Rand went on to explain about the stolen reticule and the elopement of Miss Fletcher. Catherine was relieved to note (between sobs) that he tactfully left out certain other adventures and described the events as having occurred but a few hours ago.

When he'd finished his summary and answered one or two of his sister's questions, that lady directed her gaze to her guest, who had regained a semblance of composure.

"I see," said the countess. "Max has brought you here in order that I may enact the role of Cousin Agatha."

"Oh, no! I told him I meant to go home. That is —" Catherine's colour deepened, but she swallowed her pride and went on. "I'm afraid I will need the loan of a few shillings for coach fare."

"Now if that ain't the most cowardly thing —"

"Max," Lady Andover said quietly.

"But she can't —"

"If Miss Pettigrew wishes to return, I can hardly keep her prisoner, can I?"

"Dash it all, Louisa —"

The countess turned her back upon her brother. "All the same, Miss Pettigrew," she said, "you are too overset at present for travel. You will pardon my saying so, but your colour is not good. If I were to allow you to depart now, my conscience would plague me so, *I* would become ill."

"Really, I'm quite well," Catherine protested. "I've never had good colour."

"My conscience refuses to believe you. I do apologise, my dear, but mine is a very fierce conscience. Molly will convey you to a guest chamber and bring you a fresh cup of tea — you've scarcely touched yours and it is grown cold, I'm afraid." Lady Andover's tones became commanding. "Tonight you will remain here. We will reserve further discussion until tomorrow when you are rested."

"Might as well do as she says," Lord Rand suggested, taking his cue. "M' sister's got a stubborn conscience. No use arguing."

In other circumstances, no amount of cajolery or command would have kept Catherine in Andover House. She was still in London, and every step she'd taken since coming here had hurled her into disaster. She wanted only to flee.

She knew she should press harder for the small loan that would allow her to go home immediately without having to answer embarrassing questions. By the time she'd met Lady Andover, however, Catherine was on the brink of hysteria. Miss Fletcher's elopement had been the *coup de grace* of a series of stunning calamities. A clean, comfortable bed, a maid to look after her, and a hot cup of tea to consume in private was more temptation than Catherine could withstand.

She made the feeblest of protests, to which Lady Andover proved quite deaf. Moments later, Molly was leading the unexpected guest upstairs.

4

Now that his charge was in capable hands, Max was eager to get away. He was not permitted to do so. Fortunately, Lady Andover not only ordered him to remain where he was, but invited him to sample the contents of the alluring decanters. After filling a glass and taking a long swallow, Max ambled over to the fireplace and commenced a rapt contemplation of the marble.

His sister studied him for a few moments before she spoke. "Well, dear," she said, "this is a very interesting homecoming present you've brought me. Only I'd thought it would be you welcomed back with fatted calves and such — though she isn't very fatted, is she?"

"I didn't know what else to do with her, damn it. I could hardly send her off in a coach on her own, and I couldn't go with her — bound to cause trouble with her curst father."

"Who is she, Max? Not a schoolmistress, despite that quiz of a dress. Not your mistress either, I'll wager. Wild and unconventional as you like to appear, even you have your limits. Besides, if that girl ever had a depraved thought in her life, I'll eat my new bonnet."

"What a lot of strong opinions you've acquired, considering you hardly let her open her mouth."

"I observed." The countess settled herself comfortably upon the sofa. "I don't think you'd have brought her here if you had not sensed that she is — how shall I phrase it? Out of the common way? Not what she appears or wishes to appear? Her curtsey was quite elegant. Her manners are refined — though that is not at all unusual in a governess or teacher. However, since I did not perceive the usual submissive attitude of the class, I concluded that she was gently bred. I may be mistaken, of course. She may be a radical. That is not impossible, though most unlikely."

There was relief in the countenance Lord Rand turned to his sister. "Then I did the right thing?"

"Oh, Max, you never do the right thing. Only you would take up a stray female as though she were one of those abandoned kittens you were forever bringing me. This is a bit different, I'm afraid. One cannot banish her to the kitchen to make Cook's life a misery."

"Don't tell me you mean to send her back?"

"I never know what I mean until Edgar explains it to me, dear, and he will not be home until just before dinner. I confess I am curious why you're so set against her going back. You're not in love with Miss Pettigrew, are you?"

Her brother stared at her in horror. "Gad, Louisa — a scrawny little girl like that who sermons at the drop of a hat? You ain't heard her yet. I daresay she was overawed by your magnificence, but give her half a chance and she'll be preaching at you. It was all I could do to keep a straight face . . ." He trailed off, realising he could not very well repeat to his sister the lectures he'd heard in the brothel or his lodgings.

"Then what is it to you if she returns to marry this person her papa has selected for her?"

"It's against my principles, and I won't be a party to it, anymore than I was when the old man tried to shackle you to that birdwitted old troll. It's against her principles as well. I know, because she gave me scold on that too before she ever admitted it was her own trouble."

"Principles," her ladyship repeated. "I see. Still, I must consult with Edgar. If he feels we must return her to her family, we must."

"Now, Louisa —"

"Surely you don't doubt his judgement? Was it not Edgar persuaded Papa to allow you six months to finish sowing your wild oats? And was that not because Edgar convinced Papa that you are a far better horseman than Percy and therefore much less liable to get your neck broken in the interim? That Papa has not troubled you once in these six months is all Edgar's doing, I can assure you. Between answering Prinny's every petty summons and keeping Papa in temper, poor Edgar has had not a moment to himself."

"Don't try to make me feel guilty. Andover's only had to pamper the Old Man these six months. I'll be doing that and everything else from now on. I suppose he's got my bride picked out?"

"Actually, he's picked out half a dozen. Not, I'm sure, that you'll want any of them, as Papa well knows, but he does like to feel he's doing something, poor dear."

Max groaned. "Half a dozen. And the blasted house?"

"I've taken care of that. Not a trace of Percy. I'm sure you'll be pleased."

"Oh, I wasn't afraid he'd haunt the place, if that's what you mean. Old Percy hadn't the gumption. Wouldn't have gotten himself killed if he had. Curse him, that horse could have taken the stream."

"Yes, dear, and you'd told him often enough to put more trust in his beast. Poor Percy — he never had much spirit, did he? He should have been the younger son. He might have gone quietly into orders then, and Papa would have accepted it."

"And I'd still be in the same blasted predicament. Oh, well." His lordship finished his wine and deposited the glass on the mantel. "Might as well get used to it. I'll go see the Old Man later today. But if Edgar wants to send the girl back, you must promise to tell me straight away."

"Why?"

Lord Rand bent to kiss his sister's forehead. As he straightened he said, "Because I've half a mind to go back with her anyhow. Maybe I've a choice word or two for her papa."

Catherine fretted over her dilemma while she sipped her tea. By dinnertime her host and hostess would be sure to ask unnerving questions. What on earth could she tell them?

To run away from home and travel unchaperoned was enough to soil a young lady's reputation. To have spent one night in a brothel and in a bachelor's lodgings was utter ruin.

She would earn no credit for having managed to preserve her virtue. Appearances alone would make her an outcast, a disgrace to her family — unless, as Lord Rand had advised, no one learned of the matter. At present he was the only other person who did know. Since she was merely Miss Pettigrew to him, the Pelliston name was still unsullied. She had rather keep it that way. Her homecoming would be painful enough as it was.

Besides, if she admitted her true identity, Lord and Lady Andover would never let her return home unaccompanied, and Catherine did not intend to bring witnesses to the humiliating scene with which she was certain to be greeted, especially if Papa had been summoned home from his bridal trip. He had no self-control at all, and if he was drunk, as he was bound to be — oh, there was no point thinking about that. Papa was sure to carry on in the most mortifying way.

"There, Miss," said Molly, jolting Catherine from her unhappy reverie. "You just lie down now and have a nice long nap, and I won't bother you none 'til it comes close on dinnertime. I'll clean up your dress for you and press it," the abigail added, her gaze flickering disappointedly over the grey frock draped upon a chair. "You'll be fine as fivepence and all rested too."

"Oh, no. That is hardly appropriate for dinner," was the embarrassed response. "The peach muslin will do far better."

"Beg pardon, Miss, but there weren't no peach muslin I could find, and I unpacked everything you brought. Just a brown frock and underthings and such." The maid's round, rosy face plainly expressed her bafflement at this paltry wardrobe.

Catherine had been too agitated earlier in the day to take inventory of her belongings. Now, with a faint stirring of anger, she realised that the brothelkeeper must have stolen her one good gown.

"Oh, dear," she said quickly. "I packed in such haste that I must have forgotten it. How stupid of me. Yes, I suppose the grey frock will have to do."

Molly tiptoed from the room as Catherine crawled into bed. She did not expect to sleep, not with her mind churning so, but a few hours' rest would help her think more clearly, as she should have done two months ago.

She hadn't been able to think because the hot temper she'd inherited from her papa had made her wild and blind. Though she hadn't shown it, she'd become completely irrational, just as he always had, incapable of considering consequences. At the very least she should have prepared for every eventuality. She'd had weeks to reconsider, to at least think ahead.

No wonder Lord Rand thought her an ignorant young miss. Now he thought even less of her. He'd called her a coward and a non-sensical one at that, which was no surprise considering the disgusting display of weakness she'd provided him. Twice at least she'd wept in front of him — she who abhorred tears. Was not weeping maudlin self-indulgence when done privately and a bid for pity when done in public? Aunt Deborah burst into tears at every fancied slight, which enraged Papa and filled even Catherine with exasperation.

Lord Rand must have been mightily relieved to have her off his hands. The thought set off an inner flutter of pain, and her eyes began to sting. Oh, for heaven's sake! Of all the excellent reasons she had to weep, why must the mere thought of her rescuer be the one to set her off?

Firmly she banished Lord Rand's image from her mind to concentrate instead on her hostess. The Andover name was so familiar. Was the family connected to hers? That would hardly be surprising, when half England's, even Europe's, aristocracy was related to the other. Perhaps, though, the earl's family had simply been the topic of one of Great-Aunt Eustacia's rambling dissertations on genealogy. The old lady knew her Debrett's as intimately as she knew her Bible. As Catherine recalled the long monologues in those dim, cluttered rooms, exhaustion crept over her.

Genealogy. "Hadn't time to discuss genealogy," he'd told his sister in that abrupt way of his. Actually, it was rather funny, in the circumstances.

What an odd man he was, Catherine thought vaguely as her eyelids grew too heavy to keep open. Lost, of course, with his drinking and wenching, like Papa, but young . . . and handsome . . . and so strong. He'd lifted her up as easily as if she'd been one of her bandboxes.

He must have been shocked, when he had sobered himself, to realise what he'd brought home with him. Perhaps that would teach him to exercise moderation in future. With this pious thought, Catherine drifted off to sleep.

"Now who in blazes are you?" Lord Rand demanded, surveying the small, slim man before him.

His lordship had already had two nasty surprises. The first was a butler even taller than himself, whose accents hinted an intimate acquaintance with the bells of St. Mary Le Bow: a Cockney butler named Gidgeon, of all things. The second was a chef who spoke not a word of English, thereby forcing Lord Rand to rake the recesses of his mind for the French he'd determined to bury there forever along with Greek and Latin.

In front of him at present stood a mournful

creature who'd been dogging the viscount's footsteps all the way down the long hall.

"Hill, My Lord," said the little man sadly.

"Hill," Lord Rand repeated. "And what do *you* do?"

"Your secretary, My Lord."

"What the devil do I want a secretary for? Ain't there enough here as it is? The bloody place is crawling with servants. I'll wager there ain't been such a crowd in one place since Prinny married that fat cousin of his."

"Yes, My Lord. A tragic business, that," Hill gloomily agreed.

"You don't know the half of it," his lordship grumbled. "Well, what is it you do, exactly?"

"Her ladyship — Lady Andover, that is — indicated that you required assistance in managing your paperwork, My Lord. Now that you are in residence there will be a daily supply of invitations requiring responses."

"I ain't going to any of those fusty affairs."

"Very good, My Lord. You are aware, I trust, that you are engaged to dine this evening with Lord and Lady St. Denys?"

"Tonight? Already? Plague take him. The Old Man don't give me a minute to catch my breath. How the devil did he know I was back?"

"It is a regrettable fact, My Lord, that servants' gossip travels at an alarming rate," said Mr. Hill in dismal tones. "His lordship's summons arrived an hour ago. I am afraid the invitation is indeed for this evening."

"Of course it is. They can't wait to clap the irons on me." The viscount muttered something unintelligible, then said more distinctly, "Very well. Might as well get it over with."

Considering the matter closed, he was about to continue on his way, but the secretary seemed to be in melancholy expectation of something more.

"Is that all?" the master asked impatiently.

"Her ladyship also mentioned that there would be numerous matters claiming your attention, though scarcely worthy of it. She indicated that I was, insofar as possible, to relieve you of the more trivial."

Lord Rand sighed. "Such as?"

"Your valet, My Lord."

"Don't want a valet. Can't stand someone poking about my things."

"Quite so, My Lord. Therefore I have screened the applicants in advance and reduced their number to three, in hopes of sparing you some trouble in seeking one worthy of your employ."

"Didn't I just tell you I don't want a valet?"

"Yes, indeed, My Lord. So I will explain to the man you select."

"I don't want to select anybody, damn it.

I can dress myself. I ain't a baby."

"Very good, My Lord." The secretary stared dolefully at his master's scuffed boots. "I suppose, then, one of the lower servants will attend to your footwear? In that case, I will ask Mr. Gidgeon whether such a person might be spared from the present staff."

Lord Rand fought back a wild urge to bash either his own or his secretary's head against the door frame. "Where are these prodigies? I suppose they are here or you wouldn't be badgering me about it."

"In the hall outside your lordship's study. If you will be so kind as to ring when you're prepared, I shall send the first candidate in."

"No," snapped the employer as he stormed down the hall. "I'll see 'em all at once."

Half an hour later, the disagreeable task was done, the viscount having quickly settled on the one candidate whose serene countenance promised intermittent relief from the lugubrious Hill. Lord Rand was further heartened some hours later when Blackwood (for such was the name of this gentleman's gentleman), having accompanied his master to the latter's private chambers, volunteered the information that he'd recently been invalided home.

"A soldier," said Lord Rand, breaking into

a smile for the first time since he'd entered the house. "Where?"

"Peninsula, My Lord. I caught a ball in my leg, and being of no further military use, had to take up my old work."

So it happened that amid the exchange of stories, the one talking of the Old World and the other of the New, Lord Rand forgot most of his objections to having someone poking about his belongings and gave utterance to only one mild oath when the valet laid out dinner clothes.

"Confound it," his lordship muttered. "I'd almost forgotten the kind of rigout I'd be stuffed into for dinner. With the Old Man, no less. You could stand a regiment on his neck-cloth and the blasted thing wouldn't so much as crease. Wouldn't dare."

"Likes everything in order, does he, My Lord?" the valet asked as he gathered up his employer's scattered belongings.

"And can't for the life of him figure out how he sired such a disorderly brute of a son."

"If you'll pardon my free speech, My Lord, I must disagree with that assessment. It's a pleasure to a man of simple tastes like myself to attend to a gentleman who wants neither padding nor corsets nor any sort of artifice to look as he should."

5

That he looked as he should, and better than he had ever done in his life before, was of small comfort to the Viscount Rand some time later when he endured his mother's effusive welcome and his father's frigid greeting.

Lord Rand's neck-cloth began to grow rather snug, in fact, as the dinner conversation turned to his domestic responsibilities and, in particular, his need for a wife.

"Lady Julia is very sweet," his mother told him. "Raleforth's youngest girl, you know."

"Simpers," said Lord St. Denys.

"Miss Millbanke does not simper, Frederick. Very clever, too, they say."

"Blue-stocking. Worse, she's a prig. From what I hear, the family wants to shackle her to that one with the bad foot that fancies himself a poet."

Lord Rand fought down his annoyance, though he could not keep the challenge from his tone when he spoke. "I daresay, m'lord, you've someone particular in mind."

"No," the earl replied without looking up from his plate.

"No?" the son echoed in some astonishment.

"But Frederick, what about Miss —?"

"No," the earl repeated. "It's none of our affair, Letitia. The lad is perfectly capable of finding his own wife."

"Why, yes, of course," Lady St. Denys agreed as she turned apologetically to her son. "I never meant to imply, dear, that you were not. Only — that you go about so little in Society —"

"Doesn't go about at all," her husband interrupted.

"Why, yes, dear, and that is just the point. If he does not go about in Society, how is he to find a suitable girl?"

"Perhaps, Mother, I ought to advertise, and ask my secretary to screen the applicants for the position. Worked well enough for finding a valet."

"Oh, Max," the countess gasped.

"Got a valet, have you? I thought you appeared more presentable than usual."

"But, Frederick, he can hardly advertise for a wife as one does for a servant. What would people think?"

"How should I know? None of our set's ever done it before."

"Oh, Frederick, I believe you're roasting

me. And you too, Max. You wicked creatures." The countess smiled indulgently and returned her attention to her dinner.

Baffled by his father's uncharacteristic behaviour, the viscount had trouble concentrating on his meal. Never in Max Demowery's twenty-eight years had his parent shown any confidence whatsoever in his younger son's judgement.

The father had the same tall, strong Demowery physique. However, his features were haughtier, more aquiline and forbidding, and maturity had added distinguished grey to his thick hair. That and the extra stone or so of girth made him a formidable figure — one, in fact, of a man accustomed to command. The Earl of St. Denys was indeed so accustomed, having inherited his title at a very early age. His voice rang out in the Lords as he enumerated with sonorous regularity his colleagues' errors. That same voice resounded with equal force through his household. The Old Man, Max often complained, had never noticed that his children had graduated from leading strings.

Lord St. Denys had not permitted his eldest son to take orders, though that was what Percy wanted and what everyone knew him best fitted for. The earl had also tried to choose his daughter's husband. Fortunately, unlike

Percy, Louisa had not inherited her mother's meekness. She'd refused. Threatened with being locked in her room until she could work herself into a compliant frame of mind, she bolted, dragging a reluctant abigail with her, to take refuge with the one human being her papa could not command — his formidable Cousin Agatha.

In this Louisa had followed the example of her younger brother, who'd been running away from everyone and everything since his little legs were strong enough to carry him. Max had run away from home innumerable times. At the age of ten he'd fled Eton and would certainly have found other ways to make himself unwelcome there after being dragged back had not a young, perceptive master taken the restless boy under his wing and found work to challenge him.

Max had managed his Oxford career with a few scrapes, but without disgrace. Immediately upon quitting that institution he'd enlisted under a false name as a common soldier. The earl had eventually tracked him down and gotten him discharged. Less than a year later, Max smuggled himself on board a ship bound for the New World.

There he'd have contentedly remained had Percy not met with the riding accident. Rebellious as Max was, even he was no match for the claims of eight centuries of Demowerys. Even he could not ignore this one great duty, especially after the earl had effectively sundered the one tie that might have kept his new heir in that raw, wild, young country. The place had suited Max. It appealed to his restless nature, his impatience with convention. He had learned there that he could make his own way. He could achieve success without depending upon either his social station or his father's largess.

Max returned from his sojourn in the wilderness with a fortune of his own. That was some consolation for having to embark upon a life he'd always detested among people whose narrow-mindedness, rigid rules of behaviour, and arrant hypocrisy made him seethe with frustration. He might have to accept the responsibilities of an heir, but at least he need not beg his managing father for money. He owed the earl nothing.

So the heir had meant to assert as soon as Lord St. Denys embarked upon the hated topic of marriage and producing heirs — several, preferably. After all, as Percy's accident had demonstrated, a nobleman could never be certain he wouldn't require spares.

Now the viscount felt the wind had been taken out of his sails. He'd looked forward to another blowup with his father. The heir's townhouse, with its army of servants and its spotless, tasteful furnishings, had seemed so cool and proper and polite that it suffocated him. The prospect of living there as the lone master oppressed his spirits.

In the past when he'd felt stifled, he'd always run away. Since he couldn't do that now, he wanted to take out his frustration on the Old Man. Lord Rand wanted, as well, distraction from the odd female whose eyes and voice persistently intruded upon his thoughts. A quarrel about the future viscountess was just the thing — only it seemed he was to be forestalled in that too.

Refusing to give up hope altogether, the viscount raised the subject again after his mother had left the two men to their port.

"I confess I'm puzzled, My Lord. Louisa told me today that you had half a dozen suitable brides picked out for me — but just a while ago you claimed you hadn't any."

"Oh, I do," said the earl. "Five, actually."

Max's blue eyes gleamed, and he felt a rush of exaltation as the old animosity blazed up within him.

"Only five?"

"Yes, but I'm not going to tell you who they are."

The son put down the glass he'd just raised to his lips. "I beg your pardon?"

"I said I won't tell you. What sort of fool do you take me for? As soon as I breathe a young woman's name you'll take her in dislike, sight unseen, simply because *I* suggested it. No, as I see it, the only way my opinions stand a chance is to keep them to myself."

"Do you mean to say that you think I'll approve one of these five?"

"I'm not saying anything, as I just told you. It's your affair, and if I come poking in with my opinions, you're bound to go contrary on me, as you always do, Max. Since the day you were born, I think."

Lord St. Denys took an appreciative sip from his refilled glass. "Still, you're no longer a child, as my son-in-law has pointed out repeatedly," he went on while absently turning the goblet in his hands. "Edgar claimed you'd be back at the end of your six months, ready to do your duty. So you are, punctual to the minute. I have no doubt you'll do your duty in the matter of finding a bride. More than that a parent has no right to ask."

Had Lord Rand not been staring perplexedly into his own glass, he might have caught the suspicious twinkle that lit his father's eyes. As it was, the viscount was aware only of a surging frustration — and a resultant need to find some topic on which the two might loudly disagree.

"Except, I suppose, that I do this duty at the earliest opportunity," the son suggested.

"Whenever," was the provoking answer. "Plenty of time, plenty of fish in the sea. If you never do get around to it before you reach your dotage, there's always your Cousin Roland. Serena — his wife, you know — just produced their fifth, I hear. No danger of the title dying with you."

Max ground his teeth. He detested his sanctimonious Cousin Roland and suspected his father did as well. The idea of Roland or one of his puling brats becoming Earl of St. Denys was more than one could stomach, even if one didn't give a damn about titles and thought the whole business of primogeniture a poisonous carryover from barbaric times and the aristocracy itself a cancer on the body politic.

"I thought you'd rather see the line die out than have it carried on by Roland and that stupid cow he married," he could not help reminding.

"Won't matter to me, will it, when I'm six feet beneath the earth?"

This altogether unsatisfactory conversation ended shortly thereafter when the gentlemen rose to join Lady St. Denys in the drawing-room.

Consequently, as soon as he'd taken leave of his parents, Lord Rand marched himself directly to White's, confident that he would be denied entrance to that bastion of Torydom and might, in response, instigate a riot in St. James's.

Lord Rand had reckoned without Mr. George Brummell. That gentleman, upon learning of a brewing altercation upon the club's outer steps, and finding himself holding a singularly poor hand, put down his cards and strolled to his usual place at the famous Bow Window to join his colleagues in watching the scene.

"Who is that tall, noble-looking fellow?" he enquired of his neighbour.

"Wh-why — L-Lord Rand, sir," stammered Sir Matthew Melbrook, his poise knocked to pieces at being addressed by the Great Beau. "A r-radical — and a great r-ruffian."

"Ah, yes. Viscount Vagabond. His neck-cloth is a work of art," said Society's arbiter of fashion. He turned away and sauntered back to the card table.

In less than a minute his pronouncement had made its way out to St. James's Street. A gentleman who'd been endeavouring to lay his hands upon that same neck-cloth — apparently intending to throttle his adversary with it — backed away, and Lord Rand, to his astonishment, was invited to enter the club.

"I ain't a member," he challenged loudly as he stomped inside.

"'Fraid you are," drawled Lord Alvanley while he surveyed the newcomer with appreciative amusement. "Have been this twelvemonth. Andover sponsored you and the decision was unanimous. Apparently some of our lads forgot that small matter. I would have spoken up sooner myself, but I hated to spoil the entertainment you were so kind to offer us."

"Confound it," the viscount complained as Lord Alvanley ambled away. "Has everyone in Town taken leave of his senses?"

"If you mean the warm welcome," came a voice behind him, "it must be they suddenly remembered what a dull old stick Percy was. Either that or the fact that Brummell admired your cravat." The voice's owner, a good-looking young man with dreamy grey eyes and rumpled brown hair, moved to Lord Rand's side. "Don't you remember me, Max? Langdon. We were at Oxford together."

"So we were, Jack," said the viscount, a smile finally breaking through his clouded countenance. "Only how was I to know you without a book in front of your nose? Damme if I didn't think they grew there."

"Oh, these suspicious fellows won't let me read when we're at cards. They claim I keep a spare deck between the pages. But come. As your brother-in-law isn't here to do the honours, let me introduce you around."

His humour partially restored by the presence of his old school chum, Max submitted with good grace. Whatever remained of his rage soon evaporated in the convivial atmosphere of gambling, drinking, and increasingly raucous conversation as the night wore on. So convivial was the company that Lord Rand had to be carried out to a hackney shortly before dawn, from which vehicle he was removed by a brace of footmen, who carried him to his bedroom. There Blackwood succeeded to the honours of attending to his happily unconscious lordship.

While Lord Rand had been trying to ascertain whether an alien spirit had taken possession of his father's body, Miss Pelliston had been having an equally baffling evening with her host and hostess. Catherine had expected an interrogation. When that did not occur during a dinner she was far too agitated to eat, she anxiously awaited it later, when Lord Andover, after a quarter hour alone with his port, rejoined his wife and guest.

No attempt was made, however, to ascertain just what exactly this odd young woman was doing in the Earl of Andover's noble townhouse. Catherine was sure her pristinely elegant host must think her odd, given the occasional pained glance he dropped upon her grey frock.

Whatever he thought, he was scrupulously polite and thoroughly charming. Conversation through dinner focused on politics, and after dinner on books, the earl having quickly discerned his guest's keen appetite for literature.

While she inwardly cursed her cowardice, Catherine could not bring herself to open the subject so courteously ignored, though she did wince every time her host addressed her as "Miss Pettigrew."

It must be as the countess had said, Catherine told herself later, while Molly brushed her hair. The matter was reserved for discussion on the morrow. She did wish she might have some peace and quiet in the meantime, so that she could decide at last what to do. Unfortunately, Molly talked incessantly from the time she entered the bedchamber until the time she left.

The abigail's main subject was Lord Rand, with whom she unblushingly admitted she was infatuated.

"Not but what I knows, of course, that he'd never notice me — or should, either. Still, a cat may look at a king," she paraphrased in response to Catherine's startled expression.

"Once when her ladyship took me with her to a picture gallery I fell in love with a picture of a foreign gent what had on no clothes to speak of, just a bit of cloth. And so long as he was only paint on a bit of cloth himself there's no harm in it. Same with him — My Lord Rand, I mean — like a great handsome statue, because *he* wouldn't be pinching a girl, either, no more than the statue would. Not like some I could mention, who if you so much as smile the least bit they grows another dozen hands all at once, I declare."

Catherine's attempts to distract Molly from discussion of the roving hands of males of all classes only led to further enlightenment about the idol. He had not returned to England, according to Molly, until eighteen months after his brother's death.

"It weren't so long a voyage as all that, Miss, either, but that he didn't want to come back on any account, as he already had a sweetheart there and was planning to marry her and stay there forever, living among the wild Indians."

"I collect," Catherine faintly responded, "the lady changed her mind."

"Say Lord St. Denys changed it for her, rather. Mum's been with Lady St. Denys since afore her ladyship married and she was at the house when Mr. Max come back. Mum said he was arguing so loud with his papa you could hear it down at the stables. She says everyone in the house heard him yelling that his papa had sent the girl money to break it off. Not but it wasn't the right thing, you know, her being a nobody and a foreigner at that. Mr. Max — his lordship, I mean — couldn't hardly bring back some poor farmer girl and take her to meet the Queen, now could he?"

From what Miss Pelliston knew of his lordship, she was convinced that he could very well introduce a farmer's daughter at court — and in pattens, no less. Had he not introduced to the Countess of Andover a girl he'd found in a brothel?

"I suppose that would be rather awkward," said Catherine. "Especially when our two nations are at war."

Molly, who knew nothing of international politics and who believed the United States was located somewhere in China or Africa, wisely ignored this remark.

"Anyhow, I know he never did get over it," she went on. "He hasn't spoke a word to Lord St. Denys six months now — nor anyone else, either. Until today, that is. Why, you could have knocked me over with a feather when I come into the drawing-room and seen him sitting there, chatting with her ladyship just as easy as if he'd been here every day, and her ladyship no more amazed than if he had been."

Having doggedly brushed Catherine's hair the required two hundred strokes — Catherine had kept count as a means of steadying her nerves — the abigail stood back to admire the results. "What splendid hair you have, Miss. I declare when I first saw it I was sure I was in for a long night of it — curly hair do tangle so — but yours is soft as a baby's. Such a handsome colour too. There's folks'd pay a pretty penny for it."

Miss Pelliston had been contemplating, in spite of herself, Lord Rand's tribulations. Now she came abruptly to attention. "Pay?" she asked. "Not money, surely? Or did you simply mean that some would be envious?"

"Brown hair is common enough, but not light and soft and curly as yours. Oh, I'd expect plenty would like to have it, Miss."

"You mean for wigs? But surely those have been out of fashion for years."

"That don't mean a hairpiece don't come in handy for some folks. Monsoor Franzwuz, what does her ladyship's hair, could tell you stories about that. Nor I don't mean *her*," the maid hastily explained. "Every bit of what's on her head is her own, and no curlpapers, neither. Now then, Miss, shall I bring you a nice warm cup of milk?"

This Catherine politely declined.

"Really, I think you should, Miss. Tom says you never touched your dinner hardly and if you'll pardon my saying so, you'll be all hair and eyes if you keep on at this rate."

Touched by this concern, Catherine acquiesced, though when the milk arrived she found it difficult to swallow enough to satisfy the well-meaning abigail. Miss Pelliston was too excited about the alternative that had suddenly presented itself to care about nourishment, and the prospect of becoming all hair and eyes did not alarm her in the least.

"Well, Edgar," said the countess as her husband settled himself among the pillows and took his book from the nightstand, "what do you recommend we do about her?"

"Burn that dress," he replied. "It frightened me out of my wits. And do something about her hair. That knot is a crime against nature."

"Then you believe we should take her in?"

"Have to," said his lordship as he opened his book. "Pelliston's chit."

Her ladyship, who'd also snuggled comfortably against her pillows, bolted upright. "What? Who?"

"How many times have I told you, Louisa, not to make sudden movements? You've made me lose my place."

"Stop teasing, you wretched man. Are you

telling me you know her?"

"Not personally. I believe her mama was my mother's second or third cousin." He returned his attention to the Bard.

"Edgar!"

"Yes, my precious?"

Lady Andover jerked the book from her husband's hands. "If you do not explain this instant, I shall tear the curst thing to pieces."

The earl breathed a sigh. "Ten years, and I have never been able to teach you patience. Still, what's a mere decade to centuries of impatient Demowerys? I see you intend to beat me over the head with poor Will's work if I cannot satisfy your all-consuming curiosity." He gazed sadly at the bedclothes.

"Well, then?"

"I met her some months before that blissful day when we two were united —"

"Edgar!"

"Ten years ago. Our families have never been close, but Pelliston is known for his hounds and I meant to make a gift of a pair to your papa."

"And you recognised her after all these years?"

"She closely resembles her mama, especially in the eyes — most unusual, very like Eleanor's."

"No wonder you never questioned her. I

expected to see you work your subtle arts upon her, extracting information without her ever realising. Still, I'm surprised she didn't recognise you," the countess added fondly as she admired her husband's wavy black hair and classically sculpted features.

"Her father had a crowd of his cronies rampaging about the place. To her I think we were all one noisy, unwanted crowd. Besides, she kept her eyes on her papa. I found her intriguing. She behaved as she did tonight, stiffly proper and courteous, but with that wild, pent-up look in her eyes. I was waiting for her to explode. She never did, though her papa was provoking enough."

"Apparently, he has provoked her at last."

"Yes. I'm not surprised he wants to marry her to one of his loutish friends, if his behaviour that day was typical. Still, I know little enough about them. In fact, it's only because my dear mama pointed out Pelliston's wedding announcement in the paper that I made the connection. He and his doings were already in my mind when I met the girl tonight."

"If her papa is the ogre he sounds, I can understand the false name," said Louisa, "but then why is she so adamant about returning home?"

"We needn't understand everything this minute. Tomorrow you can tactfully explain that we know all. I'll write her father."

"To say what?"

"Why, that you wish to bring my cousin out. Since fate — or your brother, actually — has dropped her upon our doorstep, we might as well keep her. I am not blind, Louisa. You are itching to get your hands on the girl. Potential there, you think?"

"Oh, yes. How convenient that she's a relation, however distant. My motives will seem of the purest. How considerate of Max, don't you think, darling?"

6

Lord Rand eyed with distaste the murky liquid in the glass his valet offered him. "What's that filthy mess? You don't mean me to drink it?"

"I highly recommend it, My Lord. Guaranteed to eliminate the aftereffects."

Either the aftereffects or the cure would kill him, the viscount was certain. He groped for the glass, brought it to his lips, held his nose, and drank.

"Ugh," he croaked. "That's the vilest-tasting stuff I ever swallowed in my life."

"Yes, My Lord, I'm afraid so. However, I thought you would require a prompt-acting restorative, as the Countess of Andover has sent a message requesting your immediate attendance."

"She can go to blazes," his lordship groaned, sinking back onto his pillow.

"She sent this," the valet said, holding up a note.

Lord Rand shut his eyes. "Tell me what it says."

Blackwood unfolded the sheet of paper and read aloud: "'The cat has bolted. Please come at once.'"

The viscount let loose a stream of colourful oaths while his valet busied himself with arranging shaving materials.

"Yes, indeed, sir," Blackwood agreed, when his master stopped to catch his breath. "Your bath is ready, and I have laid out the brown coat and fawn pantaloons."

Not long after, Lord Rand stormed unannounced into the breakfast room of Andover House, where the earl and countess sat, their heads bent close together as they perused what appeared to be a very long epistle.

"There you are, Max," Lord Andover said, looking up with a faint frown. "Seems our guest has fled. Apparently," he went on calmly, oblivious to the thunderclouds gathering upon his brother-in-law's brow, "she slipped out shortly after Jeffers unlocked the doors — before the rest of the household was up."

"Then why the devil ain't you out looking for her?"

"Because we were waiting for you," Lady Andover answered. "Edgar has already dispatched nearly all the menservants to comb the streets, so there is no need to stand there scowling. Do sit down, Max. Perhaps you can help. We were rereading her note in hopes of discovering some clue as to where she's gone."

Lord Rand snatched up the letter and read it. "Oh, the bloody little fool," he muttered when he'd finished.

"I do wish you'd speak more respectfully of my relations," said the earl. "'Poor, misguided creature' would be rather more like it, I should think."

"Relations? What the devil are you talking about?"

"My cousin — at least I believe she is the daughter of my mama's second or third cousin — but you will have to ask Mama about that. By the time it gets to second cousins and times removed I lose all ability to concentrate."

Lord Rand sat down abruptly.

"Her name," said Louisa, "is Catherine Pelliston — not Pettigrew. Her papa, according to Edgar, is the Baron Pelliston of Wilberstone."

"Why that deceitful little b —"

"If you persist in insulting my cousin, Max, I shall be forced to call you out, and that will be a great pity, as you are the better shot and Louisa has grown rather accustomed to me, I think."

"Your cousin can go to the devil," Lord Rand retorted. "How dare she pretend to be a poor little schoolmistress, playing me for a fool —"

"As easily as you pretended to be some low-born lout, I suppose," his sister interrupted.

"Perhaps," said the earl, "she suspected that you might hold her for ransom if she admitted her identity. You did not, I understand, admit yours, and Pelliston's rich as Croesus. At any rate, I was intending to question Molly as soon as she recovered from her hysterics. Care to join me, Max?"

Lord Rand maintained crossly that he didn't give a damn what became of a spoiled debutante and an ingrate at that, not to mention she was an ignorant little prig. His brother-in-law took no heed of these or any of the other contradictory animadversions which followed regarding the young lady's character, motives, and eventual dismal and well-deserved end. When the viscount had finished raving, Lord Andover merely nodded politely, then rose and left the room. Grumbling, Lord Rand followed him.

The Viscount Rand was too restless a man to be much given to introspection. All the same he was not stupid, as his Eton master or Oxford tutors would have, though some of them grudgingly, admitted. He was therefore vaguely aware that his invectives upon Miss Pelliston were a tad irrational.

Although she'd had no reason to trust him with her true identity — just as Edgar said — Lord Rand felt she'd betrayed him somehow, which was very odd. His chosen course of life had resulted in what he called "a tough hide." Even Jenny's defection had not penetrated his cynical armor — he was too used to having careers and friends bought off by his interfering father. He'd had a wonderful row with the Old Man about it, of course, but inwardly he'd felt nothing more than a twinge of disappointment in his American friend.

Though he told himself he had far less reason to be disturbed about Miss Pelliston, the viscount was disturbed all the same. He was worried about her — she was far too naive — and he hated being worried, so he was furious with her.

Unfortunately for his temper, Molly was worse than useless. When asked about her conversations with the young houseguest, the loquacious abigail became mute. She was not about to admit having discussed Lord Rand's private life in vivid detail, and was so conscious of her indiscretion in doing so that she could remember nothing else she'd said.

"She gave no hint of her intentions?" the earl asked patiently. "Did she seem distraught or frightened?"

"Oh, no," said Molly. "She didn't say much of anything. Shy-like, My Lord. Even when I admired her hair she acted like she didn't believe me, poor thing," the abigail added as tears welled up in her eyes. "It weren't no flattery, either. Curly and soft it was, like a baby's, and as easy to brush as if it was silk."

"You needn't carry on as if she was dead," Max snapped, agitated anew by the tears streaming down the maid's round, rosy cheeks.

The earl quickly intervened. "Very well, Molly. Thank you," he said, patting the girl's shoulder. "Now do go wash your face and compose yourself. You will not wish to distress her ladyship, I am sure."

Molly dutifully wiped her eyes with her apron and, without daring another peek at her idol, curtsied and hurried from the study.

"That," said Lord Rand, "was a complete waste of time. I'm going to the coaching inns."

"She can't board a coach without money, Max."

"I know that and you know that, but she's just ignorant enough to throw herself on the mercy of the coachmen. The little idiot trusts everyone."

With that, he stomped out.

The little idiot was at the moment trying

to understand how she'd lost her way twenty times in one morning. A milliner had given her clear directions to Monsieur Francois's establishment. At least they'd seemed clear at the time. The trouble was, there were so many turns, so many lanes and ways and roads and streets bearing similar names, and so many other people contradicting each previous set of instructions that by now she had no idea whether she was any closer to her destination than when she'd started.

Catherine was tired, hungry, and miserable, and wished she could sit down — but a lady could not plunk herself down upon a cobbler's doorstep. She had been able to reduce her luggage to one bandbox, thanks to the stolen peach muslin and a few other missing items. Now she transferred the box to her other hand and tried to straighten her stiff shoulders.

"Got a penny, Miss?" a childish voice enquired from behind her.

She looked around. A very untidy boy was studying her gravely.

"No," she said. "Not a farthing."

The boy shrugged and turned to a nearby lamppost, which he gave a savage kick.

"I don't suppose," Catherine said, "you know where Monsieur Francois's shop is?"

"I don't know nuffink." He scowled and kicked the lamppost again.

"Don't know anything," Catherine corrected automatically, half to herself. "Is there anyone in this wretched city who can speak without murdering the King's English?" Dispirited, she stared about her. Where on earth was the horrid hairdresser's shop?

The urchin followed her gaze. "You ain't batty, 'er you?"

Catherine met his scrutiny and sighed. "Not yet, though it is likely I will soon descend to that state. No one," she went on wearily, "knows anything. Or if they do, they will only vouchsafe the information in the most esoteric formula possible. Or else they may as well be speaking Turkish for all one can comprehend of their dialects and cant."

The urchin nodded wisely, though Catherine was certain that her words had been Turkish to him. "I thought you wuz batty on account of you wuz talkin' to yourself. SHE talks to herself. Only SHE says it's on account of Aggeration."

"I hope that is not your mother to whom you refer so disrespectfully," she said.

"Me mum's dead."

"Oh, dear, I am so sorry."

"I ain't sorry," was the shocking response. "Beat me sumfin' fierce she did — when she could cotch me."

"Good heavens!"

"Well, she don't any more, as 'at Blue Ruin killed her."

"Oh, my! And have you no papa?"

"No. Only HER."

This odd conversation was bringing her no nearer her destination. There was nothing for it but to continue walking. Catherine turned the corner. To her surprise, the boy followed. Evidently, having begun to talk, he had no inclination to leave off, but chattered amiably as he accompanied her down the street.

SHE, it turned out, was Missus, who kept a shop where she made clothes for the gentry. This morning, according to the boy, Missus was in a state of Aggeration on account of someone named Annie.

Since Missus was not a hairdresser, she was certainly not going to be any help. Catherine's throat began to ache. She would very much like to sit down on the curb and cry her heart out. It must be past noon by now. If she didn't make her transaction soon, she'd miss the coach that could take her home before dark.

"Are you sure you don't know where Monsieur Francois's shop is?" she asked in desperation. "A hairdresser? I was told he would buy my hair — and I do need the money."

The boy frowned as he studied her drab bonnet. "Oh, you mean 'at wig man. Won't do you no good. Gone to do a wedding. I got" — he bent to stick one grimy finger into a shoe a full size too large for his foot — "tuppence. What SHE give me to go away and not Aggerate her. We could get a meat pie."

Catherine needed a moment to understand that the scruffy child was offering to share his worldly wealth with her. When she did grasp his import, she was touched almost to tears. "Oh, dear, how very generous of you, but one pie will scarcely feed a strong, growing boy like yourself."

"Oh, SHE'll give me suffink arter she's done Aggeratin' herself. I knows a place," he added with a conspiratorial wink that required the cooperation of all the muscles of his face and made him look like a goblin. "Pies as big as my head. Come along," the urchin said impatiently, as his invited guest hesitated. "Ain't you hungry?"

Catherine was very hungry and she could not remember when she had ever felt so desolate. She gazed down at the round face and smiled ruefully.

"Yes," she said. "I am very hungry."

The boy nodded, satisfied, then took her by the hand to lead her to the establishment where one might find a meat pie as big as his head.

While they ate he grew more confiding. He

introduced himself as Jemmy, and explained that Missus had taken him in after his mother's death — the *modiste* being, Catherine guessed, a charitable soul who had some employment for the child which might keep him from the rookeries and flash houses with which he appeared to be appallingly familiar.

Jemmy ran his mistress's errands and swept the floors, but was primarily left to educate and amuse himself, which he did by wandering about the city streets.

Even as she wondered at this unchildlike existence, Catherine found herself confiding her own tale, reduced to the essentials of stolen reticule and absent friend.

At this the lad shook his head and looked as wise as it is possible for a boy of eight or nine years to do. He told her that she must be a "green 'un" not to keep better watch on her belongings.

"Yes," Catherine ruefully agreed. "I fear I am very green indeed."

"Why, 'em knucklers and buzmen ken fence a handkercher easier wot you ken wipe yer nose. Wonder is you still got yer box 'n' all."

Catherine glanced at the bandbox beside her and considered. If a handkerchief was of such value to these persons Jemmy spoke of, surely she must have something she could pawn for her coach fare. While she meditated, she could not help but note the longing with which her young host eyed a large fruit pastry being served to a fat gentleman at the next table.

She opened the bandbox and rummaged in it. "I wonder, Jemmy," she said finally, holding up a peach-coloured ribbon, "whether this would buy us one of those pastries."

The boy's eyes widened. "Oh, I'd say, Miss —" Then he subdued himself. "But you hadn't orter."

"Oh, yes I ought. You take this ribbon to your cook friend and ask if she will accept it in trade."

The boy dashed off with his treasure to the shop's owner, whereupon a discussion ensued, nothing of which Catherine could hear over the loud voices and clatter about her. When she saw the cook look questioningly at her, Miss Pelliston responded with a smile and a nod. The cook shrugged, turned away briefly, then presented Jemmy with a plate upon which reposed two plump, mouthwatering fruit tarts.

"She says," Jemmy explained as he deposited the feast upon the rough table, "as she'll only hold it some 'til you can pay her."

Jemmy's companion tasted only a bit of her dessert before declaring she was too full to enjoy it. She insisted that he not let it go to waste. As he disposed of her portion,

106

Jemmy's round face grew thoughtful.

Catherine waited until he was done before asking if he would direct her to the nearest pawnshop.

"What for?" he demanded.

"I need money," she bluntly explained. "That seems to be the only way left to get some."

Unfortunately, Jemmy didn't know nuffink about pawnshops, except perhaps those around Petticoat Lane, an area he was quick to explain was no place for green females. He volunteered instead to take his new acquaintance to Missus, who could answer her questions better than he could.

Missus's Aggerations must have dissipated somewhat, because when Jemmy returned to the shop he was clasped in a welcoming hug, then grasped by the shoulders and shaken affectionately as the plump *modiste* demanded to know what mischief he'd been up to, worrying her sick all this time. Only after she had done scolding the boy and telling him what a naughty little wretch he was did she take notice of the young woman in the dowdy grey frock who stood by the door.

As Catherine stepped forward to introduce herself and make her enquiry regarding pawnshops, she was startled to hear Jemmy announce, "I told her as how Annie took a fever and you wanted a girl and she wants a job, and so I brung her."

7

Missus, it turned out, was Madame Germaine, a woman of strong sentiments and changeable mood. Though her temperament might be considered Gallic, her only claim to the nationality was her late husband's name. Madame was no more French than Miss Pelliston — less, in fact, for the former's ancestors had not entered England with the Conqueror.

The *modiste* wanted but a moment to study Catherine's pale, thin face before her susceptible heart softened. This was hardly surprising in a woman who had taken in a budding delinquent the instant she'd learned of his plight from a beadle's wife.

Still, Madame would never have achieved her current prosperity if she had not been an astute businesswoman. She discerned at once that the despised grey frock was extremely well cut, neatly sewn, and altogether modestly becoming in a respectable working woman. That she wanted desperately to see a respectable working woman may have urged the dressmaker to her speedy resolution. Whatever the cause, she led Catherine to her office, plied the young woman with tea and biscuits, and immediately embarked upon an interview to which Miss Pelliston, oddly enough, responded just as though she had been seeking a position.

She too had made a speedy decision. There was nothing but misery for her at home. Aunt Deborah would never let her forget how she'd disgraced them all, and Papa would make certain his daughter lived to regret her rebellious act — if, that is, he didn't drive her from the house with a horse-whip.

On the other hand, here was an opportunity to begin a new life under a new identity. When her conscience insisted she deserved the punishment awaiting her at home, she answered that working was more productive penance than passive submission to endless reproaches and abuse. Providence, after all, "judgeth according to every man's work," she told herself as she accepted Madame's offer.

Catherine Pelliston — now Pennyman — would earn her own way in the world, enduring the hardships of her lot as other less privileged women did. She was thankful that she had done the rather dreary duties of the lady of the manor, taking supplies to ailing villagers and sewing endlessly for the needy. All those hours of sewing would provide her means of survival from now on.

She wondered anew at the little boy who'd led her to this momentous decision. He'd apparently taken to her immediately, and he'd never heard of the Baron Pelliston. To Jemmy she was another waif like himself, in need of useful work and shelter.

Shelter. Good heavens. Where would she live?

"Madame Germaine," she began hesitantly, "I wonder if, before I begin working, you might direct me to the nearest pawnshop."

When Catherine explained to the startled *modiste* that she required funds in order to obtain lodgings, and went on to admit that she had no idea where to find said lodgings, Jemmy cut in.

"Din't I tell you wot a green 'un she is? You orter put her upstairs wif Betty, Missus."

"Oh, no," Catherine cried, seeing the doubts writ plain on the dressmaker's face. "I would never impose in such a way."

Jemmy's dire predictions regarding what would happen to Miz Kaffy if she were let loose upon the streets combined with the new employee's dignified refusal of charity to erase Madame's doubts. With an empty bed in the housemaid Betty's attic chamber, there was no reason Miss Pennyman could not be accommodated until she'd received her wages and might seek proper lodgings.

After lengthy debate and many direr predictions from Jemmy, Catherine acquiesced — on condition, she said, that she might repay the favour. Her eyes on the little boy, she proposed to tutor Jemmy in the rudiments of reading and writing.

Madame snatched at the suggestion as though Miss Pennyman had showered gold upon her.

"Why, that's just the thing! What a clever, kind girl you are to think of it. You can see for yourself what an ignorant creature he is. I cannot trust him to go to school as he should — nor spare the time to teach him myself. And though I do my best to keep him tidy, he is such a restless little devil, always into something, that in half an hour one would think he never saw soap or water in his life. How he manages to tear his clothes to ribbons in such a short space of time I shall never know. I would need half a dozen more girls just to keep him patched. Isn't that so, you young ruffian?" she asked, pulling Jemmy to her for yet another fierce embrace.

"Wot's she going to do to me?" Jemmy asked, scowling at the hug, though he otherwise bore it manfully.

"Why, teach you the alphabet, you ignorant child. Do you know what that is?"

Jemmy didn't know nuffink and didn't want to know nuffink, especially if it had to do with soap and water. The *modiste*'s excited monologue had led him to conclude that reading and writing were somehow connected with bathing.

Catherine hastened to explain, pointing out the advantages of being able to read signs and shopkeepers' bills without assistance. She was not certain how much the boy understood, but he seemed to trust her and eventually agreed to "try it some and see as he liked it."

A just Providence must look favourably upon efforts to lead this young soul out of the darkness of illiteracy, Catherine assured herself later as she sat working with the other seamstresses. Surely that must compensate in part for the disobedient act to which she'd been driven.

She was far less easy in her mind concerning the family she'd run away from this morning. She had written a long letter of apology, though, hadn't she? Besides, Lord and Lady Andover had more important concerns than the fate of the lowly member of the working classes they must have taken her for. They'd probably decided, just as Lord Rand had remarked the other night, that Catherine was either insane or horribly ungrateful. By now they'd all ceased thinking about her altogether. She only wished she could stop thinking about *him*.

Well, strong personalities were very difficult to ignore — look at Papa — and whatever one thought of Lord Rand's unfortunate habits, one must admit he had an overwhelming sort of presence. When he was in the same room one became oblivious to everything else. He was also mind-numbingly handsome. His deep blue eyes alone were enough to stop one's brain dead in its tracks. Add to that a face and physique like a Greek god and a mop of wavy golden hair . . . yes, indeed, he was just as Molly had said, like a great handsome statue. Any person of any aesthetic sensitivity must be impressed.

Handsome is as handsome does, Catherine reminded herself as she threaded a needle. She would never see the man again, and that was fortunate, because he was evidently embarked upon the same dissolute courses as Papa, and in a few years those godlike features would degenerate. In time Lord Rand's face would match his character, a conclusion she had rather not witness. She sighed softly. What a terrible waste.

The search for Miss Pelliston was not brought to the speedy conclusion Lord Rand had hoped for. He'd expected to find her the same afternoon, cowering in a corner of the inn yard, or else — as he imagined in a more lighthearted moment — delivering one of her scolds to a giant, red-faced coachman.

Three days later he was still seeking her. When enquiries at coaching inns proved futile, he had, sick at heart, descended into the seamier environs in which he'd first found her. He'd even stormed Miss Grendle's establishiment, where he was met with mocking assurances that the "ungrateful young person" was warming the bed of some rich nob.

The viscount learned no more in London's underworld than he had at the inns. The only news he acquired in those three days was from a tavern keeper. The man had not seen the young lady, but had heard her described by another "gentry cove." The description of this man — a tall, thin, middle-aged redhead — bore no resemblance to anyone with whom Max or Lord Andover was acquainted.

"The fellow's not her father," Lord Rand confided to his valet. It was daybreak of the fourth day since Miss Pelliston had run away, and his lordship had made another of his brief visits home for a bath, an hour's rest, and a change of clothes. "Andover says the old brute's short and shaped like a pear. Besides which he's in the Lake District on his bridal trip. Must be the confounded fiance."

"That tells us the young lady has not returned to her family," Blackwood replied.

"I wish she *had*, damn her. At least then we'd know she was safe and could forget about her, the stupid chit."

Blackwood, who'd learned somewhat more about the missing lady than his master had intended to relate, had begun to have some ideas of his own. While his employer lay down for a short nap, the valet noiselessly exited the chamber, donned his hat and gloves, and departed for Andover House.

In the same quietly efficient manner in which he'd taken charge of his employer, Blackwood insinuated his way into the heart of the Andover household, eliciting from Jeffers, the earl's butler, an invitation to stop belowstairs to "take a bite of breakfast" with the others.

As Blackwood had hoped, the very same Molly his employer had characterised (though in more vivid terms) as incapable of intelligent speech was enjoying an early repast with her colleagues. The valet's openly appreciative gaze won him a place at her side and a scowl from Tom, the footman. Mr. Blackwood's charm did the rest. Lord Rand would have

116

been amazed to find what an entertaining fellow his inscrutable valet could be. That was because his lordship did not know what Blackwood quickly learned: that added to his own winning personality was the considerable advantage of personal attendance upon Molly's idol.

Molly's infatuation with Lord Rand was a household joke, and a grim provocation to Tom, who was equally besotted with the rosy-cheeked abigail.

"Why, all he had to do was look at her or anywhere's near her an' she busts out bawling. Didn't you, then?" he accused his beloved. "An' wasn't no help at all, an' his lordship's cousin lost now an' his lordship up all hours looking for her."

"I'm sure Miss Jones faithfully reported all she could," said Mr. Blackwood, bestowing a compassionate smile on the maid. "Though it must have been very trying indeed having to answer two gentlemen's questions at once."

"Oh, don't you know it, Mr. Blackwood. Here was my master asking me a hundred things and Mr. Max — his lordship, I mean — frowning and grumbling like I stole her myself. And all I ever did was explain about his lordship being away all that time and tell her what nice hair she had. As even you said yourself, Tom Fetters, and was carrying on so about her eyes as made a body wonder what you was thinking of."

Blackwood smoothly stepped in to prevent the angry retort forming on Tom's lips. "Ah, yes," Lord Rand's gentleman said, "even ladies of quality do not object to being reminded of their assets from time to time."

"Well, I don't know about that," Molly said frankly. "She looked like she didn't believe a word of it — as if I was the kind to flatter in hopes of getting something by it," she added scornfully.

"You strike me," said Blackwood, "as the soul of honesty. She ought to have believed you."

"I should say so. Don't I know that Lady Littlewaite's paid as much for a set of curls like that as she did for a ball gown? Nor they didn't match properly neither, but was the best Monsoor Franzwuz could do on short notice, when the other one fell into the turtle soup. Which it never would have done, he says, if she wasn't always flirting and tossing her head like she was a girl of eighteen instead of a grandmama."

Blackwood listened carefully, his precise mind examining, selecting, and discarding as Molly continued talking. He had come because he knew Lord Andover's servants would speak more freely to one of their own kind than to their masters. In their less guarded speech might be a clue to Miss Pelliston's whereabouts. A remembered word or phrase might offer some inkling of her plans.

Now he sorted out two facts that appeared significant. Miss Pelliston had come to Andover House penniless, and, according to his master, desperate to go home. Molly had talked to her of the buying and selling of hair. This, perhaps, was the clue he wanted.

"Sold her hair?" Max repeated, aghast, when the valet presented his report. "That glorious —" He stopped short, equally horrified at what he'd been about to say. "That's ridiculous," he snapped. "If she'd done it, then why ain't she home? Why didn't anyone remember her at the coaching inns?"

"A confused mind is a vacillating mind, My Lord. Perhaps she changed her mind about returning. If she managed to acquire money, she may have sought temporary shelter in London."

"Or maybe someone changed her mind for her," was the angry response. "Confound the woman! Why couldn't she stay put? Did you ever hear of such a henwit?"

Blackwood wisely refrained from responding to this. Silently he handed a snowy white length of linen to his employer.

"Damn it, man, I haven't time to fool with that thing. Takes me half a dozen to do it right, and I'm in no mood to bear those pained looks you give me when I do it wrong, as though I'd just put a ball through your other leg. I'll wear one of the old ones that don't feel like such a noose about my neck."

"With the Bath superfine, My Lord?" the valet stoically enquired.

Lord Rand looked at his coat, then back at the neck-cloth the valet held. "I suppose," he said after a moment, "if we do meet up with the wretched girl, you think the combination will drive her off again."

"Rather excessive for a young lady's sensibilities, I do believe, sir."

"Very well," said the defeated employer. "The gibbet it is. Only you had better tie it, unless you mean to see your master garrote himself."

"Bit early in the day for this sort of thing, ain't it? Sun ain't even set," said Lord Browdie as his companion led him through the door into a red velvet-draped vestibule.

"Ah, you're getting old, Browdie. Time was you were ready for a bit of fun morning, noon, and night. Or is it you're afraid of being disappointed? No fear of that. Granny's gals'll tend to you, day or night — and cheaper than

120

the kind you usually spend your money on."

On no account did Lord Browdie care to be reminded of his age. If his dark red hair had origins more pharmaceutical than natural, that was a secret between his manservant and himself, as were the yards of buckram padding that filled out his chest, shoulders, and calves. These features were no secret to a host of low females of his acquaintance, either, but he regarded their opinions no more than he regarded their sensibilities.

Might as well have a bit of fun, he thought, as he was led to meet his hostess. Damned tiresome business, this. He'd been in London four days and not a trace of his fiancee could he discover.

He had, moreover, met with a great deal of discourtesy. The frigid crone at the school had disclaimed all knowledge of Miss Pelliston and had been notably unforthcoming regarding the blasted governess. A man-hater, that one. He'd had to bribe a maid to learn what little he now knew — that a young woman answering his description had come calling, but had stayed only a short time.

The maid, who'd been daydreaming out a window instead of attending to her work, had seen the young lady meet up with a tall gentleman, but no, she couldn't say who that was. The two had met up on the opposite side of the square, and that was too far away to see what the man looked like.

When Catherine turned out not to be where she was supposed to be, Lord Browdie was stymied. He hadn't the faintest idea how to find her. Thus he spent most of his time in diverse taverns and coffeehouses, occasionally remembered to enquire about the girl, and generally convinced himself he was diligently seeking her.

"— and this is Lynnette."

Lord Browdie looked up from his musings to behold a shapely brunette wearing a great deal of paint, cheap jewelry, and a bizarrely demure peach-colored gown from whose narrow bodice her ample bosom threatened to burst any minute. The woman seemed vaguely familiar.

"Don't I know you?" he asked a few minutes later as she led him upstairs.

"I don't think so, sir," she said, with a naughty grin. "I'd remember a handsome face like yours, I'm sure."

If Lynnette might have had what she wished, she would have wished for a younger patron who was a tad more considerate. Being ambitious, however, and not overly fastidious, she left wishes to dreamy idealists. She had risen from the Covent Garden alleys to this house. It was not the best sort of house but it wasn't the worst, either. At any rate, she would not remain longer than necessary. She meant to have an abode of her own, paid for by a wealthy gentleman, as would be the myriad gowns and jewels that normally accompanied such transactions.

Being an astute judge of character, she knew what her customer wanted and proceeded to fulfill his fantasies. Lord Browdie, who was not overly generous, was sufficiently moved by the experience to offer a bit extra compensation. He promised to see her again very soon.

"Thought you looked familiar," he said as she helped him on with his coat. "Now I know why. You're the gal of my dreams, ain't you, my lovely?"

Not until the next afternoon, in a rare interval of sobriety, did Lord Browdie realise that it hadn't been the female who was familiar, but the gown. The experience of remembering a woman's frock was so unusual that he actually puzzled over the matter for some minutes. Then his crony, Sir Reginald Aspinwal, appeared, the sober interval abruptly concluded, and Lord Browdie forgot all about frocks.

Catherine had adapted remarkably well to her new life, despite its obvious deficiencies.

No one waited on her, willingly or otherwise. She dined simply in the workroom with either her fellow employees or Jemmy. She had neither fine clothes nor elegant accessories nor even the pin money to buy a single ribbon. On the other hand, she had not to cope with a drunken papa wreaking constant havoc with her attempts to keep the household in order, finding fault with everything she did and didn't do, and making her feel — despite what reason told her — that she was worthless, unlikable, and ought never to have been born.

The other seamstresses seemed to accept her as one of themselves. Though Madame was inclined to be emotional and easily provoked by demanding customers, she indulged her aggerations in the solitude of her office. She treated her employees kindly, realising that good health and even tempers were as critical to the creation of exquisite finery as were quality fabrics, well-lit work areas, and carefully maintained tools.

Yes, she had been most fortunate to meet up with Jemmy that day, Catherine thought, as she watched the little boy who sat with her at the worktable. At present he was stabbing viciously with his stubby pencil at a grimy piece of foolscap.

If she had not met him, she'd be home now and utterly wretched. She would never marry

Lord Browdie. Now, being unable to provide a respectable accounting of her disappearance, she could never marry at all.

Perhaps Aunt Deborah was worried about her. Perhaps even Papa was concerned. If so, their concern was mainly pride. If they'd truly cared about her, she would never have gotten into this fix in the first place. How could they possibly have expected her to give her property and person into the keeping of that odious *roué?*

Good heavens, even her employer showed more compassion — and Jemmy seemed genuinely fond of her. He was so determined to please Miz Kaffy that he would drag out his foolscap and pencil the instant the other seamstresses rose to leave for the day. They were all gone now except Madame, who was in the showroom attempting to rid herself courteously of the inconsiderate customer who was staying well past closing time.

"No, dear," Catherine said as she gently extracted the pencil from her student's grasp. "You do not clutch it in your fist as though it were a weapon. You hold it thus, between your fingers." She demonstrated.

Jemmy complained that the pencil wriggled like a worm. "You must show it who is master. You are a great, growing boy and this is only a small pencil. Here, I'll help you." She inserted the instrument between his grubby fingers and guided them with her own. "There. That is 'J.'"

"J," the boy repeated, gazing soberly at the mark he'd just made.

"Isn't that grand? I'll warrant none of the other boys you know can do that."

"No," he agreed. "Too ing'rant."

Catherine stifled a smile. "You, on the other hand, are very clever. In just a few days you've made all the letters in the alphabet as far as 'J.' Do you realise that's nearly halfway?"

Jemmy groaned. "More still? Ain't 'ere never no end to 'm fings?"

"*Those things* — and 'ain't' is not a proper word. Sixteen more to go. Then," she quickly added, noting the expression of profound discouragement upon his round features, "you will have enough letters to make every word you ever heard of — even your own name. By this time next week you'll be writing your whole name all by yourself."

"Show me wot it looks like," Jemmy ordered, offering her the pencil.

Miss Pennyman agreed on condition he help her. Once more she placed the pencil between his fingers and guided them.

"Miss Pelliston, I presume?"

The "y" of "Jemmy" trailed off into a long

crazy scrawl as Catherine dropped the child's hand.

At the sound of the familiar voice all the muscles in her neck stiffened. Slowly, painfully, she turned her head in the direction of the voice. In the same stiffly painful way, she became aware of gleaming boots, light-coloured trousers, a darker coat, and the blinding contrast of white linen as her gaze travelled up from the floor to his face, to be pinioned by the deep piercing blue of his eyes.

Blue . . . and angry. He had never seemed so tall and overpowering as he did now, his long, rugged form filling the narrow doorway.

8

Jemmy stared as well. As he took in his teacher's shocked white face, he waxed indignant. "Here now," he sharply informed the stranger, "you can't bust in here."

The stranger ignored him. "Miss Catherine Pelliston of Wilberstone, perhaps?"

Jemmy leapt from his chair to confront the aggravating visitor. "Din't I jest tell you you wuzn't allowed here? 'At ain't her name, neither, so you just be on yer way, sir, as you's had too much to drink nor what's good fer you." Apparently unaware that he was addressing the stranger's waistband, Jemmy endeavoured to turn the man around and push him on his way.

Lord Rand caught the child by the collar. "Settle down, boy," he said. "I've business with this young lady."

Jemmy did not settle down. He immediately began pounding the man with his fists and shouting threats, along with loud advice to Missus to call the Watch.

Lord Rand, whose short store of patience was quickly deserting him, gave the boy a light cuff on the shoulder and bade him be still. This adjuration proving ineffective, he picked the child up and slung him across his hip, in which position Jemmy, undaunted, flailed and kicked, mainly at empty air.

"Oh, do stop!" Catherine cried, rising from her chair. "Jemmy, you leave off that noise this instant and stop striking his lordship. And you, My Lord — how dare you bully that child!"

"The little beast is bullying me, in case you hadn't noticed." Nonetheless, Lord Rand released the boy, who ran back to shield his teacher. The urchin stood in front of her, scowling fearlessly at the giant. The teacher's great hazel eyes flashed fire.

"Is this your latest protector, ma'am? If so, I'd advise you not to stand too close. I daresay the wretch has lice."

In response, Miss Pelliston put her arm about the boy's shoulder and drew him closer to her. "I suppose, My Lord, you are provoked with me," she said stiffly. "I will not deny you may have reason. That is no excuse for picking on a helpless child."

"He's about as helpless as a rabid cur. Little beast *bit* me," Lord Rand grumbled.

"'N'll do it agin if you don't go away," Jemmy retorted.

"Very well," his lordship replied. "I do mean to go away — but not without your lady friend."

At this Jemmy set up a screeching that brought Madame to the workroom door. "Heavens, what is the child howling about?" she cried. "Jemmy, you stop that racket this minute, do you hear? Whatever will his lordship think? And poor Miss Pennyman — Miss Pelliston, I mean — you dreadful boy. Isn't she ill enough without your giving her the headache besides?"

Lord Rand moved aside to let the *modiste* enter the room.

"My dear," said Madame, taking Catherine's hand, "I had no notion. Such a shock it must be for you — but my poor brother had the same trouble. Knocked over by a farmer's cart and when he came to he didn't know who he was. Thought he was a farmer himself. It was two days before he came to his senses."

"I beg your pardon, but I am in full possession of my wits," said a baffled Catherine.

"Yes, dear, so he thought too. It's the amnesia, you know. If I hadn't been by to help him, he might have wandered off just as you did and none of us would ever have known what became of him."

"Amnesia?" Catherine faintly repeated.

"Yes," said the viscount as his face quickly assumed a mask of concern. "Apparently you tripped on the stairs the other morning and hit your head. Of course you don't remember, Miss Pelliston," he added, as she opened her mouth to contradict. "But I described to Madame the bandbox you'd packed with old clothes for the parish needy and she tells me you arrived carrying the very one."

The dressmaker nodded her agreement.

"Evidently you got muddled in your brain, ma'am, and thought it was your own luggage. Naturally, one understands how your confused mind perceived it."

Miss Pelliston's enormous eyes opened wider at this arrant falsehood. "My mind was — is — not in the least confused —"

"There, there," Madame comforted. "Just as my brother kept insisting. But his lordship is here to take you home now, and in a day or so you'll be right as a trivet. I shall miss you terribly, though. I never did see such fine, neat stitches as you make, dear, and never wasting a scrap of fabric."

Jemmy, who understood nothing but that his teacher was to be carried off by this evil giant, began objecting loudly. Catherine hastened to comfort him. She bent to embrace him and murmur soothing remarks, most to the effect that she would never desert him.

Jemmy was a child wise in the ways of the world. He knew that tall, fancy dressed gentlemen always got exactly their way in that world, and most especially when they were addressed as "My Lord." He refused to be consoled.

Catherine gazed up pleadingly at her erstwhile rescuer. "My Lord, I am sure there is some misunderstanding. You've confused me with someone else —"

"It's you who's confused. I'm only getting a headache is what. Drat it — can't you stifle the little b — lad?"

"He doesn't understand what's happening. Oh, please go away. Don't you see?" she begged. "He needs me. Madame needs me as well, as she just said. Oh, do go away, please."

The viscount, who'd expected to be greeted with every possible expression of gratitude, was confounded. An hour earlier, Blackwood had found a pastry cook who had not only seen the young lady the valet described, but was in possession of a length of ribbon belonging to her. The cook having volunteered directions to Jemmy's place of employment, Blackwood had hastened across the street to inform his master, who was questioning a chemist.

On the way to the dressmaker's, Blackwood had tactfully reminded his impetuous employer of the need for discretion if the young lady was found. After all, hadn't Lord Andover refused to call in Bow Street, fearing that a scandal would result? It was the valet who'd suggested the tale of amnesia.

Now there seemed to be prospects of precisely the to-do Lord Rand had promised to avoid. The boy's shrieking was loud enough to raise the Watch, if not the dead, and Miss Pelliston had got that mutinous expression on her thin face. Even the seamstress was beginning to look doubtful.

The valet, who'd been waiting in the showroom, now appeared. "There seems to be a difficulty, My Lord," he said in as low a voice as possible, given the noise the child was making.

"The brat's taking fits, and so she won't come," was the frustrated response.

"Indeed. If you'll permit me, My Lord?"

Lord Rand shrugged. Blackwood moved past him to approach Jemmy.

"Here, now, my lad. What's all this fuss?"

Forgetting all Miz Kaffy's lessons in grammar and elocution, Jemmy burst out with a stream of loud outrage and complaint in cant so thick that none of his listeners could comprehend a word he said. None, that is, but Blackwood.

"And is that what makes a great strong boy like yourself cry like a baby?"

"I ain't no baby," was the angry retort.

"In that case, perhaps you would express your objections calmly to his lordship — man to man, so to speak."

Jemmy considered this while Catherine wiped his nose with her handkerchief.

"'N' I will too," he said, looking round at the company. He marched up to Lord Rand, gave him a fierce glare, and spoke.

"Miz Kaffy is learnin' me to write all 'em hundred letters and now you come to take her away and we just got to 'J' and there's a pile more arter. 'N' who sez anyhow 'at's all wot you say?" the boy demanded. "How does we know you don't mean bad for her? She ain't one of 'em wicked ones, you know. Miz Kaffy's a lady and knows all 'em letters and eats wif her fork and all. 'N' she tole you to go away besides," the child summed up with his most unanswerable argument.

Lord Rand, as has been noted, was not a stupid man. He had been a bold, angry little boy himself once. He'd had precious scraps of treasure torn from him and burnt as trash, had been ordered to do and whipped for not doing a great many things without being given any comprehensible reason. Even as an adult, he'd had someone he cared for driven away from him. He knelt to look the urchin in the eye.

"Of course your friend is a lady," he answered. "That is why I've come to fetch her. You know, don't you, that ladies don't work for a living?"

Jemmy nodded grudgingly.

"I realise you'll miss her," his lordship went on, "but her relatives have been missing her several days now, and they've been very worried about her. They'll be most grateful to learn what good care you and Madame Germaine have taken of her in the meantime."

The boy's face grew very still, except for the tears that welled up in his eyes. "But 'ey'll — they'll — have her back and I won't see her no more and we only got to 'J.'" His voice quavered.

"Yes, that is a problem." Lord Rand stood up, darting a glance at Miss Pelliston, whose own eyes were filling. Gad, but her eyes were extraordinary — a great, unfathomable world seemed to exist there.

Lord Rand made a hasty decision, precisely as he was accustomed to do. "Suppose then, Jemmy, you come back with us to see where Miss Pelliston's relations live, so you can be sure everything's right and respectable. You can ride with the coachman," he offered.

The boy's eyes lit up. "Ken I?"

"Yes — if you assure Miss Pelliston that you won't raise any more fuss and will be as brave as you can. Maybe then she'll come by to visit you from time to time."

"You knew I had no choice but to come," Catherine accused as the carriage rattled down the street. "Nonetheless, I cannot condone your methods, My Lord. You bribed that poor child with the promise of a ride on a fancy coach."

"Miss Pelliston, you are the most contrary woman I've ever met. Did you honestly intend to work as a seamstress the rest of your days?"

"Yes. I was content — and it was honest work."

Max studied her narrow face. Was it his imagination or was her color better? Somehow she didn't seem as tired and drawn as before, yet she must have been working ten, eleven, twelve hours a day. What a mystifying creature she was.

Aloud he said, "I'll be sure to mention that to Louisa. Perhaps she'll set you to embroidering her gowns — or making your own. I suppose that would spare all those tiresome visits to dressmakers. She can boast that you're the only debutante in London who's made every stitch of her Season's wardrobe."

Miss Pelliston, who'd been staring dismally at her hands, looked up. "I am not, as you well know, My Lord, a debutante. I am engaged to be married — or I was. Perhaps he won't want me now," she added with a faint, rueful smile. "Then at least something good will have come of all this."

"Sorry to upset your happy fantasies, ma'am, but I don't think your fiance has anything to say in the matter. Louisa's determined to bring you out, and once Louisa's determined on something there's nothing and no one can stand in her way. Certainly not irate papas or broken-hearted bridegrooms."

"Bring me out? Where? Why? What on earth are you talking about?" She leaned forward eagerly in her seat only to find Lord Rand's blue-eyed gaze rather too close for rational thought. Abruptly she sat back, her heart thumping wildly.

"Oh," she said. "You're talking nonsense. I didn't think you were inebriated, but one can never be certain. I suppose you have a very hard head." She winced as soon as she'd finished speaking, realising that, as usual, she'd been quite tactless.

Lord Rand smiled. "Bless me if you don't have the oddest way of flattering a man. I can hardly wait to see the other fellows' reactions when you treat them to some of your compliments."

To his satisfaction, her face turned pink.

"Yes, I do have a hard head, Miss Pelliston, but the fact is I'm sober as a judge at the moment. Dash it, didn't the Andover name ring any bells with you? Probably not. Country's crawling with relations — who's going to keep track of a lot of third and fourth cousins?"

"Oh, dear," she said softly as she took his meaning. "They are relations. I was afraid of that."

"You weren't afraid of slaving your life away for a miserable handful of shillings a week. What's so terrifying about Andover?"

"I know it will sound cowardly to you," Catherine began reluctantly, "but I didn't want anyone to know who I was. People treat one so differently. . . . I mean, they would have felt obliged to go out of their way on my account and I'd be obliged to accept, even though it would make matters worse."

"With your family, you mean? But how? They don't come any more respectable than Andover. Even the Old Man — my father, that is — can't find fault with the fellow, though he's tried hard enough for ten years."

"I' mean," Miss Pelliston said so softly that Lord Rand had to bend closer to hear her,

"I had rather face Papa alone — not before strangers."

Lord Rand began to think he understood. She must have expected a perfectly horrendous homecoming if she'd elected to work for the miserable wages of a seamstress instead. The rage and frustration that had been building in him for days abruptly dissipated. She was gallant in her way, wasn't she? He remembered the girl clutching a coverlet about her as she sought help from a wild, drunken vagabond. Brave then too.

"Miss Pelliston, I assure you I'm not the least foxed," he said more kindly. "Edgar and Louisa intended to tell you the very next morning, after you'd had time to recover from your — experiences. No," he added hastily in response to her horrified look. "They know nothing of Granny Grendle or how you spent that night and they'll never know of it, I promise you."

"Thank you," she whispered.

"Anyhow, my brother-in-law's no stranger, and no one intends to make you face your papa at all, because Louisa's set on keeping you with her in London. You don't know my sister, Miss Pelliston. She's got scads of energy and intelligence and no productive use for 'em. She wanted dozens of children and would have been happily employed dom-

139

ineering them, but she's been unlucky that way. She needs to take charge of someone. She took to you right off, and that's all the reason she needs. I do wish you'd give her half a chance — you'd be doing her more of a favour than you would yourself."

That last was a stroke of inspiration. Catherine might have persuaded herself that she did not deserve to be rewarded for undutiful, ungrateful behaviour with a Season. She was not proof, however, against a plea on another's behalf.

Lord Rand seemed to believe his sister needed her, and Catherine wanted badly to be needed. Though she was distressed to abandon Jemmy and Madame, and thought that they — Jemmy especially — being less privileged folk were more entitled to her help, she knew that she'd never be allowed to return to work. She was not certain she could possibly do the self-possessed, breathtakingly beautiful Lady Andover any good, but Lord Rand claimed she could.

"If matters are as you say, My Lord, I would be both ungrateful and un-Christian to object. I am deeply sorry now that I behaved so rashly."

"Oh, never mind that," his lordship answered generously. "I like a bit of rash behaviour now and again. Keeps things interesting, don't you think?"

Lord Pelliston had spent a most enjoyable fortnight touring the Lake District with his bride. So enjoyable was the experience that more often than not he forgot to have recourse to his usual several bottles of strong spirits per diem. He had no idea he was being managed and would have scoffed at anyone who had the temerity to advance such a ridiculous notion.

His new wife had helped him forget a great many things, actually, including his dismal sister and waspish daughter. Now he had a letter from the Earl of Andover and one from his sister, in both of which Catherine's name seemed to appear repeatedly. He was not altogether certain of this fact because he was too vain to wear the spectacles he needed or allow his new wife to see how far away from his face he must hold the epistles in order to peruse them.

He glanced at his helpmeet, who was tying the ribbons of a most fetching bonnet under her dimpled chin. She was a dashed handsome woman. Just as important, she understood a man and talked sense.

Lady Pelliston turned to meet his gaze.

"Why so thoughtful, my dear? You don't like the bonnet? Say so at once and I shall toss it on the fire."

"No, it's the da — dratted letters. Don't anyone know how to write legible any more?"

His wife smiled and held out her hand. "Let me see them," she offered. "I seem to have a knack for deciphering anything."

A few minutes later she looked up. "Well," she said. "Well, well."

"Can you make 'em out?"

"Yes, dear. How I wish you'd explained matters to me more fully. I might have talked to the girl . . . but there, it is no business of mine. Catherine is your daughter and I do not like to interfere."

"With what? What's Andover palavering on about?"

"My dear, I believe you need a glass of wine." Lady Pelliston knew he'd prefer a few bottles, after which he would become unpleasant. This was her idea of a compromise.

Not until after he'd been supplied with refreshment did she set to work. "Catherine is not a strong girl, I take it?"

"If you mean in will, she's obstinate as a mule. If you mean body strength, well, what does she expect? Plays with her food instead of eating it and then goes gadding about among a lot of whining peasants, poking her nose where it don't belong or else locked up in her room with her infernal books. Plagues the life out of me," the baron complained.

"I see." The baroness rapidly readjusted her previous estimation of her stepdaughter. "Apparently, these unfortunate habits resulted in unsettled nerves. She ran away on our wedding day and left a note for your sister saying she was driven to it because she could not abide Lord Browdie."

"Ran off! There now — didn't I just tell you what a stubborn, plaguey gal she was? Ran off where? As if she had any place to go, the little bedlamite." Lord Pelliston polished off his glass of wine, muttering to himself between gulps.

"Evidently, she did not get far. Lord and Lady Andover happened to run across her. He does not say where, but he does remark that Catherine was quite beside herself. Very ill, he says, and terrified half out of her mind. I hope, James, it was not Lord Browdie who terrified her. His rather brusque ways are liable to intimidate a delicate lady. Particularly one," she hastened to add, "accustomed to more refined treatment from her papa."

"That's ridiculous. Browdie tells me that if he so much as says a word to the gal she glares at him like she meant to turn him to stone."

"As a Pelliston, she would scorn to show her fear, whatever she felt within," the baroness flattered. "Dear me, I had no idea she objected so to the match. Though I daresay," she quickly corrected, "that was mere missishness. How I wish I had been her mama and might have talked to her — but I am not and it is none of my affair. What do you mean to do, James?"

"Fetch her back, curse her. She ain't back, is she?" he asked hopefully.

"No, she is in London with her cousin and his wife."

"Cousin — fah! Family's never had a word to say to me unless they wanted hounds. Sold Andover a fine pair too, years ago, and that was the last I heard of him. Why the devil didn't he take her home again? Now we must be traipsing off to London — filthy, stinking hole that it is. Where's that bottle, Clare?"

Lady Pelliston was a young woman, and she did not mean to waste her remaining youth buried in a remote country village. She had every intention of visiting London in the near future. She meant, in fact, to spend every Season there until she grew too decrepit to stand upright. Interrupting her bridal trip in order to drag an unwilling stepdaughter to the altar was not part of these plans.

The situation was bound to be unpleasant, and Lady Pelliston hated unpleasantness. Also, she knew that the action would not win her husband — and herself by association —

the earl's esteem. She had taken into account the Andover connection as systematically as she had all Lord Pelliston's other assets, and meant to use it to her advantage. The baroness was a practical woman.

Lord Andover wrote of his wife's intention to bring Catherine out. That was very odd of them, to be sure, but the Earl and Countess of Andover must be indulged their eccentricities. Lady Pelliston was not about to permit her spouse to interfere with those plans and thus wreak havoc upon her own. Accordingly, she removed her bonnet, poured her husband another glass of wine, and set about the formidable task of making him see reason.

9

Lord Browdie frowned at the heavily embossed sheet of vellum in his hand. Old Reggie had procured him the invitation to Lady Littlewaite's ball, thinking to do his friend a favour. Reggie had been visiting the day Pelliston's note arrived, and Lord Browdie being at the time more drunk than discreet had shared its contents with his friend. A good thing too. He might have dropped into a sulk if he'd been alone.

Fortunately, Reggie had been there to rally him, repeating his red-haired crony's many complaints about the girl's sour disposition and physical inadequacies. She had told her papa she couldn't abide Lord Browdie. Well, she'd soon learn that no one could abide *her*, and in a few months her papa would be apologising again and begging Browdie to take the shrew back.

Lord Browdie thought this unlikely. Lady Pelliston must have engineered the betrothal's end, just as she had instigated its beginning.

146

Pelliston, he told Reggie, had been henpecked before he ever reached the altar. Pitiful, it was.

"Don't waste your pity on him," Reggie had argued. "He'll be feeling sorry for himself soon enough. You're a free man again — in London in the Season — with a hundred pleasanter females ripe for the plucking. What better time and place to find a wife? They're all here, my boy, from the baby-faced misses fresh from the schoolroom to the lonely widows who know what they're missing."

Hence the invitation. The trouble was, Lord Browdie had far rather spend his time with the accommodating Lynnette than at the tedious work of courting either innocent misses or less innocent widows. He was even beginning to think seriously of setting Lynnette up in a modest house in Town. Though that would be a deal more expensive than what he now paid for her company, he'd have that company whenever the mood seized him, instead of having to cool his heels in Granny Grendle's garish parlour while his ladybird entertained another fellow.

Lynnette was greatly in demand. If he did not remove her from the premises soon, some other chap might. Still, no reason a man mightn't eat his cake and have it too. He'd take a look at Lady Littlewaite's display of potential breeders. If nothing there appealed to him, he'd pay Lynnette a visit. Meanwhile, he'd better see about that house.

"What in blazes is that?" Lord Rand demanded, staring out the window.

Blackwood looked out as well. "Jemmy, My Lord."

"I know it's Jemmy. What the devil is he doing there?"

"Sweeping the steps, My Lord."

"May a man ask why he is sweeping my steps when I have a regiment of servants already stumbling over one another looking for something to do?"

"Gidgeon set him to it, My Lord. The boy's been haunting the neighbourhood this past week, and the footmen complain that they hardly dare step out the door for fear of tripping over him."

Lord Rand sighed. "Doesn't the brat have work enough at the dressmaker's? Why must he haunt my house?"

"Apparently, sir, he's spying on you."

"Oh, give me strength." The viscount ran his fingers through his golden hair.

"Indeed, sir. It seems Mr. Hill was endeavouring to chase the boy away a few days ago. Mr. Gidgeon, who doesn't care for interference in household matters, took the lad's part in consequence. They had rather a row about it, and what must Mr. Gidgeon do but call Jemmy in for a talking to and tell him we wouldn't have vagrants hanging about. Mr. Gidgeon handed the boy a broom. Mr. Hill was fit to be tied."

"No wonder Hill's been sulking. I was missing his funereal pronouncements. So Jemmy's watching me, is he? Does he think I'm one of Buonaparte's spies?"

"No, My Lord. He wishes to assure himself that you do not attempt to spirit Miss Pelliston away to your domicile 'for no wicked biznez,' as he puts it."

The viscount decided it was high time to have a talk with young Jemmy.

When Lord Rand opened the door, he found Jemmy diligently cleaning the railings. "Don't the maids do it well enough for you?" his lordship asked.

"Me hand's smaller," was the sullen reply. "I ken get in 'em — them — those little places."

"Don't you have work to do for Madame Germaine?"

"Not in the arternoons. Besides, SHE'S in one of 'em Aggerations. Allus is now, wif Miz Kaffy gone and Annie still sick."

Jemmy threw the viscount a reproachful glance before returning to his work.

"I suppose you haven't seen your friend in some time now?"

"Not since you took her off."

"Would you like to see her today?"

The urchin nodded, though he kept his focus on the railing.

"Shall I take you, then?"

A pair of brown eyes squinted suspiciously at the viscount. "You don't mean 'at — that."

His lordship uttered a small sigh. "I'm afraid I do. Only I can't take you to my sister's looking like a dirty climbing boy. Go down to the kitchen and ask Girard to give you something to eat," he ordered, breaking into a grin as he envisioned Jemmy's confrontation with the temperamental Gallic cook. "I'll see whether Blackwood can find you a better rigout."

Despite his vociferous objections, Jemmy was given a bath by a pair of housemaids assisted by a footman. Following that ordeal, the boy was dressed by Lord Rand's own valet in a brand-new suit of clothes, and his brown hair was brushed until it shone. Jemmy's own mother, even if sober, wouldn't have known him. He endured these diverse insults to his person only because, according to his lordship, they were necessary sacrifices.

"Look at me," Lord Rand said. "D'you think I let Blackwood strangle me with this blasted neck-cloth because I *like* it? Ladies are very difficult to please," he explained.

Had he been so inclined, the viscount might have also mentioned that he'd like to take a look at Miz Kaffy himself. He'd not seen her since he'd removed her from the dressmaker's shop — more than ten days ago.

Miss Pelliston had been nowhere in view whenever he'd called, and his sister had refused to bring her into sight, claiming that Max would have to wait, as everyone else must, until Miss Pelliston was fully prepared for her entrance into Society. Lord Rand was not, however, inclined to explain this to Jemmy.

When their respective sartorial tortures finally ended, the two males marched bravely to Andover House and into the glittering presence of Lady Andover.

"I believe you've heard something of Jemmy," the viscount said to his sister.

"Oh, indeed I have." She smiled at the boy. "Catherine has told me all about you."

"Where is she?" Jemmy demanded, not at all intimidated by Lady Andover's grandeur, though he thought her very fine indeed.

"She'll be down in a moment," the countess said easily, making Max want to slap her. "Perhaps you'd like some biscuits and milk to sustain you while you wait."

Though Jemmy had been very well sustained at the viscount's establishment, he was not fully recovered from his recent ordeal. He was, moreover, a growing boy, and like others of the species hungry all the time. He nodded eagerly.

He had just plunged a third biscuit into his mouth when Catherine appeared. He nearly choked on it, so great was his astonishment. Lord Rand, who had not been eating biscuits, only blinked and wondered if he'd been drinking all day without realising the fact.

In place of the prim schoolteacher he'd expected was a delicate-featured young lady in a fashionable lavender gown. Her light brown hair was a confection of curls, some of which framed her face and softened its narrow features, while the others were held back in an airy cloud by a lavender ribbon.

He stared speechless at her as she made a graceful curtsey. She darted one nervous glance at his face, then hurried forward to clasp Jemmy in her arms.

"How happy I am to see you," she said. "And how fine you look."

"He made me do it," Jemmy answered, recovering quickly from his surprise. "Made me have a bath 'n' everything."

"Oh, my. Was that very dreadful, dear?"

"It wuz horrid. But I done it cuz he said he wouldn't bring me if I didn't. *He* had to be strangled, he sez."

Lord Rand did strangle an oath before hurriedly explaining, "I was referring at the time to my neck-cloth. Blackwood claims it is a Mathematical. I call it a Pesticidal myself. Feel like a curst mummy."

"You look very well for all that," said his sister. "This Blackwood must be an extraordinary fellow from all I've heard — and seen," she added, eyeing her brother up and down.

"Yes. Drives me terribly. He has interesting notions about who is master. Just like the rest of the household. Not a one of them does anything but what he pleases. My butler drops his aitches and sets young vagrants to sweeping my steps. I'm hanged if there's one of them ever hears a word I say."

"If they listened to you, Max, the house would be a shambles and yourself the sad wreck you were but two weeks ago. Was he not a sad wreck, Catherine? Was he not falling to pieces before our very eyes, and that because he'd spent six months doing exactly as he pleased? Now that he does his duty instead, he's almost presentable, don't you think?"

Though Miss Pelliston had led Jemmy to the sofa in order to talk quietly with him, she had not missed any of the preceding discussion. She glanced at the viscount, then looked quickly down at her hands when she felt heat rushing to her cheeks.

She had never thought him a sad wreck, except perhaps morally, and now he was so tidy and elegant that one must have a very discerning eye indeed to detect the crumbling moral fiber within. One certainly could not detect it in his eyes, which were no longer shadowed and bloodshot. There had never been any lines of dissipation about his mouth, as there were about Papa's, nor was Lord Rand's long, straight nose webbed with red, spidery veins.

Still, Papa was past fifty and Lord Rand not even thirty and it was perfectly absurd to sit here tongue-tied like a shy little rustic, she told herself angrily.

She raised her head to meet the viscount's unnerving blue gaze. His lips twitched. Was he laughing at her?

"His lordship and I are so recently acquainted that I have no basis for forming an opinion on that subject," she answered. "At any rate, I do believe some years of concentrated effort are needed for a healthy young man to reduce himself to a sad wreck. The human body is amazingly resilient." Then, in spite of herself, she winced.

Lord Rand's blue eyes gleamed. "Right you are, Miss Pelliston. I told my family six months wasn't nearly enough time. Some years, did you say? How many do you suggest?"

"I suggested nothing of the sort. Certainly I would never undertake to advise anyone upon methods of self-destruction."

"No? Well, that's a relief. I'd hate to have it get about that a young lady of one and twenty had to instruct me in dissipation. Most lowering, don't you think?"

"I should say so. I hope I know nothing whatever about it."

"Catherine, you must not take Max so seriously. He is bamming you."

"I was not. I thought for once I had someone on my side."

"You have your valet on your side, dear, and that is all a man requires, according to Edgar."

"Can't be. Miss Pelliston has neatly avoided answering your question about my presentability, so I can only suspect the blackguard has failed me."

"I beg your pardon, My Lord. I had no idea you sought reassurance," Catherine responded with a trace of irritation. "I assumed your glass must have told you that your appearance is altogether satisfactory."

"Is it? Kind of you to say so. Did your own glass tell you that you look like a spray of lilac?"

If this was more teasing, Catherine was at a complete loss how to respond. Her face grew hot.

"Here now," Jemmy cut in. "Wot's he about?"

Haven't the vaguest idea, Max answered inwardly. Aloud he said, "I was telling Miss Pelliston how lovely she is. Don't you agree?"

Jemmy gazed consideringly at his friend for a moment. Then he nodded. "Why'd you go all red, 'en?" he asked her.

"I was embarrassed," was the frank reply.

While Jemmy was deciding whether or not he approved this state of affairs, Lady Andover hastened to Catherine's rescue. "My dear, you must become accustomed to compliments. You will hear a deal more tomorrow at Lady Littlewaite's ball."

"Still, she might blush all she likes," said the provoking Max. "The chaps will love it."

"Since you know nothing whatever about how gentlemen behave at these affairs, I beg you keep your opinions to yourself," the countess retorted dampeningly.

"Being a chap myself, I expect I know more about it than you do," her brother rejoined before returning his attention to

Miss Pelliston. "So that's to be your first foray into Society?"

"Yes. I did not wish to take any steps before we were certain Papa would not object. Lord Andover just received his letter a few days ago. Apparently, Papa has reconsidered — about Lord Browdie, I mean."

"Browdie. So that's the old goat's name. Never heard of him."

"You never heard of anybody higher in the social scale than a tapster, Max. The Baron Browdie is not precisely an old goat, as you so poetically put it, though he does have nearly three decades' advantage of Catherine. He is also reputed to lack refinement. According to Edgar's mama, Lord Browdie's company is not coveted by Society's hostesses, though he is tolerated."

"Better and better," said Max. "Means you're not likely to be running into him very often. That is, if he's in London at all."

"That we don't know," the countess answered, before Catherine could look up from her conversation with Jemmy. "Lord Pelliston wrote that Lord Browdie had come to Town looking for Catherine but would be receiving written notice that the engagement was off."

"There now, Miss Pelliston. Didn't I tell you to put your faith in Louisa?"

Miss Pelliston, who had not yet fully recovered from her previous exchange with his lordship, had much rather talk to Jemmy. She answered, a tad distractedly, "Oh, yes — certainly. Still, I can scarcely believe it. Even when Lord Andover let me read Papa's letter, I couldn't believe it. It was so unlike — I mean to say, I mustn't have expressed myself plainly enough —"

"Oh, of course," Lord Rand sweetly replied. "Never mind that Andover can talk the horns off a charging bull. Don't you know that's what they're always wanting him for at Whitehall? If he ain't persuading Prinny's ministers he must be persuading Prinny himself."

"I did not mean to discount Lord Andover's efforts. I agree that I should have listened to you in the first place, My Lord." Catherine's gaze dropped to the child sitting beside her. "Yet if I had, I would never have met Jemmy. I cannot be sorry for *that*, whatever hundred other things I am sorry for."

Though much of the conversation was beyond his comprehension, this Jemmy grasped.

"So why don't you come see me?" the boy demanded.

"I will. Tomorrow afternoon when Lady Andover takes me to order the rest of my wardrobe from Madame," Catherine promised. "The dress I'm wearing had to be made up in rather a hurry, I'm afraid, along with a gown for tomorrow night, and I didn't want to impose on her, knowing how very busy she must be."

"Will you show me more letters when you come?"

"I will show you some now, if her ladyship and his lordship will excuse us," Catherine answered, so eagerly that Lord Rand frowned.

"Well, Max, you do look fine," said her ladyship after teacher and student had exited, "but you are no match for Jemmy's sartorial splendour."

"No, despite my fine feathers, Miss Pelliston knows I'm a bull in a china shop. Leastways she looks at me as if she thought any minute I might step on her or crash into her or I don't know what. Am I that clumsy, Louisa?"

Lady Andover studied her brother for a moment before answering quietly, "I don't think anyone's ever teased her before, Max. She is rather fragile in some ways."

"Bull in a china shop, just as I said. Well, then, as long as she's out of the room, why don't you tell me your plans for your innocent victim? Has she the least idea what she's in for?"

Some hours later, as he recalled his conversation with Miss Pelliston, Max grimaced. Like it or no, he seemed to be undergoing a transformation, and that annoyed him. In the first place, he thought, glaring into the cheval glass, there was his appearance. When he'd first returned to England, he'd let his sister coax him into ordering two new suits of clothing. These he'd promptly abandoned after the battle with his father and the truce allowing the heir six months' freedom.

Max had considered two new costumes sufficient, even when he assumed his rightful position in Society, since he most certainly had no intention of gadding about with a lot of dim-witted macaronis. Yet the day after he'd returned Miss Pelliston to his sister's care, he'd made a long visit to Mr. Weston. There and at the establishments of Mr. Hoby, the bootmaker; Mr. Lock, the hatter; and diverse others, Lord Rand had ordered enough masculine attire to fit out Lord Wellington's Peninsular Army for the next decade.

A person would think he was well on his way to becoming a damned fop, he mused scornfully.

In the second place, there was his behaviour. *A spray of lilac.* What the devil had he been thinking of? That was just the kind of trite gallantry that had always filled him with disgust and that was one of the reasons he avoided Fashionable Society. Young misses expected such treacle and one must be endlessly cudgelling one's brains for some effusive compliment or other, even if the miss had a squint and spots and interspersed her sentences with incessant Oh, la's.

It didn't matter that Miss Pelliston had neither squint nor spots and was perfectly capable of intelligent conversation. It was the principle of the thing, dash it!

That she'd left off her prim, buttoned-up, spinster costume was no reason to pour smarmy sludge upon her. Obviously his new *ensembles* had gone to his head. Because he looked like a fop, he'd tried to act like one. Clothes make the man.

Apparently, they made the woman as well. Perhaps he might not have taken leave of his wits if he hadn't been so very surprised at her transformation. The lavender gown and soft hairstyle had brought out a subtle, delicate beauty that no one but Louisa would have realised the girl possessed.

Idly he wondered, whether other men would appreciate it, and if they did, what they would make of the curious character beneath. Not that most men would waste much time evaluating her appearance or personality when they learned who her papa was. She would be prey to fortune hunters, naturally, but Louisa and Edgar would protect her.

Miss Pelliston was in good hands. All the same, he might as well pop in briefly to Lady Littlewaite's "do" tomorrow night. If other fellows turned out to be slow to recognise Miss Pelliston's attributes, she would need a partner. Though Max had little taste for the convoluted intricacies that passed for dancing, he knew all the steps just the same. He would dance with her and appear captivated and Edgar would do the same and eventually some other chaps would notice.

The ball, of course, would be tedious, stuffy, and hot, as such affairs always were. Still, he had only to do his duty by the young lady, then take his leave.

It occurred to him that he hadn't addressed certain needs in nearly a month. About time he turned his mind to that issue. After he left the ball, he'd drop by the theater and see what the Green Room had to offer.

Lord Rand accosted his lugubrious secretary and ordered the startled Hill to convey his Lordship's acceptance of Lady Littlewaite's invitation.

"Excuse me, My Lord, but I sent your regrets, as you requested, three days ago."

"Then unsend 'em," came the imperious reply. "Apologise for the mistake or whatever. *She* ain't going to argue. They always want those affairs well-stocked with bachelors, don't they? Daresay she wouldn't turn a hair if I towed you along with me — or Jemmy, for that matter," the viscount added wickedly.

10

"That's all that's left," said Miss Pelliston, examining in some surprise the names scrawled upon her fan, "except for the waltzes, and I mayn't dance those until I receive permission from Almack's patronesses."

"You seem to be the belle of the ball," said Lord Rand.

"There seems to be a shortage of ladies, rather. Nearly everyone who attended Lady Shergood's musicale the other night is ill," she explained. "Fortunately, hers was a most select affair or I daresay this ballroom would be deserted."

"Don't be ridiculous. The house is crawling with females. You underestimate your attractions."

"Hardly that. It's my papa, you know. Though he's only a baron, the title is an old one. You see, his ancestor, named Palais D'Onne, arrived in England with the Conqueror. Thus we are quite ancient," the lady recited, precisely as her great-aunt had taught

164

her. "People put much stock in such things, though one does wonder why. I had not noted that human beings were bred for speed or endurance as horses or hounds are. I suppose it is because ancient titles are so rare nowadays."

"Indeed," her attentive student soberly replied. "If Charles II had not been so generous to his illegitimate offspring, we would speak of the Upper Ten, rather than the Upper Ten Thousand. So you conclude that your rarity accounts for your popularity?" Lord Rand asked, sternly suppressing a smile.

"Not entirely. I'm sure Papa's money and the property I inherited are considered as well."

As perhaps must the fact that she looked like a pink rose, Lord Rand thought. Her eyes sparkled with happiness, her cheeks were flushed, and her pink muslin gown with its delicate embroidery fit her to perfection. That much he'd noticed from halfway across the crowded ballroom.

Now it struck him that she appeared a deal healthier overall. She had gained some weight. He hadn't realised that yesterday. He decided the addition became her, and felt somewhat relieved that life with his domineering sister was proving agreeable — physically at least — for the young lady. What she wanted now was a tad more self-confidence. Ancient titles, bloodlines — she knew as well as he what rubbish that was!

"I mean to debate this issue with you, ma'am, at length," he answered. "But later, when your next partner is not bearing down on me. Will you save me the country dance and sit out one waltz?"

"Oh, you really needn't —," she began, but he'd turned and left, and her partner had come to claim her.

Really, he was too obliging, she thought as Sir Somebody led her to the dance floor. All the women in the room were ogling the viscount as though they were half-starved and he a holiday banquet. In his simple evening garb — black coat, dove grey unmentionables, and snowy white linen — he was more striking and handsome than ever.

How graceful he was. For all his great height and those broad shoulders, he was well-proportioned, as the perfect tailoring of his coat clearly demonstrated. Well, he was an active man, and such men seemed to have an inborn grace — the natural result of physical self-confidence. In plain point of fact, he was splendid, and certainly needn't waste a waltz on her when she couldn't even dance it and there were scores of beautiful women who could.

He had asked her, though, and did not seem drunk. He would probably fluster her — he already had — but that was because she was unused to the ways of elegant gentlemen. One could not avoid every new experience simply because it was new or one would never develop intellectually.

"Dash it, Mother, I ain't a baby to be hauled about by the ear," Lord Rand complained as Lady St. Denys clutched his arm.

"My dear, no one ever led you by the ear — at least I should hope not, or if they did it must have been because you were doing what you oughtn't, and no one would have done so at any rate when you were a baby and couldn't walk at all until you were nearly two years old and then it was run, run, run."

She paused to catch her breath and Max was about to order her to let go of his sleeve when he found himself confronting a statuesque blonde whose light blue eyes were nearly level with his own. Dimly he heard his mother rambling on at the fair goddess's mama and then babbling at the goddess herself. He shook out of his daze in time to hear the introductions. Lady Diana Glencove. She even had the name of a goddess.

He heard himself uttering all the inane imbecilities he despised, and couldn't stop them from dribbling off his tongue. The goddess seemed to accept them as her due. After she'd made some gracious reply, she asked, in throaty tones that made his brain whirl, what he had thought of North America.

At the moment, Max knew as little of the New World as Molly did. It seemed to exist, along with everything else but this fair Juno, in another galaxy. With a mighty effort he wrenched his mind back to answer as rationally as he could. Then at last — blessed relief — he had to talk no more, for she'd agreed to dance with him.

That, Catherine thought as she watched the two tall fair ones take their places in the set, was exactly as it should be. They matched perfectly, Lord Rand and the beautiful unknown, like a pair of Norse deities. If her own face had suddenly grown overwarm, that was because the way he looked at his partner could not be quite proper. Though Catherine was unsophisticated, she was quite certain a gentleman ought not stare at a lady as though he were a famished horse and she a bucket of oats. Goodness, she was full of dietary similes this evening!

Catherine decided she was hungry. Lately her appetite astonished her. She, who normally picked wearily at her meals, had just this morning accepted Tom's offer of a second helping, and she blushed to recall how many of those delicious tiny sandwiches she'd consumed at tea. She would grow out of her new wardrobe before Madame had finished cutting the pattern pieces.

When the viscount came later to claim her for the country dance, Catherine forgot all about being famished. The steps were a tad too complicated — especially for one who'd just learned them — to permit concentration on much else, and the movements too energetic to permit witty repartee. She did miss a step when he told her she was in looks, but she reminded herself about intellectual development and managed a faint smile.

She returned to Lady Andover feeling rather pleased with herself and somewhat awed at the novel sensation. Catherine knew she was not, as Lord Rand had flattered, the belle of the ball. She had not expected to be.

Still, Papa's lineage and wealth counted for something, and she was grateful that they offered her a chance to find a more agreeable husband than Lord Browdie. None of the gentlemen she'd met so far appeared irritated or bored with her company, and she had managed to control her sharp tongue. She'd acquitted herself reasonably well, she thought, even with the one man who could unsettle her with a glance. London was not such a terrifying place after all.

Her new-won confidence and optimism helped her through the rather difficult few moments that ensued between Lord Rand's relinquishing her to Lady Andover and Mr. Langdon's appearance to claim Miss Pelliston for the next set. During these few minutes she found herself face to face with the hated Lord Browdie.

The shocked look that creature bestowed upon her gave Catherine some grim satisfaction. He had always made unpleasantly jocular remarks about her appearance. "Skinny as a broomstick" was not her idea of a witty compliment, any more than his blunt advice that she put some meat on her bones had ever sounded like affectionate concern. He had always spoken to her precisely as he spoke of his horses and hounds — except that he considered the beasts with far greater warmth. If he'd had his way he'd surely have put her in the care of a stableman who'd have made her eat her corn.

Now, though she found the way he leered at her bodice highly objectionable, she bore his clumsy compliments with frigid composure. Looking, she reminded herself, was all he'd ever be able to do.

She was delighted that she could decline

his request for the next two dances without uttering any falsehood. Her pleasure would have been unalloyed had he not gone on to ask for the supper dance. She had hoped the somewhat absentminded Mr. Langdon would remember to ask her about that. He was very attractive, and his soft voice was so calming. Now she darted a pleading glance at Lady Andover, who promptly came to her rescue.

"So sorry, My Lord," the countess told Lord Browdie with a cold smile. "Another gentleman has won that honour."

Mr. Langdon appeared in time to hear this exchange. When he led Miss Pelliston out, he expressed his disappointment. He looked so forlorn that Catherine had to stifle a maternal urge to brush his hair back from his forehead and murmur something soothing. She too was disappointed. Mr. Langdon seemed so gentle and intelligent. She would have enjoyed talking quietly with him during supper. Now she would dine partnerless — though that was hardly a tragedy. Her cousin and his wife would be with her and they were both most entertaining — and had she not already achieved undreamed-of success?

Having dragged six debutantes about the dance floor, Lord Rand decided he'd done his duty. In fact, he might be on his way to fulfilling the most unnerving duty of all.

He'd never expected to meet in elevated company a woman whose physical attributes so perfectly met his ideals. Not only was Lady Diana in no danger of breaking if one touched her, but she was generously formed and stunningly beautiful. Her throaty voice was a merciful relief from the usual high-pitched nasalities. She did not chatter endlessly about nothing and certainly didn't lecture about everything. Actually, she'd said very little, he now realised. Instead, she'd encouraged him to talk, and upon a subject she seemed to find as fascinating as he did.

The viscount's obligation to marry and get heirs began to seem less onerous. Tall, fair Junos were a rarity, even in the crowded London Marriage Mart. Courting Lady Diana would not be a punishment . . . still, he needn't make so weighty a decision this instant.

Nudging duty aside for the moment, Lord Rand headed for the card room. There he had the dubious honour of being introduced to Lord Browdie and the satisfaction of finding the brute as contemptible as he'd imagined. The viscount's enjoyment of the evening was further heightened when he proceeded to relieve Lord Browdie of a respectable sum of money, despite the rather paltry stakes.

Lord Browdie was a poor loser. Though he

managed to put on a swaggering show of hilarity at the outcome, he decided he disliked Lord Rand. After the card game broke up and its participants filed out to supper, dislike grew into loathing. Lord Browdie watched the blond viscount saunter confidently up to the Earl and Countess of Andover, make some remark that caused the couple to smile, and offer his arm to Miss Pelliston.

Lord Browdie had expected to find Catherine languishing at the sidelines with the other antidotes. To discover her dancing her feet off the entire evening was a greater shock than her improved appearance. He felt he'd been villainously deceived and ill-used, and though his feelings for her were no more affectionate at present than they'd ever been, he remembered her property and dowry with every sort of tenderness. He recalled as well the numerous rebuffs he'd borne this evening from all those other females Reggie had claimed were panting to breed Browdie heirs.

How he'd like to wipe that insipid smile off her sharp little face, and how he'd love to put that grinning, yellow-haired Exquisite in his place. Much as he would have enjoyed these innocent diversions, Lord Browdie had no idea how to bring them about. He decided, therefore, to leave the party and get roaring drunk in more congenial surroundings.

★ ★ ★

"You see, Catherine?" Lady Andover was saying. "We spoke no falsehood to Lord Browdie. My instincts must have told me Max would forget to ask anyone to sup with him. Though that's hardly complimentary to you, perhaps he'll contrive to be entertaining enough to make you forget the insult." The countess took her husband's arm and they preceded Max and Catherine to the supper room.

"Never mind what she says," Max told his partner. "Browdie was deuced generous to confound all the other fellows' hopes for your company. Because of him, my own lack of virtue is rewarded. If I'd been playing the proper gentleman, I'd have to sup with someone else."

Miss Pelliston found herself more pleased than she wished to be with the way the supper issue had resolved itself. Self-annoyance made her face rather stiff as she answered, "Since taking a lady into supper is hardly a moral obligation, your argument is unsound. In the first place, you committed no crime. In the second, if you had, there are a number of ladies here whose company far better qualifies as 'rewarding.' Your argument for the rewards of wickedness is specious, sir," she concluded with satisfaction.

"I'm a Sophist, am I? Oh, don't look so

amazed," he added as her wide hazel eyes opened wider. "I learnt philosophy as well as the next chap, I suppose. Which is how I know that your logic is shaky. You don't know a thing about those other ladies, yet you claim them more rewarding company than yourself. Shall we take a poll of the gentlemen, Miss Pelliston?"

"No, of course not. It was a pretty compliment. I would not have argued if you had not used it to defend an immoral philosophy — though I would be forced to admit that virtue is not always rewarded in this world and wickedness often is. But you see, you were merely forgetful, not wicked."

"Then you'll allow the pretty compliment to stand?"

She bit her lip. "I suppose I must, for you have twisted the issues so that . . . well, never mind. You are only trying to divert me, as her ladyship suggested, and I have no business scolding you for it."

"Of course not. You never scolded Jack Langdon, I'm sure. Why, he spent at least ten minutes raving about you. Then he forgot all about it and wandered off to find his book. I'm amazed he didn't have it with him when he danced with you. Often does, you know."

"Yes, Lady Andover mentioned that he was a tad eccentric. Still, I found his comments on the Medes and Persians most intriguing, though I'm afraid my ancient history is rather weak."

They'd reached the room where a very large number of very small tables had been set out to accommodate hungry guests. Lord Rand drew out a chair for Miss Pelliston. As she sat down, he leaned over her shoulder and said in a low voice, "I'm sure he was too busy talking himself and staring into your lovely eyes to notice your scholarly failings. Or if he did, he's far more levelheaded than he should be. You look like a pink rose."

Miss Pelliston turned pink enough. Lord Rand stared blankly at her for a moment before he remembered where he was and hastily took his seat beside her. Why had he uttered that revolting treacle?

He now wished he hadn't offered to sit out the waltz with her. That would not take place until sometime after supper and he wanted out of this confounded menagerie now, before every last vestige of his common sense was stifled by etiquette.

Meanwhile, if he didn't want her to get the wrong idea, he'd better bring the conversation into more impersonal channels.

"Miss Pelliston, you are behaving very badly," he lightly chided.

"Why, what have I done? This is the proper

spoon, I'm sure," said Miss Pelliston, surveying her silverware in some alarm.

"You were supposed to make a clever retort to my compliment."

"I know — but I just couldn't think of a single thing," she confessed with chagrin.

"I'll think of it for you. You must warn me of your thorns."

She considered. "Thorns — that seems apt enough. And the part about my eyes?" she asked, focusing those brilliant orbs upon him.

He leaned a hairsbreadth closer. "Yes," he said, wondering why he felt as though he were in quicksand, "your eyes are lovely."

"That's what you told me," his disciple reminded patiently. "What must I answer?"

He hauled his attention back to his plate. "Why, that they're sharp enough to detect the wicked truths lurking behind honeyed words."

"That sounds rather like a scold."

"Not if you smile when you say it, and especially not if you contrive to blush at the same time. That will encourage the gentleman to declare his innocence."

Miss Pelliston sighed. "This is very complicated."

"Yes," his lordship concurred, more heartily than she could know. "Very complicated. Anyhow, you're thinking instead of eating and you'll need sustenance if you hope to dance until dawn. We'll talk of something less taxing, shall we? How long before I can expect Jemmy to begin lecturing me on the rise and fall of the Roman Empire?"

Relieved to turn the conversation from herself, Catherine responded with more of her usual poise, though her mind drifted elsewhere.

She thought she'd been handling his lordship's altogether unexpected attentions with reasonable composure — until he'd bent to whisper in her ear. Then she had become acutely aware of a faint scent — a mixture of soap and something woodsy and cheroots and wine.

Examined objectively, this should not be an aesthetically pleasing combination of aromas, the two latter ingredients being vivid reminders of masculine frailties. Lord Browdie always stank of tobacco and spirits and that, along with his other unfortunate personal habits, usually made her wish herself in another county when he was by.

Lord Rand aroused an altogether different response, a host of sensations so novel that she could not be certain what they were. She realised, however, that these feelings were not altogether objective. Turning gooseflesh all over and having to count to twenty to settle one's pulse back to normal rhythm was not her idea of aesthetic detachment.

Except for ruthless exposure to most of her father's vices, Catherine had lived a very sheltered, isolated life. She had never had a friend her own age. There was no room for sentiment or frivolity in her education. Had she not been such a voracious reader on her own, she might never have known that such a thing as flirtation existed. Any tender, silly sentiments she'd felt before had been summoned up by plays, poetry, and novels, and had always seemed to belong to a fantasy world completely unconnected with her own sober existence.

Now she began to understand — viscerally — Sophia Western's trembling when Tom Jones was near. This was troubling. One ought not be so susceptible to a few pleasing words. If she did not keep a careful lookout, she would imagine herself in love with every gentleman who flattered her.

Lord Rand merely did what was expected at these affairs, she reminded herself. His behaviour seemed out of character only because she'd never seen him in such an environment before. Obviously, he could not have intended that she take his remarks seriously or he would not have offered to teach her how to play the game. If, at the moment, the game seemed perilous to one's peace of mind, that was because new experiences were often unnerving. Once she mastered the necessary skills, she would go about the business as coolly as he did.

Not that she meant to become a coquette. Even if capable of so far lowering her standards, Catherine was incapable of playing the part. She'd only look ridiculous. She wished she could find some safe island between prudery and impropriety — but the Beau Monde offered no solid moral ground. Hypocrisy seemed to be the fashionable equivalent of propriety, discretion indistinguishable from morality, and the rules seemed to constantly shift on whim.

Still, that was the way of the world. If Lord Rand could navigate these treacherous waters with such skill, there was no reason an erudite young lady could not.

11

As long as he'd already plunged into the turbulent waters of the Beau Monde, Lord Rand decided he might as well swim the distance. Dutifully he called the following day upon the young ladies with whom he'd danced. Among these was Lady Diana, whose mama beamed as the viscount entered her ornate drawing-room.

The young lady was fortunate, Max thought, to have been built to such generous proportions; otherwise she'd have been lost among the bric-a-brac. The room was large enough, but so thickly furnished with ancestral wealth that it seemed a museum whose collection had outgrown it. The walls suffocated under the weight of heavy tapestries and massive paintings, the latter encased in thickly carved gilded frames. Everywhere was gilt and ornate carving — chairs and tables so ponderous that any one would require a dozen strong men to lift it.

Lady Diana managed to hold her own

among this gilded magnificence. She accepted with quiet graciousness his tribute of compliments and all the other nonsense he uttered about the pleasure of her company the previous evening. As he found himself speaking mainly with her mama, the disloyal thought occurred that perhaps gracious acceptance was the sum of Lady Diana's conversational talents.

Her mother must have had the same thought. Out of the corner of his eye Lord Rand noted the minatory glance Lady Glencove shot her daughter.

"My Lord, I am so glad you found a moment to stop with us," Lady Diana obediently began. "I had been endeavouring without success to locate upon Papa's maps the town you described so beautifully last night. Is it part of the United States proper?"

Lord Rand ought to have been flattered that the young lady had exerted herself to examine maps. It did not occur to him to be flattered. Between his starched neck-cloth and the oppressive room he was certain he would be asphyxiated, and his mind was fixed on getting out to the street where he might loosen his cravat and breathe.

Not until he'd left the temple of the goddess and arrived at his sister's residence did the viscount realise he'd forgotten to invite Lady Diana to drive with him. Oh, time enough for that. He'd stop in again one day soon.

When he entered the saloon, he found Jack Langdon entertaining the ladies. At Max's entrance, Jack glanced at the clock and exclaimed, "Good grief, you sweet creatures have let me run on well past my time. Miss Pelliston, you must not ask such thorny questions about Herodotus when a fellow's allowed only a few minutes' visit," he gently chided, looking thoroughly embarrassed.

"I suppose you'd have answered well enough if I hadn't kept interrupting," said Miss Pelliston.

"If you hadn't, Jack wouldn't have let you get a word in edgeways," Lord Rand put in. "We once spent four hours debating Herodotus's explanation for the difference between the Persian and Egyptian skulls."

Miss Pelliston's obvious astonishment at this hint of his erudition would have put Max completely out of temper if her blank look had not immediately given way to one of dawning respect. He barely heard, therefore, Jack's overlong leave-taking, and scarcely noticed his exit. Max was too busy scrambling through the recesses of his mind for the section labelled Ancient Authors to even notice himself dropping into the chair nearest the young lady instead of that next his sister.

"What is your opinion, Miss Pelliston?" he asked. "You have an abiding interest in hard heads, I recall. D'you think the Egyptians did have thicker skulls than the Persians, and that it was on account of shaving their scalps?"

"Really, Max, must we discuss such morbid topics?" said his sister with a ladylike shudder. "Skulls and scalps, indeed."

Catherine intervened. "Actually, I was curious about just that matter. Perhaps it is morbid of me — but that is not Lord Rand's fault."

"Oh, everything's my fault," he answered carelessly. "You aren't morbid at all, Miss Pelliston. Your interest is scientific. You seek wisdom."

"Then she seeks at the wrong fount," said her ladyship. The viscount threw his sister a quelling glance which was utterly wasted.

"Louisa refuses to hear our speculations about the effects of exposure to the elements upon the human skull. We'll have to talk about the elements themselves, I'm afraid."

Miss Pelliston looked disappointed, but bravely took up the subject. "Very well. A lovely day, is it not? Rather warm for this time of year." She frowned. "That was not very scintillating, was it?"

"Of course not. How in blazes can talk of

184

the weather be scintillating? Oh, you do it well enough, Louisa, but then you've scads of practice. M' sister," he explained to Miss Pelliston, "has had years to develop the art of making the dullest topics sound horribly scandalous. I suppose you'll learn all that in time, but I'd rather you studied it with some other fellow. Shall I take you driving, so that we can talk morbidly to our hearts' content without offending her delicate sensibilities?"

A pair of startled hazel eyes met his gaze. "Driving?" she echoed faintly.

"Max, you're impossible. Catherine can't just dash out of the house at your whim."

"Why? Have you got an appointment with another chap?"

"Oh, no, My Lord."

"She's expecting callers, you inconsiderate beast."

"I see." Of course she'd have more callers. Bound to, when she'd danced until the wee hours. He had no reason to wish the whole lot of capering jackanapes at the Devil.

"Then what about tomorrow?" he asked.

Tomorrow the two ladies were promised to the Dowager Countess of Andover.

"Then the next day," he suggested.

That would not do, either. They must meet with Mrs. Drummond-Burrell in order to satisfy that august personage as to Miss

Pelliston's eligibility for vouchers to Almack's. After that, they had an appointment with Madame Germaine.

"Then the day after," Lord Rand persisted.

"Yes, I suppose that's all right, if, Catherine, you have no objections? Max is an excellent whip, so you need have no fear for your safety."

A rather stunned Miss Pelliston had no objections she could voice. A time was settled upon, and shortly thereafter the viscount took his leave.

"That was very obliging of him," said Catherine when he was gone. Frowning, she studied the lace at her wrists.

"Max is never obliging if he can help it, dear. I rather think he enjoys your conversation."

Miss Pelliston expressed disagreement and began to fuss with the lace.

"Well, at least you do not make him impatient," said the countess. "Not once during supper last night did I see that caged animal expression he normally wears in fine company."

Lady Andover's glance dropped from her protégée's face to the hand tugging nervously at the delicate fabric. "Obliging or not," she continued, "you must contrive not to look so thunderstruck when a gentleman seeks your company, my dear. It makes them conceited. At any rate, being seen with Max will do you considerable good — though of course I would not say so before him. People may call him Viscount Vagabond, but he's a great catch for all that. Your driving with him will arouse the competitive instincts of the other gentlemen."

Catherine had no opportunity to rebut, because at that moment the Duke of Argoyne was announced.

"Invited her for a drive?" Lord Andover repeated. "All on his own? You never had to drop a hint?"

The countess shook her head as she draped her dressing gown over a chair.

"Amazing," said her husband. "Should I demand his intentions, then? In loco parentis, I mean. As you told her, Max is an excellent catch . . . though I was certain he'd set his mind on that great gawk of a girl of Glencove's. She's the right altitude for him, certainly, even if she hasn't a thought in her head that wasn't put there by her mama first."

"Regardless her size, Lady Diana is a fair catch herself."

"Oh, I daresay. She has certainly developed well enough, and the Glencoves are prolific, are they not? Five sons and two daughters."

"You needn't be vulgar, Edgar. I know precisely why Lady Diana is one of Papa's half-dozen eligibles." Lady Andover climbed into bed and snuggled next to her husband. "I also know that she's a sweet girl. She will make an agreeable wife and a kind mama and would never give Max a moment's difficulty or disquiet."

"Now why didn't I think of that when I was looking for a wife?" his lordship asked.

The countess kindly proceeded to unravel this knotty problem for him.

At the moment Lord Rand was demanding his own intentions. How the deuce did he expect to make progress with the fair Juno when he was gallivanting about town with Miss Pelliston? She had been engaged today, and he should have let the matter drop. He'd only asked her on a whim because he'd rather talk of the Egyptians than the Americans. He'd been at the time sick to death of the Americans. Lady Diana's mama evidently knew his hobbyhorse and had ordered the girl to humour him. He hated being humoured. It made him feel like a recalcitrant little boy.

An adult ought not be coaxed into courtship as a child is coaxed to eat his peas, he thought, unconsciously paraphrasing one of Miss Pelliston's remarks. Not until he reached the entrance to White's did he realise that he *had* paraphrased her. Really, wasn't it enough that the chit had forced him to chase all over town for her? Must she now formulate his thoughts for him as well?

Two glasses of wine were required to mollify him. Then Jack accosted him and undid all the good the spirits had done.

Jack Langdon might live in a jumbled dream world haphazardly composed of history and fiction. He might be considered an eccentric. All the same, there was no denying he was a good-looking enough chap, with a more than respectable income, not to mention clear prospects of a title. He might have been married long since if only he could have kept his mind fixed on the matter. Jack Langdon, however, rarely fastened on anything in the present for more than ten minutes at a time, doubtless because his brain was too crowded with historical trivia.

Now, unfortunately, he had battened his mind on Catherine Pelliston, and Lord Rand had consequently to endure an overlong soliloquy about that young lady's perfections. Max was a man of action. He thought that if Jack was so very much taken with the female, he had much better set about taking her in fact — to the altar, if that's what he meant — instead of plaguing his friends with the young lady's views of Erasmus, Herodotus, and a lot of other fellows who'd been worm meat this last millennium.

Lord Rand shared this view with his friend.

Mr. Langdon's dreamy grey eyes grew wistful. "That's easy enough for you to say, Max. You've always been a dashing fellow. You can sweep women off their feet without even thinking about it."

"That's the secret, don't you see? Can't think about those things or you end up thinking and hesitating forever."

"Like Hamlet, you mean."

"Exactly. There he was meditating, waiting, and watching — and where does it get him? His sweetheart kills herself. Don't blame her. The chap wore out her patience."

Mr. Langdon considered this startling theory briefly, then objected to it on grounds that *Hamlet* was not first and foremost a love story. There was, after all, the matter of a father's murder to be avenged.

"On whose say-so?" Max argued. "A ghost. He had no business seeing ghosts. If he'd attended to the girl properly, he wouldn't have had time to see ghosts. If you want Miss Pelliston, my advice is to go and get her, and never mind palavering at me about it. While you're thinking, some other more enterprising chap's going to steal her out from under your nose."

Mr. Langdon stared. "Egad, you're right. There's that stuffy Argoyne and Pomprey's younger brother and Colonel —"

"Argoyne?" Max interrupted. "Lord Dryasdust? What the devil does he want with her?"

"He approves of her views on agriculture."

Jack stopped a waiter and ordered more wine before turning back to his friend. "I hear he had his face stuck in Debrett's all morning, rattling her ancestral closets for skeletons."

"Why, that pompous ass —" The viscount caught himself up short. "There you go, Jack. Three rivals already. No time to be wasted. Now, can we find ourselves a decent game in this mausoleum?"

Three days later, Catherine Pelliston was perched upon an exceedingly high vehicle pulled by two excessively high-strung horses. She was nervous, though that was the fault of neither carriage nor cattle. If the fault lay with the driver, that had less to do with his obvious skill in handling the delicate equipage than the nearness of a muscular thigh encased in snug trousers. The scent of herbs and soap, today unmixed with other aromas, seemed more overpoweringly masculine than ever. At least she hadn't to cope with the viscount's intense blue-eyed gaze as well, because he had to keep his eyes on the crammed pathway.

They had discussed Egyptian customs between the inevitable interruptions of stopping to greet acquaintances. These were short delays, Lord Rand having scant patience with the gentlemen who stopped them from time to time to pay their compliments to Miss Pelliston.

"Curse them," he muttered after the fifth interruption. "Can't they do their flirting at parties instead of holding up vehicles in both directions?"

"Oh, they weren't flirting." Catherine coloured slightly under Lord Rand's incredulous gaze. "Were they?"

"They meant to if given half a chance. Only I don't mean to give it them, inconsiderate clods. Good Lord, is all of London here?"

"It's past five o'clock, My Lord, and Lady Andover says everyone parades in Hyde Park at five o'clock."

"Like a pack of sheep."

"Very like," she agreed. "This is one of the places one comes to see and be seen. At least we are not at the theatre and they are not rudely ignoring the performance. Really, how provoking for the actors it must be to find their best efforts — their genius, even — utterly thrown away upon ninety percent of their audience."

"I'll wager you'd like to stand up and read them a lecture, Miss Pelliston."

"I should like, actually, to heave them all out at once. I'm sure my thoughts last night were as murderous as those of Lady Macbeth."

"Do you often have murderous thoughts, ma'am?"

"Yes." She stared at the toe of her shoe.

"Such as?"

"I'd rather not say."

"They must be quite wicked, then."

"Yes."

"Are they? That is very exciting. Do tell."

"You are teasing me," she reproached.

"Of course I am. I know you never had a truly wicked thought in your whole life. Not even a naughty one, I'll wager. You don't even know when a fellow's flirting with you. If that ain't innocence, I don't know what is."

"That is lack of sophistication."

"Then enlighten me, Madam Choplogic. What is wickedness?"

"You know perfectly well. Besides, I thought you considered it lowering to be instructed in wickedness by a girl of one and twenty."

"In dissipation, perhaps. But I won't tell if you won't. Come," he coaxed, "tell me a murderous, wicked thought."

She scowled at her shoe. "I have wanted to strangle my papa," she muttered.

"Egad! Patricide. Well, that's a relief," said he with a grin. "I thought I was the only one. Still, you probably had more provocation. My father at least never tried to force me to marry someone twice my age, and one who don't bathe regularly to boot. That Browdie is a revolting brute, I must say. I wonder you didn't run off the same day you got the happy news."

"I would have," she grimly confessed, "only I had no idea where to go and needed time to plan it out. I thought I had planned so carefully."

Max gazed at her in growing admiration as she went on with his encouragement to describe her elaborate arrangements — the governess's garments she'd sewn with her own hands, the route she'd planned that would get her to the coaching inn unremarked, the weary trudging through fields and little-used back lanes.

Had he been in her place, with her upbringing, he wondered where he'd have found the courage to embark upon so complicated and hazardous an enterprise. Why, Louisa had gone off with her maid in tow, in her own father's carriage, and only a few miles at that. This young woman had no adoring relative to hide with, only a prim governess who might send the girl right back to her papa.

"I never thought about what slaves to propriety women of the upper classes are," he admitted. "But there's really nothing you can do unchaperoned, is there? I can drive you in the park in an open carriage or take you to Gunther's for ices . . . and that's about the sum of it. Confound it, if I were a female, I'd want to strangle *everybody*."

"Fortunately, you are not. You may do and think what you like, for the most part. The world tolerates a great deal from a man."

"Oh, yes. We can drink ourselves blind, gamble away the family inheritance, beat our wives and cheat on 'em and no one turns a hair. Is that what you mean?"

She nodded.

"We live, Miss Pelliston, in a corrupt, unjust, hypocritical world. In the circumstances, you're justified in thinking murderous thoughts. If you didn't, I'd have to suspect your powers of reason."

He was at present suspecting his own. What did he know of injustice? He'd spent his life raging over what he now saw were a few paltry duties, minor irritations in a life of virtually uninterrupted freedom. She, on the other hand, had attempted one small rebellion — an act he'd engaged in repeatedly since childhood — and had very nearly been destroyed.

She'd never have survived Grendle's. Though she had the courage, she lacked the skill — because no gently bred female was allowed to acquire the necessary experience.

Now he wondered if she had the skill — sophistication, as she put it — to manage the petty treacheries of the Beau Monde. Not that her beaux weren't respectable. Andover would make sure of that. Still, she should not settle merely for respectability. She needed someone who'd not only allow her, but would teach her how to be free, how to find expression for the wild tumult always churning in her eyes.

He didn't realise he'd stopped the carriage and was staring fixedly into those eyes, because he was preoccupied with wondering what he saw there that made him feel he was whirling in a maelstrom.

"My Lord," she said somewhat breathlessly, "we've stopped."

She jerked her own gaze away to stare past him. Then her eyes widened in shock and her face paled and froze. Lord Rand looked in the same direction to discover Lord Browdie, in company with a female Miss Pelliston had better not know, bearing down upon them.

"Don't let on you see them," Max warned. "If the fool knows what's what, he won't dare acknowledge you — not with that demirep beside him." He urged the horses into motion.

Miss Pelliston lifted her chin and gazed straight ahead. Browdie and his barque of frailty clattered past, both of them staring boldly at the pair opposite.

"Now if that didn't look like a chariot from hell, with a couple of brazen demons in it," said Lord Rand when the vehicle had passed. "Him with his painted head and his trollop with her painted face. What a nerve the brute has to gawk at you — Miss Pelliston, are you ill?" he asked in sudden alarm. She'd gone very white indeed and was trembling.

"N-no," she gasped. "Please. Get me out of here."

12

They had reached the Hyde Park Corner gates. Lord Rand steered the horses through them and on to Green Park. The place was nearly deserted. He stopped the carriage by a stand of trees and turned to his companion.

"What is it?" he asked. "Are you ill? Or was it that disgusting fellow leering at you?"

"I know that woman. I thought I'd dreamed her, but there she was, real — and — dear heaven! — she was wearing my peach muslin dress! Oh, Lord," she cried. "I am undone. She knew me — I could see it. Didn't you see the way she smiled?"

Lord Rand saw at the moment only that Miss Pelliston was beside herself with grief. Since she was also beside him, he did what any gallant gentleman would do. He put his arms around her in a comforting, brotherly sort of way. He experienced a shock.

At that moment, Miss Pelliston looked up at him, her eyes very bright with unshed tears. His grip tightened slightly. His head bent and his lips touched hers. He experienced another shock as a wave of most unbrotherly feeling coursed through him.

Miss Pelliston made a tiny, strangled sound and pushed him away.

Lord Rand stared at her. She stared back. Her eyes were very wild indeed, he thought, as he resumed his grip on the reins and restored the horses to order. Perhaps she would knock him senseless. He wished she would. He had much rather be senseless at the moment. He did not like what he was feeling. Why the devil didn't she box his ears at least? He would settle for pain if insensibility was out of the question.

"I'm sorry," he made himself say, though he suspected he wasn't remotely sorry. "Something came over me."

"Oh, dear," said Miss Pelliston, turning away. She was also turning pink, and that at least was an improvement. "How very awkward."

"I'm sorry," he repeated stupidly. "I couldn't help it."

"How could you not help it?" she demanded. "What came over you?" She turned to look at him and he thought he saw in her eyes . . . was it fear?

"Miss Pelliston, you were in distress. I meant to comfort you, but I'm afraid my —

my baser instincts got the better of me. As you know, I'm rather impetuous — drat it." He felt like a fool. What on earth had possessed him to kiss Catherine Pelliston of all people?

Her eyes were still distraught, though her voice sounded calmer. "My Lord, there are times when honesty is preferable to tact. I have come to think of you as a friend. I hope, therefore, you will be quite frank with me. Did I . . . did I do or say anything to — to encourage you?"

"No, of course not. It was all my own doing, I assure you," he answered with some pique.

Her face cleared. "Well, that's all right then."

Taken aback, he spoke without thinking. "Is it? Does that mean you wouldn't object if I did it again?" But he didn't mean to do it again, he told himself.

"Oh, I must object, of course."

"'Must'? Only because you're supposed to?" he asked, though he wasn't at all sure he wanted to hear the answer.

She bit her lip. "My Lord, I asked you to be frank. I will return the favour. You are a very attractive man and I am completely inexperienced. No gentleman has ever kissed me before — at least no one who wasn't kin — and that was on the cheek. I think — I believe I'm . . . flattered. All the same, I am not *fast*," she added.

"Of course you're not."

"Therefore I had rather you didn't flatter me again, My Lord. Right now I have enough on my mind without having to question my morals as well. In fact," she went on sadly, "it looks as though the whole world will be questioning my morals soon enough."

"There's nothing to fear," Max answered, firmly thrusting the image of a blonde Juno from his mind. "I'll marry you."

"What?" she gasped.

"Isn't it obvious? We should have done it at the outset. You can't expect to hang about in brothels and spend a night in my lodgings without some trouble coming of it. It's our duty to marry, Miss Pelliston."

Miss Pelliston's colour heightened. "With all due respect, My Lord, that is out of the question. It is perfectly ridiculous, in fact."

"With all due respect, it's you who's ridiculous. The tart is wearing your dress. She's with Browdie. If she's recognised you, she'll tell him, and since he's no gentleman, he'll carry the tale. The only way to spike his guns is to marry me. Then, if he so much as hints scandal, I'll call him out and put a bullet through his painted head. It's quite simple."

Catherine grew irritated. She had not escaped a drunken tyrant of a father in order to acquire an overbearing rakehell of a husband. She did not express her objections in precisely these terms, but object she did, and in detail. She treated the viscount to a lengthy discourse upon her views of marriage, in which suitability of temperament figured most prominently.

Lord Rand reacting to this sermon with blank indifference, she went on in some desperation to tear to pieces his rationale for proposing.

In the first place, she told him, perhaps that wasn't her dress after all, or if it was, very likely Granny Grendle had sold it to a secondhand dealer and that was how Lord Browdie's companion had come by it.

Second, Miss Pelliston could not be absolutely certain she recognised the woman. With all that paint, fallen women tended to look alike. She'd barely glimpsed any other women besides Granny during her brief time in the brothel, having been drugged for most of that time.

Third, even if the woman knew her and did tell Lord Browdie, he likely wouldn't believe it. Or if he did, he was not so foolhardy as to carry so improbable a tale, especially when that might lead to a breach — or worse — with her Papa or Lord Andover. Either might challenge Lord

Browdie to duel, and he was a great coward.

Max glared at her. "So you claim you're not in the least alarmed?"

"Not in the least," she answered spiritedly.

"Then why did you take a fit?"

"I did not take a fit. If I gave way for a moment that was because I was shocked. Possibly I overreacted."

"All the same, I've compromised you," he reminded. "Besides everything else, I just kissed you in a public park."

"Good heavens, you can't be serious. Surely you do not go about proposing marriage to every woman you kiss. In your case that would most assuredly lead to bigamy."

Catherine stared off into the distance, her spine ramrod straight and her chin high.

"I think you must be drunk," she continued. "Yes, I'm sure you are. It was your vices that entangled you in my difficulties in the first place, and though I am grateful you were there to rescue me I cannot but regret the reasons you *were* there. Just now, vice has nearly led you into a grievous error which you would have cause to regret all the rest of your days. Later, when you are sober, I hope you will consider the matter and learn from the experience. For the present, I wish you would take me home."

"There now," said Lynnette. "Didn't I tell you it was him?" Her companion appeared not to hear her. He was sulking. Lord Browdie might not care where he found his entertainment, but he had rather keep that entertainment out of public view — unless, of course, the female at his side was in great demand among Society's gentlemen and one might lord it over the competition.

Whatever degree of popularity Lynnette had achieved at Granny Grendle's, she was scarcely in the running with the Wilson sisters. She ought, therefore, to know her place and be content to abide quietly, awaiting her protector's pleasure in the modest house he'd rented for her. But no, she must be wheedling and whining at a fellow the livelong day for "a breath of fresh air." Wasn't any fresh air in London. And now Miss Prim and Proper and her uppity viscount had seen him in company with a common harlot.

"Didn't I tell you it was him?" she prodded.

"Him, who?" was the peevish response.

"The one that took the new girl off." Lynnette went on to describe the highly entertaining scene she'd unabashedly watched from the top of the stairs.

"That's how I got this dress," she said. "I saw the old witch take it from the box and made her give it me." Lynnette neglected to add that the dress was the compensation she'd demanded for having turned such a promising customer over to a mere beginner. Lynnette had deeply and loudly resented having to entertain an ugly, drunken sailor instead of a drunken Adonis.

"Fifty quid?" Lord Browdie repeated as she concluded her story. "You meant to say, the fool paid fifty quid for a scrawny country servant?"

"I never got more than a glimpse of her, but she looked all skin and bones to me. Anyhow, it was thirty for her and twenty for her things — only they never did get all her things, as I said. Then the poor man is back two days later looking for her. The ignorant thing must have run off, thinking she could do better. Some girls have no common sense at all, I declare. A viscount you said he was?" Lynnette shook her head in regret, and perhaps not all of that emotion was reserved for the poor rustic who'd tossed away a golden opportunity.

The news that Granny Grendle had so easily cozened the aggravating viscount restored Lord Browdie to good humour. When he had a moment to himself he'd turn the matter over and see what could be made of it. Rand gulled by an old bawd and then the gal bolts after all. Oh, that was rich, it was.

Had Miss Pelliston been privy to the exchange between Lord Browdie and his light o'love, she would have had the unalloyed satisfaction of knowing she had acted aright in rejecting Lord Rand's offer. She had not heard that conversation, however, and was consequently most uneasy on two counts. One, whatever assurances she'd offered the viscount, she was certain that painted face was familiar; therefore Catherine was sure Lord Browdie knew her secret. Second, she did not believe he'd keep the tale to himself. He might not want to alienate her papa or Lord Andover and he might not want to be killed in a duel, but Lord Browdie was first and foremost a drunkard, and a loud, indiscreet, talkative one.

She could expect the rumour mills to begin grinding any day now, and after a short while they would grind her reputation to dust. Her poor unsuspecting cousin and his wife — they had no idea the scandal in store.

The worst was that she couldn't warn them. Of course Lord Andover would believe in her innocence. All the same, he'd make Lord Rand marry her. Even the viscount, for all his wild ways and impatience with convention, believed that was the only solution.

Catherine trudged slowly up the stairs to her bedchamber, followed by a prattling Molly, who could not say enough about Lord

Rand's elegant carriage, prime cattle, and altogether stunning personal appearance. She declared that Miss Pelliston was the most fortunate woman in creation, having been honoured by a drive with the most splendid man in all of Christendom — and heathendom besides.

"Really, Miss, I always said as he was the handsomest man," she raved, "only that was in a rough sort of way, you know. I do think he never cared much how he looked. But, oh, when I seen the carriage come up and him sitting there like the prince in the fairy tale like the sun itself was only shining to shine on him —"

Catherine cut short this venture into the realms of poesy with the information that she was very tired and wanted a nap if she was to survive tonight's festivities in honour of Miss Gravistock's birthday.

Molly subsided. That is to say she left off talking and commenced to sighing. However, this evidence of the state of her feelings had only to be endured a quarter hour, at the end of which time she left her mistress to her "nap" — if one could call the torments of the damned a nap.

Catherine lay her head upon her pillow and immediately that head grew feverish.

He had kissed her. As kisses go, it was not

much of a kiss, but Catherine knew little of how kisses went, as she'd told him. She now wished to learn no more. What had she told him? *Flattered?* She touched her lips, then jerked her fingers away. Her whole face burned, and in her mind, where there ought to be sober reason, there was only the chaos of jolting thoughts and alien, edgy sensations.

It was only a kiss, she told herself, and only the most fleeting contact at that — but somehow the sky had changed, and that was not how it should be, not with him. Good Lord, not with *him.*

In novels, heroines got kissed, but by the heroes they would marry, which made it acceptable, if not technically proper. This was not the same, and not acceptable for her. And she had liked it, which made no sense.

Had she not met him in a brothel? Hadn't he been utterly castaway at the time? Hadn't she heard Lord Andover's ironic sympathy for the gentlemen at White's with whom Lord Rand regularly gambled? Hadn't she heard as well from several others how Lord Rand had tried to start a brawl on the very steps of that club?

Besides, he was overbearing and hasty, just like Papa. Why, the viscount even affected the speech of common ruffians, full of oaths and bad grammar. That was hardly the stuff of which heroes were made.

Yet despite the ill she knew of him, she'd pushed him away only because she'd been so startled — and immediately she'd wished she hadn't made it stop.

Who was the Catherine who'd thrilled at the muscular strength of his arms, who even now lay shuddering as she remembered the soft, moist touch of his mouth, so light — only an instant — yet somehow hinting a warm promise that made her want . . . oh, *more*. There was the clean masculine scent of him, his face so close as his dark lashes veiled the deep blue of his eyes, the warmth of his hands on her back . . . only that. It was not so much. What had it done to her — and why *him?*

If she were a true lady, she would have recoiled at his polluted touch. She hadn't, and the reason was obvious: she'd inherited her papa's depravity.

Why not? She had inherited his temper. The only difference between them was that she took the trouble — and it was a deal of trouble — to keep hers in check. Now there was yet another demon to restrain . . . and a rakehell had released it.

Lord Rand had rather a knack, didn't he, of drawing out the worst in her. Good heavens — she'd even sat there blithely chattering away about wanting to murder her father and practically boasting about her scheme to run away.

Catherine turned angrily onto her stomach and buried her hot face in the pillow.

The man was dangerous. He seemed reassuring even as he was turning the world upside down. He was already making a shambles of her neat system of values. What would he do, given the opportunity, to her morals? What would he do if he knew how easily he conjured up those demons? He could turn her into a monster of passion — like Papa — wild, angry, driven. Lord — marry him! She'd as soon plunge into a tidal wave. Never. Her reputation was precious, but so was her sanity. If the reputation needed saving, she must save it herself.

In his own way, Lord Rand was as troubled as Miss Pelliston. The fact that he'd kissed her filled him with every species of astonishment. The fact that he'd liked kissing her filled him with horror. The fact that he'd proposed to her was so utterly bizarre that he could think of no expression suitable to characterise it.

He was not, however, given to prolonged introspection. He'd taken leave of his senses, which was not at all unusual, and had behaved rashly, which was even less unusual. That was all the explanation he needed.

Regardless what had driven him to commit this afternoon's atrocities, they'd pointed out, just as Miss Pelliston had noted, that he had become entangled in her affairs. If he wanted to make progress with the blonde Juno, he'd better get himself unentangled very soon. The way to do that was to eliminate Miss Pelliston's problem.

Lord Browdie, possessed of information certain to make the blond viscount the laughingstock of the clubs, lost no time in relaying this news to his friend, Sir Reggie. The baronet's reaction was not what he'd hoped for.

"Oh, yes," said Reggie. "Heard about that from one of those fellows — Jos, I think it was. Imagine. Him and Cholly both no match for Rand — and them twice his weight and him foxed in the bargain. Broke Cholly's nose, you know."

Reggie, it turned out, was full of admiration for the viscount's prowess and thought fifty quid a cheap price for such a marvelous mill. If Granny had kept back a few of the girl's rags and trinkets, what was that to St. Denys's heir? If he wanted, he could have decked the wench like a queen and never noticed the cost.

"But the gal run away after all," Lord

Browdie reminded in desperation. "Joke's on him, don't you see?"

"Joke's on her, rather. Where's she now? Probably haunting Drury Lane. Didn't know an opportunity when it bit her on the nose. Women," the baronet muttered scornfully.

This conversation threatened to restore Lord Browdie to the foul temper in which he'd begun a day that had started with a hangover and climaxed with the humiliation of parading his tawdry mistress in front of the two people he hated most in this world.

If he broadcast the tale, he would only gild Lord Rand's reputation as a virile, dashing fellow. Lord Browdie's bitterness increased. He believed himself betrayed and ill-used on all sides.

Here he was, forced to skulk on the sidelines while the arrogant, yellow-haired viscount squired Catherine Pelliston about town. Only a few weeks before, Browdie had been the chit's affianced husband, her property and money virtually in his grasp. Now the nasty, sharp-faced female had the effrontery to declare herself not at home when he called — and he her papa's oldest friend!

Miss Prim and Proper had no time for him, not when she could be flaunting herself all over London with her pretty viscount. What would Miss High and Mighty think if she heard how her golden darling spent his leisure hours — and with whom? Did Madam Propriety think she could reform Viscount Vagabond?

Lord Browdie smiled, displaying a crooked set of brown teeth to his companion. Once again the black storm clouds drifted away and he saw the happy sunshine. He could not tell the world his tale, but he must tell her. That was his duty as her papa's oldest, dearest friend.

13

Considering the outrages to which he was inevitably goaded by Miss Pelliston's mere presence, it did not bode well for the viscount to be found dancing with her that evening at Miss Gravistock's birthday ball. Still, Lord Rand had action in mind, and that action required her assistance.

"Lead him on?" Catherine echoed in bewilderment when he began to describe her role. "Are you drunk yet?"

Her partner bit back a hasty retort. "You can't get information from Browdie unless you speak with him, which means you have to be more welcoming than you've been. Looking at a man as though he was something the horse left behind isn't the way to elicit confidences. You have to be more encouraging. You may even have to dance with him."

Whatever indignant response Catherine might have made to this is lost to posterity, the dance at that moment inconsiderately requiring that they separate.

As he watched her move away, Max decided that the rose silk gown became her nearly as well as the militant light flashing in her eyes and the faint flush of anger that tinted her cheeks. Something stirred within him and he grew edgy.

Miss Pelliston must have become edgy as well, because when she rejoined her partner she told him icily that she had no interest in Lord Browdie's confidences.

"Very well," said Lord Rand. "Trust him if you like. Maybe he doesn't know about Granny's. Maybe he won't say anything if he does know. Maybe it wouldn't help to find out where you stand so that you can make an intelligent decision about what to do."

Miss Pelliston did not deign to reply, though her deepening colour told him he'd struck home.

"Well?" he said after a moment.

"I concede your point," she said stiffly.

As he gazed down upon her rigidly composed features, the viscount wondered how quickly her expression would soften if he covered her face with kisses. Simultaneously he felt a surging desire to run — very, very far away.

Lord Browdie, it turned out, was eager to unburden himself. In fact, in his haste to claim a dance with Miss Pelliston, he elbowed aside one duke, two baronets, one colonel, and one affronted Jack Langdon, who would have called him out on the spot if Max had not been there to hear his complaints.

"Call him out?" Max exclaimed, as he drew his friend aside. "You don't know one end of a pistol from the other. I'll have to take you to Manton's shooting gallery for regular practice if you plan to take up this sort of hobby. Or did you mean to stand at twenty paces and throw books at him?"

Mr. Langdon thrust one aesthetically long hand into his already rumpled brown hair and reduced mere disorder to complete chaos. That his disheveled locks and distrait aspect made him seem more romantically poetical than ever to several ladies in the vicinity was a circumstance of which he was as sublimely unaware as he was of those ladies' existence. He could not know that his rumpled hair and absent expression made women want to take him in hand and smooth him out.

Jack knew only that he'd elbowed his way through Miss Pelliston's crowd of admirers — who seemed to be growing more numerous by the minute — and had been about to request the favour of a dance when some ugly old brute had rudely thrust him out of the way.

Jack Langdon was not by nature a violent

man. Like Max, he'd spent his childhood being bullied. Unlike Max, he had not rebelled by running away physically. Jack had quietly escaped into the pages of his books. He liked Miss Pelliston excessively because talking to her was like hiding in a book — an attractive book, to be sure, but a safe, quiet, pleasant one, where no emotional or physical demands were made of him.

At the moment, however, he was feeling homicidally unquiet. As he watched Lord Browdie lead the young lady out, Mr. Langdon knew an unfamiliar yearning to commit mayhem. Fortunately for the peace of the company, Lord Rand was able to appease his friend by offering him the supper dance with Miss Pelliston.

The viscount did not make this sacrifice out of pure compassion. He had suddenly produced an idea that involved action, instead of hovering about boring himself to tears at a hot stuffy party filled with the same dull people he met at every other hot stuffy party. This was a more reasonable explanation than that he was desperate to put as much distance as possible between himself and a rose silk gown.

"You see, Jack, I've just recalled an appointment," he explained. "The trouble is, I've already asked her, and Louisa will have my head if I abandon her. Won't you be a good fellow and take my place? I daresay Miss Pelliston will be delighted."

Lord Rand was not being deceitful. He was certain the young lady had rather Jack's company than his own — just as the viscount had rather Lady Diana's company. As a matter of fact, he couldn't understand why he hadn't asked Lady Diana for the confounded supper dance. Mayhap he'd known instinctively that he wouldn't stay long and therefore had better ask one who wouldn't miss him.

Perhaps Lord Rand's thinking was not as clear as it should be. That was his problem, however. Mr. Langdon, upon being granted supper with a book in the form of a most agreeable young lady, was instantly restored to his customary state of abstracted serenity.

While Mr. Langdon recovered from his flirtation with violence, Miss Pelliston was enduring a jovial, avuncular lecture from her former fiance. The lecture would have been altogether unendurable — Lord Browdie avuncular was not a pretty sight — if it had not brought her so much relief. The baron obviously believed the young woman purchased from the bawd was someone else.

Catherine could not appear relieved, of course. She had to feign shock at learning of

Lord Rand's sordid entertainments. Since his vices were a sorrow to her — as they must be to any right-thinking lady — this would not have been so very trying, except that the activities Lord Browdie referred to with such sanctimonious relish were precisely those with which he entertained himself.

Hypocrisy can never be agreeable to an elevated mind. Hypocrisy mouthed by a swaggering drunkard who cares nothing for Mr. Brummell's dicta concerning clean linen, soap, and hot water is not only disagreeable but unaesthetic. Catherine was disgusted. She would have hastened to Lord Rand's defense — all in a perfectly commendable battle against hypocrisy, of course — if she had not recalled Miss Fletcher's remarks about tempering justice with a dash of common sense.

Catherine had to content herself with a show of shocked dismay. She even managed to thank Lord Browdie for his kindly meant warnings. When the ordeal was over, she searched among the crowd of faces for Lord Rand, but he was nowhere to be seen. The supper dance began, bringing Mr. Langdon to her side, full of apologies for his friend's sudden departure and hopes that Miss Pelliston would not be disappointed in his substitute.

Catherine told herself she was not in the least disappointed as she offered him a welcoming smile. Mr. Langdon's company was always soothing, and now especially so, after the emotional turmoil of dealing with first a domineering, wild viscount and then an avuncular, unwashed libertine of a baron.

The only problem was that she wanted to unburden herself, to express her contempt for Lord Browdie's pious humbug and her relief that it was only pious humbug instead of scorn and insult. Unfortunately, she could confide only in her partner in crime.

"There, Diana, did I not tell you?" said Lady Glencove bitterly. "He takes no more note of you than if you had been a stick of furniture. Which you might as well be, standing in one place the livelong night and never opening your mouth."

"Yes, Mama."

"'Yes, Mama,' she says — then does precisely as she wishes. Oh, was there ever such an undutiful daughter?" Lady Glencove dabbed her omnipresent handkerchief at her eyes.

"Mama, he is gone. I can scarcely run out of the house after him."

"He would not be gone, you unnatural child, if you would make but the smallest effort. He admires your looks, for which you ought to be thankful. How many others do you think would want such an Amazon?" the countess complained, as though her daughter had deliberately grown to this abnormal height to spite her.

"My size is hardly my fault, Mama," Lady Diana answered with a touch of impatience.

"It is your manner that concerns me. If he admires your looks, you should use the advantage. Instead you stand like a dumb statue and leave me to manage the conversation. You are not a stupid girl, Diana. Why must you let him think so?"

"I had not thought the gentlemen overly concerned with female intelligence —"

"*He* is," the mama interrupted. "Instead of talking to you, he stays forever with that bluestocking — and her papa a mere baron, while you are the daughter of Glencove. If he likes bookish women, you must contrive to appear so."

"Oh, Mama!"

"Why not? She cannot be better educated than yourself."

Lady Glencove studied the woman in question, who was conversing with Jack Langdon. "She cannot be so bookish as all that," her ladyship went on, "or Argoyne would never go near her. Really, I do wonder what the men see in her. She is hardly an Incomparable."

"She listens, Mama. I'd scarcely said three sentences to her before she asked whether I was as devoted to hunting as my namesake."

Lady Glencove looked blank.

"She meant Diana, the goddess of the hunt. I said I enjoyed it immensely, and immediately she had a dozen questions for me. She is most knowledgeable, though she says the sport is not to her tastes. Her papa is famous for his hounds, you know."

Lady Glencove discovered in these remarks something more promising than Lord Pelliston's success in breeding hunting dogs. "Well, then, you and the girl have something in common. That is good." Her voice became commanding again. "Unless you wish to break your mama's heart, you will pursue the friendship."

"I wish you would make up your mind, Mama. I thought it was Lord Rand you wanted me to pursue."

The mother uttered an exasperated sigh. "How better than to be always in company with those he spends his time with? Really, Diana, I begin to believe you are stupid."

"I am always stupid in Town, Mama. I cannot breathe here and I cannot think and —"

She was cut off.

"You are not going back to Kirkby-Glenham, young lady, so just put that out of your mind. When I think of that person, my blood turns cold. But I will not think of him — and you know better than to do so, I trust. What you will do is form a closer acquaintance with Miss Pelliston."

"Yes, Mama."

Mr. Langdon was not accustomed to supping with debutantes. He liked women — worshipped them, in fact, but in the abstract and from afar. Up close they were problematic. His mother and sisters, for instance, were always pressuring him to marry, and marriageable women made him uneasy. He would always sense in them, after a few minutes, impatience, boredom, some vague irritation. He did not know how he provoked these reactions, but he had little doubt he did.

Catherine Pelliston was different. If he rambled off to ancient Greece or Renaissance Italy, she ambled along with him. No topic was too abstruse for her, and she never seemed to require that their conversation be interlaced with flirtation.

She was a kindred spirit, he thought. In his eagerness to pay tribute to the quiet pleasure she gave him, he piled her plate with enough tantalising sustenance to satiate a soldier after three days' forced march.

"Oh, Mr. Langdon," said Catherine with a

small gasp, "are you trying to fatten me up too? If I eat but a fraction of this, you shall have to push me about the dance floor in a wheelbarrow."

Mr. Langdon's fingers promptly wrought their usual havoc with his hair. How could he be so boorish, so thoughtless? One did not offer young ladies buckets of food as though they were sows. His handsome face reddened as he watched his companion. She was studying her plate as though it were a mathematical problem.

She looked up with a consoling smile. "At least you don't pretend young women live on air and nectar, like hummingbirds. All the same, I'm afraid you must come to my rescue." So saying, she took his plate from him and began apportioning the contents of hers.

A few weeks earlier, Catherine had won the affection of an eight-year-old boy with one small gesture connected to food. Mr. Langdon might have two decades' advantage of Jemmy, but his heart was equally susceptible. In a few words she had put him at ease again, and those words, like the gesture, were so fraught with overtones of domestic intimacy and tranquillity that he felt they'd been friends forever. She might have been his sister — except that any of those ladies, in like circumstances, would have either burst into tears at the imagined insult or cruelly ridiculed him.

He had no way of knowing that Catherine was accustomed to smoothing over difficulties — or at least constantly trying to do so. He knew nothing of the scenes she endured at her papa's dinner table, and the quick thinking required to spare an oversensitive aunt's feelings or distract a drunken parent from some disagreeable topic or behaviour. He did not know that she'd sensed his nervous embarrassment and had acted reflexively to remove it.

Jack knew only that he'd committed a *faux pas*. Since he'd exaggerated its importance, he likewise exaggerated the significance of her tactful response. Gazing at her with relief, he wondered if he was in love with her.

"How kind you are," he murmured as he took his place beside her. "I should know better, of course — my sisters will never take more than a mouthful in public — but everything looked so tempting."

"Yes, and all the burden of choosing is yours because you are the gentleman. Women are so difficult to please, are we not?" she asked with a faint twinkle. "If you'd left out something I fancied, I would sulk. You leave nothing out and I complain. But that is for appearances, you know," she explained, dropping her voice confidentially. "The truth is, dancing makes me so hungry I probably could eat it all — and disgrace myself in Society's eyes."

The confiding tones made Mr. Langdon feel warm and cosy. He wished they could be engaged this minute, so that he might have the privilege of squeezing one of the gentle white hands that had touched his plate.

He made do with a smile as he replied, "That is because today's modes are for sylphs. These Grecian costumes are meant for slender faeries — as you are, Miss Pelliston. If, on the other hand, this were the time of Rubens, you'd have to gorge yourself."

He took up his silverware and took a turn into the early seventeenth century, where Miss Pelliston easily followed. He was soon lost there, oblivious to the rest of the company, and not even altogether conscious of his companion. He never noticed the occasional frown that furrowed her delicate brow.

Miss Pelliston's partner in crime, meanwhile, was in the process of attempting burglary.

Some hours earlier, Max had made discreet inquiries regarding the baron. That is how he found out where Lord Browdie's love nest was. The viscount was now standing in a dark alleyway, staring up at the windows of that house.

Clarence Arthur Maximilian Demowery, Viscount Rand, had in the course of his chequered career scaled any number of edifices. To climb the walls of this house was child's play. He did not hesitate. He grasped a drainpipe, found a toehold between the bricks, and commenced to climb. In a few minutes he'd leapt over the wall of a narrow balcony and stood pressed against the side of the house near the French doors, listening.

He heard, as he'd expected, nothing. The house was dark. Obviously Lord Browdie's mistress had taken advantage of his absence. Either she was out or she'd gone to bed early. Max would have preferred knowing precisely where she was, and if she slept, how soundly she did so, but a man cannot have everything he wants in this world.

He moved silently towards the doors and tried them. They were unfastened — why not? The citizens of London's West End had a low opinion of burglars' intelligence. Perhaps the ground floor was secured, which meant the front door and servants' entrance were locked at night. Thieves obviously entered a house as everyone else did.

He quietly pushed the doors open and crept into the room. The interior being no darker than the alleyway, his eyes had already adjusted. In what dim light there was he could make out the outlines of furniture. His eyes sought a wardrobe and found it. His feet took him to it.

Only when he'd opened the wardrobe door did he note the flaw in his plans, such as they were. The small space contained several items of clothing, all of them female attire. So far, so good. However, while one might distinguish by touch silk or satin from muslin, one's touch was not so refined as to distinguish a peach-coloured frock from one of any other hue. He cursed softly to himself.

At that moment a candle flickered into light and a soft voice murmured, "If it *is* a dream, I do hope I don't wake up."

Lord Rand turned towards the bed and found himself staring down the barrel of a pistol.

14

At the other end of the weapon was a comely brunette. The candlelight was gentler upon her countenance than the grey daylight of Hyde Park, and she was not so heavily painted now. Max judged that she was pretty, though in a rather blatant way.

He smiled, the pistol notwithstanding.

"I suppose," he said calmly, "you wonder why I'm here." He had not attended Eton and Oxford for nothing. Max knew how to preserve a mask of indifference even when in the throes of the greatest inner misery. At the moment he was not miserable, only a tad concerned that the weapon might have been constructed with a hair trigger, and thus might accidentally go off . . . in his face.

"Only if I am awake," Lynnette answered, quite as calmly as if she too had known the privileges of public school education. "If I am, I expect I'd better shoot you and have it over with, because whatever the reason, it must be a wicked one. Either you're here to murder me, or . . ." Her voice trailed off invitingly.

"Then shoot me," said his lordship. "It makes no matter. When a man has lost his heart and has no hope, it makes no matter whether he lives or dies. My heart," he went on, gazing soulfully into her eyes, "is yours. Has been since I saw you yesterday. And I have no hope because" — he hesitated meaningfully, but upon perceiving the pistol shaking, quickly continued — "because you belong to another."

Lynnette was no more proof against those devastating blue eyes than any other young woman. Besides, a handsome, virile lord had entered her bedroom, like manna from the heavens. She was not so ungrateful as to question the motives of Providence.

She relented, whereupon a tender scene ensued which is better left to the memoirs she will feel compelled to write when middle age begins to fasten its clammy hands upon her person and bank account.

The scene might have proceeded with dispatch to its inevitable conclusion — thereby providing Lord Rand another black spot on his conscience — had not the young woman's protector returned earlier than expected.

Since that gentleman returned drunk — as

was his wont on all occasions — and therefore noisily, young love was not taken unawares. A mere twenty minutes after Max had arrived, he was once again clambering over the balcony, and Lynnette, her own conscience considerably clearer than she would have liked, appeared to be sleeping the sleep of innocent angels when Lord Browdie stumbled into her bedroom.

Lord Rand was not accustomed to failing in his enterprises. This time he had failed miserably, and now he thought on it, the enterprise itself had been hasty and ill-considered. Hasty he could understand. What baffled him was how he'd expected to steal a peach-coloured muslin frock from an ink-black wardrobe in an equally dark bed-chamber. Still, he told himself, had he not been interrupted, he could have taken everything that felt like muslin — though he'd have had the devil's own time climbing down from an upper storey carrying a stack of gowns. The whole business now struck him as patently ridiculous. Had this been an isolated incident, he might have put it down as one of his occasional aberrations. The trouble was, aberration seemed to be growing a habit with him lately — and it had all started, he now realised, the moment he'd met Catherine Pelliston.

An assortment of unrelated rash behaviours was normal. A string of freakish activities all connected to one female was not. The girl was dangerous.

Lord Rand began to wish, precisely as her papa often wished, that Catherine Pelliston would go away. Thence the viscount proceeded — again, like the parent — to wishing she'd never been born. To wish the latter was futile. He concentrated instead upon how to make her go away. How difficult could that be? Even her father had done it, though it had taken the old fool twenty-one years.

Lord Rand doubted that Lady Diana would wait patiently twenty-one years for him to disentangle himself. Strong measures were called for. He must frighten Miss Pestilence away, terrify her back to Wilberstone. That would be hard on Jack, but really, if Jack was so taken with her there was no reason he couldn't go to Wilberstone after her.

In pursuance of dark plans, Lord Rand betook himself to his sister's establishment the very next morning. Twinges of conscience he had none. In fact, as he met Molly upon the steps of Andover House the next morning, Max bestowed upon her such a dazzling smile that the abigail had to clutch at the railing to keep from stumbling headfirst onto the pavement.

He marched into the breakfast room in his usual unceremonious way and announced to his sister and brother-in-law that he'd come to take Miss Pelliston driving.

"Max, I don't care what Catherine says. You are a sad wreck. You took her driving yesterday, don't you remember?"

"Yes, and I've come to take her again. Where is she?" the viscount demanded.

"Max, it's scarcely nine o'clock in the morning."

"Confound it, I can tell time as well as the next chap."

"Catherine is still abed, you great blockhead," said his loving sister. "Now, you may either sit quietly and breakfast with us or you may go away."

Miss Pelliston chose that moment to enter the breakfast room.

"There you are," said Max. "Wide awake too, I see, to give the lie to my rag-mannered sister. But she's always out of sorts these days. Will you take a turn in the park with me this morning?"

"Good heavens, but you do take hold of something and worry it to death," Lady Andover complained before Catherine could recover sufficiently to make a reply. "Will you sit down and be quiet? Catherine has not breakfasted yet."

Though Max was impatient to get his nefarious enterprise over with, he did realise that he was behaving like an idiot. He subdued himself, sat down, and dined relatively quietly, waiting until Miss Pelliston's plate was empty before he renewed his invitation.

Catherine realised quickly enough that her caller would not be so insistent about her driving with him and would not have come at such an early hour if he hadn't important news for her. She was mightily curious why he'd left the party and what he'd done. Besides, she was eager to relay her own interesting news. Now that they could be sure she was in no danger, perhaps he'd leave her alone. Certainly he would not subject her to any more disquieting physical displays and mad proposals.

Catherine, in short, grew as impatient to be gone as the viscount was. She scurried to get her bonnet, and the two were out of the house before the earl and countess had time to realise they were going.

Considering the unhappy memories of aberrant behaviour the place held for him, it was curious that Lord Rand took Miss Pelliston to Green Park. Perhaps he thought in this wise to exorcise the demon that had possessed him there. Whatever his motives, he directed the horses along a path of shifting shade and dappled sunlight. No colourful flowerbeds distracted the eye from the park's green serenity, for this was the place in which Charles II's Queen had commanded no flowers ever be planted. Here at least the straying husband could not pluck bouquets for his army of mistresses.

Max brought the carriage to a halt beside a large plane tree and turned a troubled gaze upon his companion. At least he meant the gaze to be troubled, because he meant to make her anxious. Unfortunately, he found a pair of hazel eyes gazing back. Those eyes were so unfairly large and their depths disclosed such a tumultuously thrilling universe that his own features relaxed, and the only trouble he knew was a mad desire to kiss her.

He forced the kissing part from his mind and focused on the desperation: he had to get rid of her.

He began by apologising for his abrupt departure the night before. When Miss Pelliston answered graciously that Mr. Langdon had been an altogether satisfactory replacement, Lord Rand experienced a novel, and thoroughly disagreeable, sensation — one that could not be, though it was suspiciously like, jealousy.

He forgot the slightly exaggerated warnings he'd meant to frighten her with and proceeded to relate his adventures instead, describing in unnecessary detail his meeting with Lord Browdie's mistress.

"Good heavens!" Catherine cried. "Steal back my dress? Whatever were you thinking of?"

"Destroying the evidence. You must see that the dress is the only concrete proof you were ever at Granny Grendle's. Without it, everything else is just hearsay — only the word of a tart against yours."

"Well, I do wish you'd waited a bit before rushing into such a dangerous act. Wasn't it you told me to find out how much Lord Browdie knew? And then you didn't wait to hear what I learned. Which you ought to have done, you know — and perhaps would have, if you had been sober," she added, half to herself.

Lord Rand had, all his life, considered it beneath his dignity to justify his behaviour to anyone. He knew the world called him Viscount Vagabond and he was rather proud of the title than otherwise. All the same, he was heartily sick of hearing this sanctimonious female constantly ascribe his every word, practically, to the effects of spirits.

"I wasn't drunk, dash it. Why are you always

accusing me of being so?"

Being a just woman, Catherine considered the question impartially. After a moment she answered, "I suppose it is because I can think of no other explanation for your behaviour. You are very inconsistent. Sometimes you appear perfectly normal."

Max knew a dangerous wish to be enlightened. At which times, he wondered, did she consider him normal? Was it at all possible that at such times she found him pleasant company? But he didn't want to be pleasant company to her!

A light breeze rose then and a faint scent wafted to his nostrils. Violets . . . and there were no flowers in this park. There was that strange stirring, a dull ache, somewhere in his chest. Resolutely he turned to gaze straight ahead. The horses' tails restored him to objectivity.

"Consistent or not, I'm not a drunkard," he snapped. "Not yet, anyhow. But I think you'll drive me to it, Miss Pelliston. I can't open my mouth without being accused of being half-seas over. Is that some sort of hobbyhorse of yours, ma'am?"

He stole another glance in spite of himself, and his heart smote him. He had forgotten about her father. Now the wet brightness of her eyes told him he'd struck a painful spot.

He felt like a brute — a great, clumsy lummox.

"Oh, drat." His instincts told him to take her in his arms and comfort her. What remained of his rational mind told him to keep his hands to himself, no matter how they itched to touch her. The two inner voices had a violent argument, and the rational mind won out. He apologised.

He told her he was out of sorts because he'd failed regarding the dress, had made such a mess of the business, in fact, that Lord Browdie's mistress was now confidently expecting to become his.

This is not the sort of talk to which a gentleman normally treats an innocent young miss. Miss Pelliston should have been insulted. She ought, at least, have pointed out the impropriety of the subject.

Like other ladies, she knew that gentlemen kept mistresses and that in the Beau Monde this was considered in light of a duty. Other women would feign ignorance of such matters. In Catherine's case, pretence was not only impossible, but absurd — after all, the man had found her in a brothel.

This was how she justified her reaction. She did not include in that justification the conspiratorial thrill she'd experienced as the viscount told his adventures. She did not even consider the relief she'd felt upon learning that the unfortunate female was not Lord Rand's mistress *yet*.

Catherine did admit — not only to herself, but aloud — that she was touched by his efforts, ill-considered though they'd been, on her behalf.

"All the same," she added, "it wasn't necessary. Lord Browdie thinks it was some other woman you paid fifty pounds for. He was so tickled that you'd paid so much only to be cheated of the girl's belongings that I wonder he hasn't told all the world about it. What was most provoking was that, in between chortling with glee about your being made fool of, he was lecturing me on the dangers of your company."

Perhaps Lord Rand was beginning to understand how very dangerous certain company could be. Perhaps he'd begun to wish someone had warned him away weeks ago. He said nothing, however, only smiled rather bleakly.

"So there is no need to worry about the dress," Catherine went on, thinking the man was not yet convinced. "I should have realised that. Lord Browdie is not the kind of man who'd notice what a woman wore. I'm sure he never noticed any of my frocks — any more than Papa ever did."

Lord Rand's smile grew a tad more bleak. Perhaps it had occurred to him that he could, if asked, provide an accurate list of every garment he'd ever seen Miss Pelliston in, from the moment he'd seen her wrapped in a blanket.

He said, "Then we've been making mountains out of molehills — is that it? Thinking everyone sees Banquo's ghost, so to speak."

Catherine looked puzzled.

"*Macbeth*, Miss Pelliston. Shakespeare and his confounded ghosts."

"I know — only —"

"— only you thought I didn't. I suppose, besides considering me a drunkard, you also believe I'm illiterate."

"No. I'm only surprised at your not pretending to be illiterate."

A grim foreboding began to overtake him. "Let's keep that a secret, shall we? I never meant to let on. Your happy news took me by surprise and I'm afraid I let my guard down."

"Why have it up in the first place, My Lord? Why pretend to be less than you are?"

"Don't want to raise expectations, don't you know," he answered with a fine display of insouciance. "People would start expecting me to be erudite all the time, and it's confounded tiring. It's hard enough just behaving myself without adding intellectual responsibility to the lot."

"You're a very strange man, My Lord."

"'Mad, bad, and dangerous to know.' That's what Caro Lamb said about Byron — or so Louisa tells me. Still, the foolish creature got to know him anyhow, and look where that led."

Miss Pelliston's colour deepened about six shades, which must have brought her companion some enjoyment, because he grinned as he gave the horses leave to start.

Catherine was no more pleased with the smug grin than she was with the thinly veiled threat. He was warning her off, was he? Did the conceited brute think she was pursuing him?

"You forget," she began as soon as she'd crushed down an incipient urge to do him violence, "that Lady Caroline is also accounted mad. She became entangled with Lord Byron because she was not thinking rationally. A sensible woman would certainly keep away from dangerous men."

"Would she? But you don't keep away from *me*, though my character failings, according to you, are legion."

"I do try to keep away," she snapped, "but you are always there."

"May I remind you that if I hadn't always been there, you'd be languishing in a whorehouse now, or getting run down by carriages, or working your fingers to the bone in a dressmaker's shop."

"Then you may derive comfort from the fact, My Lord, that I am no longer in any sort of danger, and you need waste no more of your valuable time with heroic rescues. You are at liberty to do exactly as you like. If you have accidentally got into the habit of rescuing helpless women, perhaps you should set about rescuing the one who now has my dress. I daresay that sort of activity is more in keeping with your tastes."

"Miss Pelliston, that last smacks of jealousy."

"Oh!" she cried, stamping her foot and thus alarming the horses. "What a coxcomb you are!"

"And what a devil of a temper you have. I suppose you'd like to strike me," he said with the most infuriating grin. "No, on second thought, I recall that strangling is more to your tastes. Maybe you'd like to fasten those ladylike white fingers about my throat and choke me? Be warned that there's a deal of linen in the way. Punching me on the nose would be more efficient, though more untidy. In either case, my cravat would suffer and Blackwood would never forgive you."

"You are insufferable," she muttered,

clenching and unclenching her fists. "How I wish I were a man."

"I'm so glad you're not. Manly rage couldn't be nearly as entertaining as the present spectacle. You look like an outraged kitten. I shall have to call you 'Cat' from now on."

"I never gave you leave —"

"I never wait for leave, Miss Pelliston . . . Pettigrew . . . Pennyman . . . Catherine . . . Cat. What a lot of names you have, just like a common criminal."

With a mighty effort, Catherine controlled herself. She would have liked nothing better than to choke the breath out of him and hated him for knowing it and teasing her with it. She folded her hands in her lap.

"I see," she said with a reasonable appearance of calm, "that you are bent on provoking me. I suppose that is the most productive activity you can think of."

"No. Kissing you would be much more productive in that way. Unfortunately, being a mere male and driven by baser instincts, I'm afraid I'd provoke myself even more. Therefore I shall not kiss you, Cat, however much you beg me."

Catherine stifled a gasp and turned her gaze towards the trees shading the Queen's Walk. Their leaves stirred in the light breeze, and above them the sky was changing from blue to grey. Her heart was stirring too, more agitated than the gently swaying branches — but that was only because she was so incensed. Of course he didn't mean to kiss her. He wanted to outrage her, and she was playing into his hands. Catherine decided she'd given Lord Rand enough entertainment for one morning.

"Very well," she said. "Since you are obviously proof against all my feminine wiles, I am obliged to turn the subject. What is this I hear about Jemmy wanting to become your footman?"

Lord Rand had lost the upper hand so quickly that he felt giddy. That must account for his witty rejoinder.

"What?" he gasped.

"As you probably know, I've continued Jemmy's lessons since that day you so thoughtfully brought him by. Lady Andover has consented to my tutoring him twice a week at the shop because it seems we cannot have him coming to the house. Mr. Jeffers claims that not only does the child distract the servants, but he is sticky. Cook evidently gives him too much jam. At any rate we have hardly begun, and Jemmy tells me he knows enough because he means to be a footman. Your Mr. Gidgeon has apparently encouraged him."

Lord Rand groaned. "I should have expected it. Well, if that's what Gidgeon means, there's nothing I can do about it. My servants do exactly as they please."

"All the same, I do not see why any servant need be illiterate. I wish you would talk to Jemmy."

"I don't see where I come into it. The boy dotes on you. I'd think he'd do whatever you tell him."

"I'm afraid he puts up with the lessons only for the sake of my company. That's flattering, of course, and I would not complain except that all he wants to do is talk about the livery he'll wear one day and tell me what fine fellows Mr. Gidgeon and Mr. Blackwood are. Mere grammar cannot compete with those paragons. However, he seems to have some respect for you as well, so I ask you to use your influence."

Lord Rand had begun to think that in spite of his earlier confusion, he'd managed to make a decent start in driving Miss Pelliston off by showing her what an ill-behaved lout he was. Now she was entangling him again in what was plainly her affair. What was it to him if Jemmy was illiterate? In fact, if she had to give up this tutoring business, that would be one less commitment keeping her in London.

The trouble with her — or one of the troubles — was her obsession with being useful. She'd returned to Louisa mainly because she believed Louisa needed her. She continued teaching the boy because she believed he needed her.

What the girl truly needed was a permanent occupation — like a husband. The sooner she got one, the faster the viscount could wash his hands of her and her plaguey problems. She needed Jack Langdon, and though Jack wanted no tutoring, he did need someone to take him in hand. They were perfectly suited. They would speak of books the livelong day and night and bore everyone else but themselves to distraction.

Lord Rand smiled benignly upon his companion. "Very well," he said. "I'll talk to the br — boy."

15

Following the drive in Green Park, Lord Rand took himself to Gentleman Jackson's boxing establishment. The viscount had an excess of nervous energy and physical exertion was the obvious cure. Today the Gentleman himself deigned to accommodate his lordship. At the end of the exercise Max was pleasantly fatigued, his nervous energy dissipated in perspiration.

He even lingered for a while after, watching the other gentlemen at their labors and offering the occasional piece of unwelcome advice to his less agile fellows. Thus he had the surprise of his life. He was just preparing to leave when Jack Langdon entered.

The probability of finding Jack Langdon in a boxing saloon was approximately equivalent to that of encountering the Archbishop of Canterbury at Granny Grendle's — though the odds were rather in favour of the Archbishop.

"What the devil brings you here?" the viscount enquired of his friend.

Mr. Langdon stood for a moment looking absently about him as though in search of something he'd forgotten. "Not the most pleasantly fragrant place, is it, Max?" he noted in some wonder. "Odd. Very odd. I count three viscounts, one earl, a handful of military chaps and — good God — is that Argoyne?"

"Yes. One duke."

"All come, it seems, for the express purpose of letting some huge, muscular fellow hit them repeatedly."

"So what's *your* purpose?"

"I suppose," Mr. Langdon answered rather forlornly, "I've come to be hit."

This was insufficient explanation, as Max promptly pointed out.

"I've come to be more dashing, as you advised. I've been thinking over what you said the other day, and I concluded 'Mens sana in corpore sano,' in the words of Juvenal . . . or as Mr. Locke so aptly put it, 'A sound mind in a sound body is a short but full description of a happy state in this world.' Physical prowess accords self-confidence. Boxing is reputed not only to increase physical strength and skill but to improve one's powers of concentration. Just the thing for me, I decided."

"So you mean to leave off meditating and

hesitating and prepare yourself for action instead," said Max. "Well, they do say love works miracles."

Mr. Langdon flushed. "I was referring to what you said about throwing books at twenty paces. No reason I should be letting a gangly, decrepit drunkard twice my age push me about."

Jack plainly did not care to be teased about Miss Pelliston. If he wanted to believe that manly pride had brought him to the boxing saloon, that was perfectly acceptable. At least the chap was making an effort, and that ought to be encouraged. A hesitating, insecure Jack Langdon did not bode well for Lord Rand's plans regarding a certain young lady's future occupation.

"Right you are. No reason on earth, my lad. Wait here a minute and I'll find Mr. Jackson for you."

Lord Rand might have taken his friend to the famous boxer instead of the other way around, but he needed to talk to Mr. Jackson privately first. The viscount did not want Mr. Langdon discouraged in his first efforts, and decided to drop a gentle hint in advance regarding the care and handling of dreamy-eyed intellectuals.

Mr. Jackson proving a sympathetic soul, Jack Langdon's introduction to the manly art was considerably less debilitating than that, for instance, of an insolent young sprig of the nobility whom the professionals in the place all agreed wanted taking down a peg or two.

Mr. Langdon, in contrast, was handled with the proverbial kid gloves, and vigorously encouraged by both Max and the Gentleman. Both repeatedly pointed out that the neophyte, despite his sedentary habits, showed great promise with his fives.

At the end of his exercise, Mr. Langdon was glowing, literally and figuratively. In this malleable state he was open to every one of Lord Rand's suggestions regarding another manly art — courtship.

"Almack's tomorrow," Max reminded as they left the saloon. "It's her first time, and you have to get a waltz. More romantic, you know."

"I know. The trouble is, I have to face one of the Gorgons first and they all hate me because they heard I called them Gorgons."

"What in blazes are you talking about?"

"The waltz. The Gorgons — the patronesses — have to give her permission to waltz, and that means they pick a suitable partner and I'm not suitable. If I go up and ask them, they'll laugh in my face. The only reason they let me in the door is so they can humiliate me at their leisure."

"That's ridiculous."

"You've been away too long, Max. You don't know what cats they can be. If I ask to waltz with Miss Pelliston, they won't just refuse me. They might even not let her waltz at all with anyone, just for spite."

"They won't alienate Louisa."

"They don't care who they antagonise. Don't you know they wouldn't let Wellington in one night because he was a few minutes late? And another time because he wore trousers instead of knee breeches?"

"No, I don't know it, but I ain't surprised. Of all the dull, stuffy stupidity that passes for entertainment, Almack's is the dullest, stuffiest, and stupidest. So naturally that's where everyone wants most to be. If Society had half a grain of sense it'd shun Almack's like the plague."

"But it doesn't," said Jack. "So I can't waltz with her."

"All this means is you can't have the first one," Max answered bracingly. "I'll take care of that. Then you have to make sure you manage the rest."

What he meant by taking care of the matter was that he'd find someone who had less to fear from Almack's patronesses. Not himself, of course. Though Lord Rand was afraid of nobody, there was that nagging problem with Catherine Pelliston's proximity. He had enough trouble sitting beside her in a carriage. Whirling about a dance floor with his arm about her waist was an invitation to disaster.

He reported none of this to Jack Langdon because Jack would feel obliged to analyse the problem. Max didn't want anything analysed. He just wanted Catherine Pelliston to go away.

Having nudged Mr. Langdon gently but firmly down the path to matrimony, Lord Rand went home with equally charitable resolve to release Miss Pelliston from her onerous educational responsibilities.

Jemmy, Mr. Gidgeon reported, was belowstairs assisting Cook.

"Annoying him, you mean. Girard doesn't know any English and I'll eat my hat if the brat knows a word of French."

Mr. Gidgeon politely responded that the scrubbing of pots did not require bilingual skills. "Cleans 'em very well, My Lord, 'e does. As 'e does heverything. A most henterprising lad. Wotever we sets 'im to, 'e does it — with a vengeance, hif I may say so."

"Well, set him to come up to see me in my den — library — whatever you call it. I want a word with him. While you're at it, you might as well send a bottle along with him. My throat's dry as the Pharaoh's mummy."

Mr. Gidgeon withdrew. A few minutes later he returned with Jemmy, who bore a tray upon which reposed a decanter of Madeira and a sparkling crystal wineglass.

The boy carried the tray and set it down with a deft grace that astonished Lord Rand and brought a satisfied smile to the butler's face. Mr. Gidgeon had preceded the tray into the room in order to lend the ritual the appropriate dignity and ceremony. Now he withdrew.

Jemmy remained by the sturdy, marble-topped table upon which he'd placed the tray, and looked about him with an air as complacent and proprietary as that of the butler.

"You're a lad of many talents, Jemmy," said Lord Rand as he poured himself a drink.

"I hope I give satisfashun, sir."

His lordship blinked and put the glass down to stare at the boy, half expecting him to have miraculously sprouted whiskers and shot up two or three feet.

No, this was still an eight-year-old boy, but one doing an uncannily accurate imitation of Mr. Gidgeon, minus the misplaced aitches.

"So you mean to enter my employ, young man?" the viscount asked with like gravity.

"Yes, sir — My Lord. 'N' wear one of 'em blue coats wif shiny buttons, like Roger got."

"Exactly. Shiny buttons. I commend you on your choice of profession, Jemmy. The question is, what about your lessons?"

"Wot about 'em?" Jemmy asked, a guilty expression overtaking his grave dignity.

"Miss Pelliston tells me you don't attend as you used to. She's worried."

Jemmy sighed. "First it wuz the letters and then the words and still there's no end to it. Sentences, she says. And punk — punk —"

"Punctuation," Max supplied.

"Wot you said. 'N' grammar. Don't it *never* end?"

"I'm afraid not. After that, there's books. No end to them at all, as you see." The viscount gestured towards the bookshelves Louisa had crammed with several hundred tomes his lordship had no intention of opening.

Jemmy groaned.

"Not as interesting as the buttons, eh? Why should they be, to a lad of your talents? You have greater things awaiting you. In a few years, with diligence, you might become a footman. Or if you find your tastes don't run to fetching and carrying, perhaps you'll consider horses."

"Horses?" the boy echoed wonderingly.

"Yes. If you're as conscientious as Mr. Gidgeon says, perhaps I ought to think of training you as my tiger."

"You don't mean 'at!" The child's face glowed with excitement. Evidently he'd not dared aspire to the honour of tending his lordship's prime cattle and dashing vehicles.

"I do. But it will require a deal of work. I don't know where you'll find time for your lessons."

Gloom overtook the glow.

"What's the trouble, Jemmy? You don't care for them anyhow. You might as well give them up now and spare Miss Pelliston and yourself some pains."

"I can't," Jemmy answered in anguished tones. "'At's the only time I get to see her. 'Cept when she comes for gowns and such — and all that time she's talkin' wif HER — Missus, I mean. Or Sally or Joan."

"So the only reason you put up with these lessons is to have Miss Pelliston's undivided attention?"

Jemmy nodded dolefully, rather in the style of Mr. Hill.

Max sipped his Madeira and thought. Buttons, even shiny ones, could not compete with Miss Pelliston's undivided attention. One had better reveal the ugly truth. The child would have to face it sooner or later anyhow.

"Jemmy, I must speak with you man to man. Do you know why Miss Pelliston is in London?"

"Parties. She dresses up fancy and goes to parties, day and night."

"She is in London, going to these parties, in order to find a husband. The parties are given mainly so that unmarried young men and women can find someone to marry. Because Miss Pelliston is a very wealthy young lady of fine family, she will marry some great lord. That lord will not want his ladywife teaching anybody — not even his own children. He will hire governesses and tutors for that purpose. Do you understand?"

"No."

Lord Rand decided to take a simpler if more brutal approach. "Miss Pelliston will marry soon — possibly within the next month. When she does, I promise you will not see her again, except when she visits the shop to buy more gowns. There will be no more lessons."

To his credit, Jemmy did not reel from this blow. Instead he gazed upon the viscount with something very like suspicion. "Why din't she tell me, then?"

"I don't know. Today is your lesson day, isn't it? Ask her. I am not trying to deceive you. I am not so desperate for a tiger."

Immediately after this discussion, Jemmy sought out Mr. Blackwood. If anyone knew what was what, this gentleman did. To his distress, Jemmy learned that Lord Rand had spoken the truth. In fact, rumour had it that both Mr. Langdon and the Duke of Argoyne were vying — albeit slowly and cautiously — for Miss Pelliston's hand.

As Jemmy was aware, servants knew a deal more about what went on in the Great World than its members did. If you could not get the facts belowstairs, you couldn't get them anywhere in the kingdom.

"Wot about HIM?" Jemmy asked after he'd digested this catastrophic news.

"His lordship, you mean? What about him?"

"Is HE here to get married too?"

"It is his lordship's duty to marry at some point and get heirs to carry on the title. Whether he has set his mind to that matter yet is a question I cannot answer. I have heard some talk about Lady Diana Glencove, but no more than talk. To my knowledge, his lordship has called on her once and danced with her on occasion."

"Don't HE see Miz Kaffy too? Don't HE never dance with her?"

Mr. Blackwood studied the round face lifted enquiringly towards his. He believed he could see the inner wheels beginning to turn. Mr. Blackwood approved of turning inner wheels.

By and large the aristocracy was intelligent enough. The problem was that its members had no need to live by their wits. Thus their wits atrophied. If they could not rely upon the sharper instincts and abundant common sense of their servants, the British upper classes would destroy themselves through sheer ineptness.

That was precisely what had happened in France, and look at the result. Until very recently, most of the civilized world had been under the boot of one short, ill-tempered Corsican. Compared to Napoleon, even a mad King George III was a desirable monarch, and the fat, dissolute Regent an Alexander the Great. Mr. Blackwood was no radical.

For the survival of Britannia the turning of inner wheels must be encouraged.

"Yes, Jemmy," the valet answered, "he does see her and he does dance with her and he has, to my knowledge, taken her driving twice."

"Wot for?"

"I hope, my boy, you have abandoned the notion that his lordship has designs on the young lady's virtue." Receiving a blank look, the valet explained, "He doesn't mean anything wicked, you know."

"Then wot does he mean?"

In his pursuit of wisdom, Jemmy had followed Mr. Blackwood along the hall and up the stairs. They now stood at the door of

Lord Rand's chambers.

Mr. Blackwood glanced about him. Then he bent towards the boy and said in a low voice, "I think my lad, I had better explain something to you about the upper-class mind."

Lord Browdie sat in the bedchamber of his love nest glaring at the peach-coloured gown that lay in a heap on the floor. There Lynnette had dropped it after opening a large box containing the two monstrous overpriced gowns she'd insisted on having.

What a greedy creature she was. Worse, here he was, throwing away perfectly good money on a whore — captivating though she was — when he still hadn't found himself a wife. The only respectable willing females he'd met had turned out to have pockets to let. His affection for Catherine's property and dowry was increasing daily in consequence.

"Now isn't that better?" Lynnette asked coyly as she reentered the room. She made a slow, langorous turn so that her protector might fully appreciate every entrancing detail of the crimson gown and the shapely form upon which it was draped.

"Yes, better," the baron answered shortly, wondering what the bill would look like.

"There was a moment there I thought it wouldn't be ready after all, such a fuss there was at the mantua-maker's. That little girl," she went on while admiring herself in the glass. "You know — the one was with him that day — that tall one you said was a viscount." Lynnette knew very well the man was a viscount and she knew precisely how tall he was, but she didn't tell her protector everything she knew.

Lord Browdie was nudged out of his painful meditations. "Catherine Pelliston, you mean?"

"If you say so. With the great eyes and everything else so little," she added disparagingly. "I was going into the dressing room and she comes out with a horrid little boy holding her hand. Miss Hoity-Toity went all white," she sniffed. "The way she stared at my gown — she even had *me* thinking there was something nasty crawling on it. That one." She nodded towards the frock Lord Browdie had absently picked up while she was talking. "Which of course when I thought of it I had to give her some credit, as it didn't really suit me at all."

Lord Browdie stared at the gown as his brain slowly, ponderously creaked into motion.

"Such a stir she made. The boy starts howling and Madame comes running in and no one has a thought for me, because they must give the delicate lady the cup of tea — so she could recover from the terrible shock of seeing a fallen woman." Lynnette smiled. "Actually, I did feel sorry for her. She looked so ill and white that for a minute she put me in mind of that poor country servant I told you about — the one that cost that viscount so much money. Remember?"

"Yes." Lord Browdie's head began to throb.

"I expect Miss Prim and Proper would faint dead away if she knew she reminded me of her fine gentleman's low sweetheart."

"No," said Lord Browdie. "She's too obstinate to faint. Did she really look like the girl? Maybe that's why Rand took up with her."

"Oh, you naughty boy!" Lynnette reached out to playfully ruffle the garish red hair, then changed her mind and settled for a coquettish smile instead. "Maybe that *is* why. I told you I never saw much of her myself. You know how Granny is — never liked the girls to get together because she thought we'd plot behind her back. I couldn't say really if she's like her or not. It was just one of those odd ideas that come into your head sometimes."

Lord Browdie had a very odd idea in his head at the moment. Lynnette had connected the dress with Catherine during her monologue. Now he made his own connection.

This was the frock Catherine had donned when she'd emerged from those unspeakable mourning costumes she'd worn for her great-aunt. The warm colour had been such a relief from the ghastly blacks and half-mourning that he'd noticed. He even recalled thinking at the time that for once she didn't look like a corpse herself. No wonder he'd remembered the gown.

Catherine's gown. Now Lynnette's gown. In between it had been, briefly, Granny Grendle's — and she had stolen it from the female Lord Rand had paid fifty quid for. In a brothel.

The idea of Catherine Pelliston — the most sanctimonious of prigs — in a brothel was so outlandish that the baron would need two bottles of wine to assimilate it. He ordered Lynnette off to the milliner's. He was too taken up with his wonder to think of the bills that would result, and knew only that he needed to be alone, to think.

Lynnette promptly obliged him. She was gone before he'd opened the first bottle, in fact. Many glasses later, Lord Browdie's bewilderment had given way to the happiest of daydreams.

Another man might shrink at the prospect of a soiled wife, but Lord Browdie was not just any man and this was not just any wife. A soiled Catherine Pelliston was vulnerable, and a vulnerable Catherine Pelliston was the only female of that name who would agree to marry him — once, that is, he pointed out the alternative.

The precise name for what Lord Browdie contemplated was blackmail, but he was not overly concerned with semantics, any more than he was concerned with physical technicalities, such as virginity. That only meant he wouldn't have to endure any tiresome whining on his wedding night.

As long as she wasn't breeding already — and he'd make sure of that first — her maidenhead was of no concern to him. If she was breeding . . . he frowned briefly, but only briefly. In that case, the price of keeping her secret would be to let him enjoy the favours others had tasted — like that insolent Rand, for instance.

Lord Browdie refilled his glass and swallowed its contents with as much joy as if it had been the ambrosia of Olympus. After all, what greater happiness is there than contemplating the humiliation of one's enemies?

16

Lord Rand's plans and Mr. Langdon's hopes were doomed to disappointment. Miss Pelliston did not appear at Almack's that evening because Lady Andover had been suddenly taken ill.

The countess was better the following day, though somewhat stunned by the experience. She had never been sick a day in her life — she scorned illness, refused to have anything to do with it.

Given her attitude, it was hardly surprising that she insisted on attending the celebration of Miss Clarissa Ventcoeur's betrothal to Lord Fevis. Louisa most certainly could not lie abed all day, and if she were forced by her brute of a husband to remain at home, she would drive herself mad. The brute, who had merely suggested — in the gentlest way — that his wife indulge in a day's rest, shook off his alarm and withdrew the hateful suggestion.

Lord Rand also attended the exuberant celebration, mainly to be at hand in case Mr.

Langdon required any guidance or moral support in the pursuit of Miss Pelliston.

The party was held out of doors on the Ventcoeurs' large estate several miles from London. This meant that the guests were at liberty to join in the planned entertainments or amuse themselves by wandering about the beautiful grounds. Being at liberty to wander, Jack did so. He got into a lively debate with a literary gentleman on the merits of the Lake Poets and strolled off with him into the maze. There the two intellectuals met up with Miss Gravistock and her cousin, who promptly joined the battle.

Lord Rand decided that the mountain had better be brought to Mahomet. He found Miss Pelliston conversing with his mama and proposed that the ladies walk with him. That was perfectly acceptable — until his mother got herself lost *en route*. Lady St. Denys spied one of her friends and, in her usual fuddled manner, went where her gaze led her and forgot all about her son and the young lady.

That was when disaster struck. The maze and Mr. Langdon were due east. Due west Miss Pelliston caught sight of a Greek temple. She had never seen such an elaborate folly before, having never explored an elegantly landscaped estate. Unlike other young ladies, she was unaccustomed to discovering temples and statues, pagodas and grottoes in every nook and cranny. Instead of being overcome by ennui, she was charmed — and admitted it.

"Oh, it is like a story, isn't it?" she cried in delight. "Can one go inside, do you think?"

One could. One — or two, rather — did.

In the rotunda, she skipped from one carved deity to the next, quoting from the *Iliad* or the *Odyssey* — Lord Rand was not sure which. As she turned, smiling, to answer some wry comment he made, his heart began to thud. Her open joy warmed him.

He moved nearer and unthinkingly took her hands in his. Hers were so small and slender in their ladylike white gloves. The touch made him feel amazingly strong, but needful of something. He drew her to him.

Her smile wavered. Meaning to reassure her, he bent his head and whispered, "You're — like a happy nymph."

Her eyes grew troubled, but he was already lost, searching in her gaze for he knew not what. Even as she started to answer, his head bent closer still, and his mouth covered hers.

The lips that always scolded him — that in a moment must berate him cruelly — were soft and sweet. He meant only to taste them, but the taste was a delicious surprise, and he needed to savour it. Then he knew what the shock had been last time. Yearning that made no sense hammered in his heart as he waited for her to push him away. *Don't,* he thought. *Not yet.*

His arms slipped around her to keep her near just another moment and a thrill shot through him when he felt her hands move up to his neck. He sensed her answering shudder, and that was the last he knew of thought. What remained was the fragrance of violets, the clean scent of her skin, the tickle of frothy curls, and the dizzying warmth of her slim body melting into his arms. She was light and delicate, but to kiss her was to plunge into a summer storm, and that intoxicated him, as storms always did. He forgot she was small and fragile, and crushed her to him.

Catherine was lost. Whatever inner warnings she tried to heed at the start stilled when his lips sought hers — perhaps because that seeking was so gentle, coaxing, surprisingly tender. The taste of him, the scent of him, drew her as easily as his encircling arms.

She had not expected the gentleness or the sweetness or the sense of homecoming, still less the longing he so easily kindled. As his mouth grew more insistent, she answered helplessly. The frantic pumping of her heart warned her she was being drawn to danger, but the alarm was muffled in the sweet chaos of physical sensation. He surrounded her and she, trusting him, abandoned herself to him. The strong arms about her and the press of his hard chest secured her, even as she felt herself sinking into warm, enticing, turbulent darkness.

Falling, she thought vaguely, as her lips opened in answer to some felt command from his. Falling. Fallen. Her eyes flew open and she jerked her head back.

"Good heavens! What are you doing to me?" she asked, horrified, as reality crashed down upon her.

The viscount's blue eyes were dark as midnight. "Kissing you, Cat," he answered huskily. "Surely you remember what a kiss is. I gave you one just a few weeks ago."

"This was not at all the same thing."

"No, it wasn't," was the grave reply. "This was a deal better. This time you cooperated."

She pulled away and was alarmed to find herself still weak-kneed. Embarrassed, she glared at him. "You tricked me!"

"On the contrary, you tricked *me*. You are very deceitful. Never once have you hinted that you were passionate. You were most unsporting to take me unawares. I might have fainted."

Two bright spots of colour appeared in Miss Pelliston's cheeks.

"Passionate? How dare you!" she cried, furious with herself for the humiliating proof she'd given him. "Oh, you are the most provoking man!" She stamped her foot. Then, realising she was having a childish tantrum, she raised her chin, collected her dignity, and marched out of the ersatz temple.

Lord Rand might have been more tactful, but misery loves company. Being agitated himself, he felt obliged to vex his companion. Now, as he watched her storm off, he was torn between wanting to follow her to apologise, as he should, and remaining to dash his head against the temple's stone pillars. Though the latter course of action promised more relief, he decided he had better go after her.

Another moment's delay and he would have lost track of her. She was moving very quickly. As he hastened down the path they'd come, he saw a flash of white muslin before she turned down another pathway.

That way led to Lord Ventcoeur's man-made grotto, Max knew. He also knew that if she continued at that pace, she'd stumble and probably fall into the (also man-made) lake. The path was narrow and inclined steeply. It was meant for leisurely exploration, not foot races. Damning her temper and himself for goading it, he hurried along in pursuit.

Because of the turns and angles of the walkway, the heavy plantings and occasional rock outcroppings, she disappeared from view for a few minutes. Then he caught another glimpse of white at the grotto's entrance. At that moment, his foot slipped on a patch of moss, he lost his balance, and landed on his backside.

Cursing softly, he got up, brushed himself off, and hurried on. He had just turned towards the cave entrance when he heard a disagreeably familiar voice — Lord Browdie's — crying, "Hold a minute, Cathy. I want a word with you."

There was a muttering of male voices, then Max saw Sir Reginald Aspinwal give a shrug and turn back onto the lower path by the lake's edge.

Apologies of the sort Lord Rand contemplated cannot be made in the presence of other gentlemen. On the other hand, a gentleman cannot leave an innocent young lady — especially one in an emotional state — alone with a lecherous old sot. And, the viscount was curious what Lord Browdie wanted to talk about. Very likely he had more slander about Max, which would be entertaining. And if there was the least sign of danger to Catherine, Max would be on hand. Perhaps afterwards he would reward the brute with a broken jaw.

By now Sir Reginald was out of sight. Lord Rand took up a position under an enormous rhododendron at the grotto's entrance. He leaned back against the smooth stone, folded his arms across his chest, and eavesdropped.

In a few minutes he'd unfolded his arms and was clenching his fists.

"Me?" he heard Catherine cry in affronted disbelief. "In a — in such a place? You are mad — or drunk — I do not care which —"

"No, I ain't — and there's a peach-colour frock your Aunt Deborah'll recognise fast enough if I show it to her. Which I can, you know, if you won't be sensible."

"I will not stay and listen to this, this — I hardly know what to call it."

"I wouldn't run off if I was you, Cathy. Not unless you want the world to know what you been up to."

Lord Rand made up his mind to hear no more, but to commence immediately upon the breaking of jaws. He was about to turn into the entrance when he caught Miss Pelliston's surprising response.

"You have my leave, sirrah, to tell anyone you like. Tell them this instant, do."

Max hesitated. What was she thinking of?

"I should," Browdie growled. "After the sorry trick you've served me. If it wasn't for your papa —"

"Oh, pray don't trouble about Papa. Do tell your filthy slander to the world," Catherine urged. "I should like nothing better than to see you made the laughingstock of London."

"Ain't me they'll be laughing at, Miss Hoity-Toity, and laughing'll be the kindest of it. You won't be marrying any of your fine beaux, I promise you. Too good for me, are you? Well, you won't be good enough for anyone else, not even your randy viscount. Not that he'd marry you anyhow when he can get what he wants without."

"Now I see what this is about, My Lord. You have lost a dowry and a rich piece of property, have you not? And this is how you think to get them back."

"Your papa promised —"

"Let me make you a promise, sirrah." Catherine's voice deepened, became ominous. "Do you so much as breathe a hint of this scurrilous tale and I shall take it up and trumpet it abroad."

Max heard Browdie's outraged gasp and smiled. She had called his bluff, the clever Cat. Browdie could not publicly condemn her, then turn around and marry her after.

"Yes, I think you understand me," Catherine went on. "Even you would not wed a woman the world believes is damaged goods. Tell your slander, then. I have always lived a retired life, and if one must remain a spinster, it is best to be a rich one. Perhaps I shall bequeath my great-aunt's property to a charity. Coram's Foundling Hospital, I think. The children would do better for country air."

Lord Rand decided that it was high time to make his presence known. Catherine may have vanquished her foe, but that foe was likely infuriated enough at present to drown her. The viscount picked up a stone and skimmed it over the water. Then he sauntered into sight. Without looking towards the entrance, he picked up another flat stone and skimmed it. He was bending to find another when he heard footsteps echoing. Lord Browdie, his face an interesting display of swelling veins and maroon coloration, stomped into the sunlight.

Max feigned surprise and offered an amiable greeting to which the baron muttered some surly response before tramping away. Max turned and strolled into the grotto.

Inside were a few statues of mythological figures connected, aptly enough, with water. These were set in niches carved for that purpose. In one corner a stone nymph was reclining, her hand trailing in a shallow pool. Near her, on a seat carved into the wall, sat Miss Pelliston, her head in her hands.

"Cat," he said.

Her head went up, but she did not appear surprised to see him. "We were wrong," she said simply. "He knows everything."

"Yes. I heard."

"Oh Lord." She resumed her posture of despair.

Max moved closer. "What are you so unhappy about? You were brilliant — but I knew you had it in you, Cat. Though I did feel rather a fool, about to dash to your rescue and then finding you quite capable of rescuing yourself."

"Yes, with a great pack of lies."

"'Truly, to tell lies is not honourable, but when the truth entails tremendous ruin, to speak dishonourably is pardonable.'"

"You need not quote me Sophocles, My Lord. Even the devil can quote scripture to his purpose."

"Oh, I hadn't any purpose. Only wanted to show off my formidable knowledge, ma'am."

"I think you have shown me quite enough of your knowledge for one day," she answered tartly, apparently beginning to recover her natural waspish spirits.

"Yes, I know. I came after you to apologise. At the moment that seems anticlimactic. Besides," he went on, feeling at a loss, "I'm not sure if I am sorry."

"Why should you be?" she answered angrily. "You had your amusement and didn't even get slapped for it. I raised no objections. Why should you be sorry?"

He moved nearer still, and knelt so she would not have to crane her neck to look at him.

"Oh, Cat, you're having an attack of conscience. You let me kiss you, then you told fibs to Browdie, and now you think you're completely corrupt. Shall I make an honest woman of you? Will you marry me?"

Catherine gazed into his lean, handsome face and wished that the eyes, for this one time at least, truly were windows to the soul. If she could have but one glimpse inside, and if that glimpse could give her some reason to hope . . .

"Why?" she asked.

He glanced away at the nymph. "Because I do keep kissing you, it seems. If I keep it up, people will begin to talk."

"I have no intention of allowing you to keep it up," was the indignant answer.

"What about Browdie? You may have called his bluff this time, but surely you don't trust him to keep his tongue in his head."

"I see. You want to marry me to protect my honour. I think you are having an attack of *noblesse oblige.*"

He rose abruptly. "I wasn't brought up by wolves, if that's what you mean," he snapped. "I have got some honour, some sense of what's right. If you weren't so stubborn, you'd admit it's right. If it weren't you, but another woman in your predicament, wouldn't you advise her to marry me?"

Catherine stood up as well. Shivering, she drew her shawl more tightly about her. "That would depend upon the woman. There is some risk that Lord Browdie will repeat the tale and ruin me, but that's his gamble, as I told him. Shall you and I gamble on marriage, My Lord? Considering how ill we suit, are the stakes not excessive? Should we hazard a lifetime of wretchedness simply because there's a small chance Lord Browdie will be foolish enough to reveal my secret? If this were a card game would you risk your entire future upon it?"

"I've asked that most of my life," Max answered, his face darkening. "But we're not talking about me, are we? It's you. You're afraid of me, aren't you?"

Catherine had given her troubling feelings about him many names, but fear was not one of them. Now she realised he was right. She had met him only a month ago, yet he'd changed her. Every moment spent with him released demons. Lord, how many had escaped today? Her horrid temper. Those blustering denials and threats — she who abhorred falsehood had uttered lie upon lie.

Worst of all was the passion. He had touched her and she succumbed instantly. Even when she was away from him, he tormented her. Wicked dreams, harking back to that night at Granny Grendle's, recollections of a strong, beautiful physique, shirtless — and she in a whore's *negligee*.

It was the lust — there was no pleasanter name for it — she feared most of all. He had sensed it, as he sensed every other flaw, and would use the power it gave him over her, just as he used her other weaknesses. If not for that, she might have risked marriage, been happy to abandon her fears for her reputation, and devote her energies instead to helping him overcome his own frailties. She could never reform him altogether, and perhaps she didn't quite want that. But these were naive fantasies. She could never change him, because he could master her with the merest glance, the lightest touch.

She saw all this in an instant and answered quickly, "If you mean I am afraid of spending the rest of my life as I have the beginning, you're right."

"I ain't your father, damn it!"

"At the moment the resemblance is quite strong. He too bullies when he is contradicted."

"I'm not bullying you!" he shouted.

"How unfortunate you have not a bottle or a mug handy," said Miss Pelliston as she moved towards the entrance. "Then you might throw it at me, and the resemblance would be complete." With that, she left him.

To Catherine's relief, no one remarked her overlong absence. Lady Andover had been preoccupied with casting up her accounts and the members of her family had devoted all their anxiety to her.

When Catherine returned, therefore, she heard no awkward questions, only the brief announcement that they would be leaving as soon as the carriage was brought round. She might remain if she wished — Lady Glencove had offered to chaperone her — but Catherine had no desire to stay. At home she might look after Lady Andover, and that would help keep her miserable thoughts at bay.

If Lord Rand had any troubles of his own, he must have vanquished them after a very brief battle, because he left the grotto shortly after Miss Pelliston did, though taking a different path, and went in search of Lady Diana. When he found that goddess he was all affable gallantry and devoted so much time to her that Lady Glencove spent the next twenty-four hours in a state of paradisiacal bliss.

Gentlemen cope with rejection in different ways.

Lord Rand had all the resiliency of young manhood. After being spurned for the second time by Miss Pelliston, he decided he could take a hint and would go where he was more welcome.

Lord Browdie was not so resilient. When confronted with failure, he produced no creative alternatives. He fell into a sullen fit and his mind scraped back and forth upon the same narrow path until he wore the way so deep he could not see beyond it.

He also left the party early, in a bitter rage, vowing inwardly to publish his tale far and wide. He could not commence that publication at the Ventcoeur party because Lord Rand was too much in evidence. The fellow had aready turned up once at an inconvenient moment and might get into the habit. Lord Browdie's was not an enquiring mind. He was not eager to relive Cholly's experience of having his nose broken.

The return trip took an hour and a half, and he sulked the whole way. In the course of this exercise he experienced some doubts, one of which loomed increasingly larger the closer he got to Town. By the time he reached his love nest, the doubt had swelled to huge proportions. The little shrew had insisted she'd never been in that brothel. One would expect denials from the average lady. The trouble was, this was Catherine Pelliston, and one of her least agreeable traits was her appalling honesty.

London Society may have changed her — it changed everyone — and certainly she looked different. If she hadn't changed, though, and he started an ugly rumour that proved to be unfounded, he'd have Pelliston, Andover, Rand — and Lord only knew who else — all fighting for the privilege of putting a sword or a bullet through his heart.

There was only one way to get the truth. Accordingly, Lord Browdie had his horse stabled, then made his way by hackney to a less prosperous neighbourhood.

Fortune must have been smiling on him that day because as he was approaching the brothel he met up with Cholly, and thus avoided a far more costly confrontation with Granny herself.

A pint of gin and a single gold coin made the taciturn Cholly talkative. That is to say, he described the "country servant" in question as having great "rum ogles" of a sort of yellowish-greenish-brownish color and a rat's nest of curly hair. The girl, who had disembarked from the Bath coach, was rather small and very skinny — which Cholly had pointed out to Granny. She'd answered that the girl looked like a child, which was what plenty of the gentlemen wanted, because they believed that children wouldn't give them the pox.

"Then why, I ax you," Cholly went on in aggrieved tones, "does the old witch give her to *him* first, when she knows he likes the jolly big ones and not no babies? I knowed there was goin' to be trouble as soon as she done it, but she don't listen to me — and whose nose gets broke? Not *hers.*"

He glared at his glass. "Not as it ain't been broke afore, but that was in a good row of my own. This were all on account of that old witch thinks she's so sharp. I seed it comin' — but it's wot she pays me for. That cove," he added in mingled resentment and admiration, "got a fist like a millstone."

Lord Browdie was not a man of many ideas, but hunger for revenge, like love, works miracles. He had something like an idea, and if he worked on it — and had some help — he might end up with a real one.

"How'd you like to get even, Cholly, without so much as going near the fellow? How'd you like that, and getting yourself a nice pile of those shiners besides?" He nodded at the coin that lay between them on the rough table.

Cholly expressed the opinion that he might contrive a liking for such matters, if properly persuaded.

17

Lord Rand had survived neither his numerous youthful escapades nor his adult ones through sheer luck. His instincts were finely tuned. He knew the exact odds of his surviving any given danger because he knew how much trouble he could handle.

He could, for instance, hold his own against two great, hulking brutes determined to tear him limb from limb, as he had at Granny Grendle's. He knew the odds in his favour when a harlot pointed a gun at his head. He knew, therefore, that with Catherine Pelliston he hadn't a prayer.

He'd been upleasantly surprised by the depth of his dismay when she'd rejected his proposal again. He'd thought he was offering for exactly the reasons she'd cited. Now he realised there was more, that in spite of her being everything he thought he didn't want in a woman, he was very fond of her, and fascinated, and possibly — contrary or demented or whatever it was — well, very possibly he was rather *in love* with her, drat it.

Still, that didn't mean it wasn't a mistake or that marrying her wouldn't be a grievous error. She was right, of course: they didn't suit and one or both of them would be wretched. Besides, she didn't want him. To her he was a younger version of her papa, and she was afraid of him and despised him and that settled matters, didn't it?

Lord Rand was not one to mope. Life was filled with disappointments. He picked up his battered — but not really broken, he told himself — heart, dusted it off, and decided he might as well drop it upon the goddess's altar.

For nearly a week after the Ventcoeur party, the viscount kept clear of Miss Pelliston. If they happened to attend the same events — and that was unavoidable — he reduced their interactions to the minimum courtesy required. He stopped dancing with her and danced attendance upon Lady Diana instead.

He would have preferred to keep away from Almack's as well, but he couldn't, because he'd promised to help Jack. Besides, the goddess would be present. Accordingly, the viscount made his way to the sanctum sanctorum of snobs, that stuffiest and stupidest of places.

He arrived at Almack's earlier than he would have normally because he had to find Catherine a suitable waltz partner — as he'd promised Jack a week ago — and needed time to investigate prospective victims. Why his sister was incapable of managing so simple a matter was a question that did not occur to him.

His sister herself did not occur to him even when she was standing in front of him, offering an unsolicited opinion of his new neck-cloth arrangement, an original creation of Blackwood's. All Max saw at that point was Miss Pelliston in a white muslin gown. There was nothing remarkable in that, certainly. White muslin was the usual debutante costume. She might be a bit older than the others, but the simple innocence of her frock complemented her delicate features.

Brunettes there were aplenty at Almack's that night, as well as blondes and one unfortunate redhead, but there was no one in the cramped assembly rooms whose carefully groomed *coiffure* was such a tantalising froth, a light brown faery cloud flecked with golden light where the candles' glow caught it.

From her hair his gaze dropped to her great hazel eyes, gleaming now with the militant light that always seemed to blaze up the instant she spotted him. Thence his scrutiny proceeded to a pair of soft pink lips. He remembered how sweet they were, while his survey continued, trancelike, down the silken whiteness of her neck. It was then he realised that her neckline was cut more daringly than any she'd worn before; simultaneously he became aware of the fragrance of violets and his head began to spin. He panicked.

He mumbled some answer — he hardly knew what — to her cool greeting, then fled as quickly as he could . . . and walked straight into Sally Jersey's arms, in a manner of speaking, because he nearly knocked that lady down in his blind haste to escape.

Regardless of Jack Langdon's characterisation of Lady Jersey as one of several Almack Gorgons, she was an attractive matron, many years from her dotage, and not at all averse to having a handsome young lord fall on top of her. She offered Max an indulgent smile and waved away his apologies.

"Oh, I know what you're about," said she. "I saw you looking at Miss Pelliston and I expect you want to waltz with her. Well, come along, and I'll do the honours. It's either you or Argoyne, I suppose, though Langdon wants the same thing, but I'll see him turn to stone first, since he tells everyone I can do it, and Argoyne is such a clumsy idiot he'll trample her toes and put her off waltzing forever."

Silence Jersey had more to say on this and other subjects as she led the hapless viscount inexorably back to the peril he'd just escaped. Then the chatter ceased. Lady Jersey resumed her patroness's dignity and presented Miss Pelliston with her waltz partner.

After that there was nothing to be done because the music had started. Max led Miss Pelliston out, placed his arm about her waist, and promptly lost his mind.

The waltz, like Lord Byron, had become all the rage the previous year and was still considered by Society's more conservative element as fast at best and lewd at worst, which is more or less what these persons thought of the poet.

For the first time in his life Max wished that older and wiser heads had prevailed, and that the curst dance had been banished to benighted Germany, which had spawned it. To hold Miss Pelliston in any way was to wish to hold her closer. That was humiliating. He gazed longingly over his partner's head at the blonde Juno, who was whirling about the dance floor with a tall military gentleman.

Lord Rand looked down at Catherine. He noticed that her head came to his breast and immediately he felt a dull ache there.

"I wish you would say something," Miss Pelliston complained. "I'm still inept at small talk, but if you would help get me started, I might manage something."

"If you get *me* started, you'll be sorry. You usually are."

"Nonetheless, I shall keep a brave smile on my face, so long as we appear to be holding a conversation. At present you are wearing what your sister calls your 'caged animal' look and everyone will think I am a thoroughly disagreeable partner."

If he did feel like a trapped beast, Eton and Oxford quickly came to his rescue. "Oh, you're not disagreeable at all. Tonight, in your maidenly white, with that pink in your cheeks, you put me in mind of apple blossoms. You're as light in my arms as so many flower petals and your voice —"

"Oh, dear," she murmured.

"The sound of your voice," he went on, determined to make her as unsettled as he was, "is a breeze ruffling the leaves."

"What on earth am I to say to that?" she asked, rather breathlessly, because she was at the same time recovering from a turn that had brought her up against his hard chest. Between that and the warm gloved hand which seemed to burn all the way up her spine, Catherine felt rather like a stack of very dry kindling. These circumstances as much as his words set her cheeks aflame and made her wish fervently that she were in St. Petersburg in the dead of winter.

"Really, Cat, must I tell you everything? Haven't you told me repeatedly that you have

288

no further need of my assistance?"

"Yes, I have — and you are still there. Everywhere I go, there you are."

This was monstrous unfair — he'd kept away from her for ages, it seemed — but he chose to agree.

"Like a bad penny."

"Very like," she concurred.

How tiny her waist was. He could easily span it with his two hands, he was sure.

Aloud he said, "Actually, I'm here tonight as a favour to Jack. He'd much rather have the first waltz with you. Unfortunately he's antagonised all the great ladies, so he has to wait for the next one." Max briefly outlined Mr. Langdon's difficulties with the patronesses.

"I see," she said in a subdued voice.

"I hope you're not disappointed."

"Why should I be?" she answered a tad too quickly.

"I mean, that it's me instead of Jack."

"Well, My Lord, if you'll leave off about apple blossoms and talk of Aristophanes instead, I might more easily pretend you are Mr. Langdon."

She had recovered sufficiently to score a hit, but Lord Rand was not one to yield at the first blow.

"I wish you'd call me Max," he said, deciding distraction was the best tactic. "'My lord' always makes me feel I should be in armour, clanking about and trodding on helpless peasants. Most disconcerting when a chap's trying to be graceful."

"I most certainly cannot. That is disrespectful and far too intimate."

"If you call me Clarence Arthur Maximilian, I'll shoot you."

He heard a faint tinkling sound: Miss Pestilence was giggling!

Though she quickly squelched the giggle, she could not suppress the smile as she gazed up at him. "Clarence Arthur? No wonder you prefer Max."

"Just so." He answered the smile, despite the sudden, inexplicable thundering in his ears. "Now you've said it, I feel warm and friendly and very light on my feet."

"I wish you did not feel quite so friendly. I believe we are supposed to be twelve inches apart. Not" — she glanced down briefly — "five."

Lord St. Denys stood listening to his daughter talk, but his eyes were upon the dance floor, and, in particular, upon his son. When Louisa chided him for not attending, he smiled. "Remember the half-drowned kitten Max brought home that day? He dropped it at your feet and told you to nurse it back to life."

"I remember. The kitten. A robin. A bat. I spent my childhood nursing a menagerie."

"I was thinking how that tiny creature terrified my great mastiff out of its wits. I could not understand it then and I cannot now."

Lady Andover followed her father's gaze. "If it's any comfort, Papa, I'm sure he doesn't understand either."

"Of course he doesn't," the earl snapped. "The boy's a fool."

By the time the waltz was over and Max had relinquished his partner to Lord Argoyne, the viscount was beside himself. How dare she be so cool and proper when she made him so heated? How dare she giggle and act human for once and set off all those warm, cosy sensations and weaken his already beleaguered resistance even further?

He had weakened, he knew. For one chilling moment he would have promised anything — complete reform, a transformation into a stodgy pillar of Society, not a drop of liquor again as long as he lived, not another tavern wench — anything, if she would give him her hand and allow him to make love to her all the rest of his life.

He had stood on the brink of the precipice,

looked down, and thought, in that terrifying instant, "Very well, I'll jump." Now he drew back in horror. That awful girl could do whatever she liked with him! It was not to be borne, not by Clarence Arthur Maximilian Demowery. He would not be managed and reformed by an obstinate little prig.

Could the objective observer have looked into his mind, he or she would have concluded that Lord Rand was hysterical. Unfortunately, the viscount had no disinterested parties to point this out. Therefore, not half an hour later, when his dance with Lady Diana had concluded, he had asked for and received permission to call upon her papa the following day.

"My dear, you do deserve a severe scold, but in the circumstances, I forgive you."

Lady Diana gazed wearily out the carriage window. "Yes," she murmured, "at last you have your wish."

"All the same, you are not to dance with that man again, even after you're betrothed. The effrontery of the creature — to dare show his face at Almack's. I cannot imagine what the patronesses were thinking of, to allow that fellow entrance. It is the coat, of course. Women are altogether too susceptible to a dashing uniform."

Lady Diana said nothing.

"Still, we will say no more on that head. I'm very pleased with you, Diana," said her ladyship. "I was sure Lord Rand must come to the point soon, once you made an effort, but tomorrow is better than I expected. Lady St. Denys — just as your papa and I have always hoped." Lady Glencove sighed happily. "I can hardly think how your sister Julia can do better."

"Oh, you'll think of something, Mama, depend upon it."

Word of Lord Rand's proposal was all over London by teatime the following afternoon, Lady Glencove's servants proving even more assiduous than their mistress in relaying the momentous news. This was no doubt because the betrothal was to be kept secret until Lord Glencove might make a formal announcement at an appropriately grand party.

Catherine was told the secret by Molly, who announced it as one would an unnatural death.

"I ought to've told her ladyship first," said Molly, shaking her head in sorrow, "only she's sick again and his lordship there with her and them having a row about sending for the leech. That's the trouble with folks as are never sick. When they are, they won't believe it and act like it'd go away on that account."

What Catherine did not believe at the moment had nothing to do with Lady Andover, but with the cold sensation in the pit of her stomach. "Offered for Lady Diana? Are you certain, Molly? That is to say," she added hastily, "I would have thought he'd have mentioned his intentions to his family."

"I don't see how he could, Miss, as he never comes no more and even her ladyship says he hardly says two words when she sees him anywhere else, either." She cast a reproachful look at Miss Pelliston, who did not see it, the maid being at her back unfastening buttons.

"That will do, Molly. I can manage the rest myself."

Molly departed with the air of one following a funeral procession; and Miss Pelliston stumbled to her dressing table. Perhaps she had tripped over the truth, because she sat for a long while staring at her reflection in the glass, then spent another long while after, weeping.

That night Catherine attended a rout with her host and hostess. Lady Andover seemed to be in excellent health and spirits, despite the "shocking squeeze" that signifies a successful entertainment. She was well, that is, until they were heading home again. She climbed into the carriage wearing a very odd expression, sat down, and fainted dead away.

Sir Henry Vane, the family physician, was

sent for the following morning. Half an hour after he departed, Catherine was summoned to her cousin's study.

When she entered, the earl was standing by his desk, an odd, faint smile on his noble face as he gazed at the papers neatly arranged there.

"My Lord, is she all right?" Catherine asked immediately, forgetting her manners in her anxiety about the countess.

The earl came out of his daydream though the smile remained.

"Catherine, you are very obstinate. You have been living under my roof at least a month now. You are my cousin. Ours is a distant kinship and I know you like to be respectful, but surely you might omit my style. Louisa threatens to wash your mouth out with soap if you 'my lady' her again."

"Cousin Edgar," Catherine said obediently, "do tell me. What did Sir Henry say?"

"That is better. I had meant to save the physician for last and tell you my news in order of social consequence, but I see you have contracted the Demowery impatience. Please sit down, my dear." He indicated the chair by his desk.

Catherine sat, wishing she could shake the news out of him. Her cousin had such a fondness for roundabout preambles.

"As you must know by now," he began,

"once Louisa gets a notion, there is no preventing her putting it into action. According to Sir Henry, my lady wife has taken it into her head to commence a family. Reasoning with her is of no avail."

"I beg your pardon?"

"Louisa plans to present me with a son or daughter before Christmas. There is no stopping her, according to Sir Henry." Lord Andover did not appear in the least desirous of halting his wife's impetuous progress. His dark eyes glowed with pride and happiness.

Catherine jumped up from her chair to hug him. "Oh, that is wonderful news!" she cried. "I know how you have wished for children. How excited you must be, and how happy I am for you both. Louisa is going to have a baby." Her eyes grew moist. "That is marvelous news."

Abruptly she realised that in her enthusiasm she'd crushed her elegant cousin's neck-cloth. She let go of him with a stammering apology.

"Don't be silly, Catherine. On such an occasion even my dour valet must forgive you. Besides, Louisa has already made rather a shambles of my *ensemble,* and in all the excitement I forgot to change before sending for you. Really, this has been a very busy day. Do sit down, Cousin. I have something more to tell you."

Though Catherine had much rather dash up to her ladyship's chamber, she quelled herself and sat down once more.

"As you know, Catherine, your papa has entrusted you to my care and engaged me to act in his behalf, which was wise of him. One cannot forever be consulting him on every question. The distance is most inconvenient and his self-imposed isolation from his peers equips him ill to judge objectively."

Isolation — intoxication was more like it, Catherine thought, though she said nothing.

"While I act in his stead, there are some matters in which your opinion is paramount."

Papa would hardly thank you for that, was the silent reply — but I do.

"Lord Argoyne has asked permission to pay his addresses."

Catherine immediately abandoned all thoughts of her papa to turn a startled gaze upon her cousin.

"His timing was unfortunate," the earl continued. "I was expecting Sir Henry at any moment. I explained that my wife was ill, and in the circumstances I could not possibly give proper attention to any other subject. He seemed to find that startling. It is just as well. That is a man who wants startling at frequent intervals. He may be a duke, but he is a very dull duke. He has no business being so. It sets a bad example. I hope you have not conceived a *tendresse* for him, Cousin. I should, of course, accede to your wishes, since it is you who would have to marry him. Still I must warn you that if you do, Louisa and I cannot possibly visit you above once a decade."

"Good heavens — a duke — offered for me — why, I hardly know him."

"That is just as well. He does not improve upon acquaintance. I take it, then, I might tell him to go to blazes?"

Catherine thought rapidly. "It is a very good match. He might have looked much higher. Perhaps I'd better have him. I can scarcely expect a more advantageous offer — or even another," she added, frowning.

She had rather have Mr. Langdon, she thought, ruthlessly banishing another image from her mind. He was most attentive, but he was so shy and so preoccupied with matters literary that likely he'd never come to the point this century. She began to wish she'd acquired a few of those feminine arts she'd always scorned. Sometimes men required firm guidance. Now, with Louisa *enceinte*, there was no time to waste. Catherine could not expect to reside with her cousin forever, and Louisa would soon be unable to chaperone her.

"Maybe it would be best to accept him,"

she said with a dreary sigh.

"Catherine, it is most unlike you to be so silly. Argoyne only wanted to be ahead of the other fellows. I must say I find his haste indecent. You have only been out a few weeks. Perhaps he takes his example from my impetuous brother-in-law."

He must have noticed Catherine's wince, because he added, "Still, as you appear so terrified of finding yourself on the shelf, I shall ask him to call again in another month or so if he is still of the same mind."

With that, and reassurances about Louisa's health, and further assurances that the Dowager Countess of Andover would be delighted to take over as chaperone whenever Louisa was prevented by her condition, the earl dismissed his cousin.

18

"Where the devil's Jemmy? I haven't seen him in days."

Lord Rand tore off his coat, neck-cloth, and waistcoat, and flung himself onto the bed. He had not drunk an unusual quantity of wine, but lately he did not require very much alcohol to become dizzy and tired. Perhaps that was because he'd spent the past eight nights thrashing among the bedclothes instead of sleeping like a good Christian.

"I couldn't say, My Lord. Evidently, Madame Germaine is extremely busy these days. He has not been by since — " The valet hesitated.

"Since when?"

"I beg your pardon, My Lord. As there has been no formal announcement in the papers, the matter at present is mere household gossip."

"What matter? What in blazes are you talking about?"

Blackwood bent to retrieve the abandoned

articles from the floor. "There is word that your lordship has contracted an alliance with one of England's great families."

"Oh, that." Lord Rand scowled at the bed-post.

"When Jemmy received that word, he left the house. He has not been seen since." Black-wood straightened and draped the garments over his arm.

"Just like that — not a word?"

"Actually, My Lord, he had a great deal to say on that occasion. If you'll excuse me, I'd rather not repeat it."

The viscount transferred his scowl from bedpost to servant. "No, I won't excuse you. What did the brat say?"

"He found fault with your thinking processes, My Lord."

"None of your euphemistic translations, Blackwood. What did he say?"

"His words, as I recall, were, 'He's got no more brains 'an 'at shoe.' He pointed to his footwear. He followed that with a long, not entirely coherent speech about his education, in which Miss Pelliston's name recurred repeatedly. He expressed doubts regarding a profession as a tiger. Mr. Gidgeon pointed out alternatives, to which Jemmy responded he'd rather live in the Hulks."

"Spoiled," said the master. "That's what comes of indulging the whims of — of maternal butlers. You're excused, Blackwood. Wait — where are you going with my clothes? I'm going out again."

"Yes, My Lord. I was taking them away to clean them. There is a spot of wine on your coat and what seems to be a gravy stain on your waistcoat."

"Well, what do you expect? I'm a barbarian, ain't I? Barely civilized, you know. Brought up by wolves. And illiterate. Not to mention a drunkard."

A light flickered very briefly in the valet's eyes, but his face was otherwise expressionless as he responded, "I beg leave to disagree, My Lord."

The figure sprawled on the bed heaved a great sigh.

"You're loyal, Blackwood, besides being a paragon. Because you're loyal, I'll share my secret with you. There's been no announcement in the papers because the girl's parents want to bore everyone to death with another overcrowded party where they'll make the announcement and expect the world to be astounded. Ask Hill when that is — I don't remember. End of the week, I think. In short, I am engaged to be married to Lady Diana Glencove."

"Then may I take leave to wish you happy, My Lord?"

"You may wish," the viscount answered gloomily, "all you like."

To find Lady Diana Glencove in the drawing-room was hardly surprising. She was, after all, engaged — though unofficially at present — to Lady Andover's brother. What did surprise Catherine when she joined the sisters-to-be was that Lord Rand's fiancee had stopped by primarily to ask Miss Pelliston to accompany her to Hatchard's.

"Lord Rand tells me you are a prodigious reader," Lady Diana explained. "It would be a great pleasure to have the company of one who shares my fondness for books."

To refuse would be rude, to make excuses cowardly. Catherine had no reason, she told herself, to avoid Lady Diana's company. Lady Andover having an errand or two to be performed in Piccadilly, the matter was speedily settled. Catherine would shop for a while with Lady Diana before going on to Madame's for her regular Wednesday appointment with Jemmy. The Andover carriage would retrieve her at the usual time.

When they reached Hatchard's, Lady Diana suggested that her abigail perform Lady Andover's errands.

As soon as the reluctant maid departed, Lady Diana turned to Catherine and said in a low voice, "I'm afraid I asked you here under false pretences, Miss Pelliston. The plain fact is that I am in need of a friend at the moment. Lord Rand has spoken so highly of you. Your efforts on behalf of that poor orphaned boy I found particularly touching."

Catherine abruptly realised that her mouth was hanging open. She shut it, but continued to stare in bewilderment at her statuesque companion.

"That is why," the goddess continued, "I dared hope that perhaps you would act the part of a friend for me."

Catherine stammered something that must have sounded like agreement, because Lady Diana quickly explained her difficulty. There was a gentleman, a member of her brother's regiment, who had formed an attachment for her some months ago. Unaware that her parents had ordered her to see him no more, he had followed her to London.

"It is very difficult to explain, Miss Pelliston, but I must speak with him. My engagement came as a shock to him, and I feel I owe him a proper good-bye."

Catherine might have made a speech about filial duty, but her heart was not in it. She only nodded sympathetically and pointed out to her companion that they could not remain whispering in the street.

The fair Juno glanced over her shoulder, then led the way into the bookshop and stopped in an unoccupied corner.

"He is waiting for me near the theological books. I will be no more than five minutes. I would not involve you, Miss Pelliston, but Mama has set my maid spying on me. If Jane comes back too soon, I had rather she didn't see me with him. Will you help me?"

Catherine examined her conscience. She did not understand what needed explaining to the fellow. Wasn't Lady Diana's betrothal to another gentleman sufficient? Still, the lady wanted only five minutes and her disappointed suitor might be entitled to a kindly farewell. Miss Pelliston agreed to help. She would wait by the door. If the abigail made an unwelcome appearance, Catherine would distract her, loudly enough to alert Lady Diana. Would that do?

"Oh, yes. Bless you, Miss Pelliston." Lady Diana squeezed her companion's hand, then hurried off to the religious works.

The kind farewell took nearly half an hour, and Catherine grew mad with frustration. After reading the titles displayed by the door at least a hundred times, she lost all patience with Lady Diana and her thickheaded suitor.

Miss Pelliston was also most displeased with Lord Rand. If he had not praised her to his fiancee, Catherine would not be in this awkward position now.

Lady Diana should not be meeting clandestinely with other men, regardless the reason. It was improper and equivocal. She should not engage in any behaviour that might trigger nasty gossip, that would make vicious-minded people laugh at or kinder hearts pity her affianced husband.

Not that Catherine pitied him, she thought, glaring at an innocent volume of the recently published *Pride and Prejudice*. His fiancee was beautiful. She did as her parents commanded and all the world knew they'd ordered her to have the future Earl of St. Denys. He would marry her and do as he pleased, and so would she, after presenting him with the requisite male offspring. They would live as others in the Great World did — serene and comfortable. There would be no battles of will and none of that passion that gnawed at one and frightened one and made one so very unhappy.

Lady Diana finally approached, carrying two of Hannah More's pious works. The tall fair one had time only to assure Miss Pelliston that "everything was settled" before Jane appeared, her face a mask of suspicion. Not another word could be uttered on the subject after that, because the abigail was at their elbows all the rest of the time they shopped.

As previously arranged, Lord Glencove's carriage deposited Catherine at the dressmaker's. The coachman was about to start the horses again when his mistress cried out to him to wait. She turned to her maid.

"Go see if my bonnet is ready, Jane," the lady ordered, indicating the milliner's shop opposite.

"If it please your ladyship, Mrs. Flora did say it wouldn't be ready until Monday."

"Well, I have a mind to wear it tomorrow. See if you can hurry her."

The sullen maid took herself across the street and disappeared into the milliner's shop.

"Oh dear," Lady Diana exclaimed. "I forgot to tell her about the ribbon." She disembarked. "We may be rather a while, John," she told the coachman. "Perhaps you would like to walk the horses."

John would like, actually, to stop at a friendly place around the corner and refresh his palate with a pint of something. Visits to milliners, he knew, consumed at least half an hour. He smiled and drove down the street.

Lady Diana Glencove gave one quick glance towards the milliner's, another at the window of Madame Germaine's, then hastened off down the street in the direction opposite the one her papa's carriage took.

Miss Pelliston had entered the dressmaker's shop in no pleasant temper. In the last hour she had come to a most distressing — and maddening — realisation. The maddening part was that her distress was all her own doing.

The sight of Madame Germaine in a fit of hysterics being comforted by the odious Lord Browdie was not calculated to lift her spirits. Madame sat in a chair talking agitatedly as tears streamed down her cheeks. Lord Browdie was alternately patting her elbow and clumsily waving sal volatile under her chin.

"What are you doing to that poor woman?" Catherine shrieked, hastening to Madame's side.

"Oh, Miss Pelliston, how glad I am you've come," the *modiste* gasped. Impatiently she brushed the man away. "It's Jemmy. One of those dreadful street boys came running in — not ten minutes ago, was it, My Lord? When you had come to pick up that cerise gown for —" She stopped abruptly, having recollected, evidently, that as far as young ladies were concerned, gentlemen's mistresses did not exist.

"One of those boys came running in," she repeated, turning back to Catherine, "and said

Jemmy was taken up as a thief — a thief, Miss Pelliston!" Madame's voice rose. "Which of course he is no such thing, and it is a terrible mistake, but what am I to do with Lady Ashfolly coming any minute and Miss Ventcoeur's *trousseau* scarcely begun and that dreadful contessa quarrelling about the silk —"

"There, there," Lord Browdie interrupted. "No need to trouble yourself. I'll just pop down to the magistrate and see everything sorted out. Have the boy back before you can wipe your nose."

Catherine stared at her ex-fiance in disbelief. Lord Browdie had never in his life rushed to the rescue of anything, except perhaps a bottle in danger of toppling.

"You?" she asked incredulously, having already abandoned all pretence of politeness.

"Certainly. Can't have an innocent lad tossed in with a lot of thieves and cutthroats, and his poor mistress breaking her kind heart. Just tell me what he looks like and I'll be off."

Madame's description was rather skimpy on physiology and elaborate in details of attire.

"Brown hair, brown eyes, and about so high?" Lord Browdie gestured at a level with his belly. He shook his head. "To tell the truth, that sounds like anybody. There's bound to be dozens of boys —

309

always is — and he could be any of 'em."

Catherine sighed in exasperation. The man was obviously incompetent. Why could it not have been Lord Rand in the shop? That was just like him, wasn't it? Always there when he had no business to be and not there when you truly needed him. Which of course was monstrous unfair, but Miss Pelliston was not in an impartial frame of mind.

"I had better go with you," she said. "Every minute we stand here giving you particulars is another minute wasted, and I will not have that child thrust among the lowest sort of criminals."

Lord Browdie objected that the criminal court was no place for a young lady.

That was all Catherine needed to hear. If he would not take her, she snapped, she'd go alone. It was a fine Christian world, wasn't it, when a poor helpless boy, little more than a baby, must be left to languish among London's foulest vermin while one stood idly by on pretext of being a lady.

Madame protested that Miss Pelliston truly must not go. Madame would go herself. She would close up the shop. She hoped she was as much a Christian as anyone else.

Catherine, however, had already worked herself up into the fury of an avenging angel. She was prepared to tear apart the temples of justice with her own bare hands if need be. She swept out of the shop. Lord Browdie hurried after her.

"Afraid we'll have to take a hackney," he said apologetically. "My carriage is in for repairs."

Miss Pelliston did not care if they rode donkeys, so long as they went *now*.

"Well," said Max, peering owlishly over his glass at the gentleman who'd just entered his study. "Well. There you are."

Mr. Langdon took in the owlish expression and the empty champagne bottle standing on the desk. "You're foxed," he said.

"I'm celebrating," the viscount announced, waving his glass airily. "Now we can celebrate together. I'm going to be married. Ring for Gidgeon, Jack. We want another bottle. 'Fraid I couldn't wait for you. Too impetuous, you know."

"No, I think I'd better not. You're going to have a devilish head by nightfall as it is, and I thought we were going to the theatre."

Lord Rand hauled himself out of his seat and yanked on the rope. A minute later Mr. Gidgeon appeared, bearing a fresh bottle of champagne. In response to orders, he uncorked it with all due solemnity, though he cast a worried glance at his master. He shot another worried look at Mr. Langdon before exiting.

Mr. Langdon had no choice but to accept the glass thrust in his face. "All right, then," he said. "Congratulations."

"Don't you want to know who the lucky bride is?"

"All London knows. Alvanley has lost a pony to Worcester on account of your haste. He gave you another week."

"No matter. Somebody will propose to somebody in another week. You, maybe, Jack. Why don't you offer for Cat?"

Mr. Langdon's posture stiffened. "I presume you mean Miss Pelliston."

"As you say — Miss Pestilence. I expect she's well? Preachy as ever?" The viscount stared dolourously at his glass. "I ain't seen her in seven days. Couldn't, you know. Had to sit in what's-her-name's pocket. Minerva. Athena. One of 'em. Diana," he said gloomily.

"Lady Diana Glencove," the friend reminded. "What on earth is the matter, Max?"

"Nothing. Couldn't be happier. She's just in my style. Tall, you know. I like to look a girl right in the eye. Small women give me a crick in the neck. And a headache," he added, tapping his chest, having apparently misplaced his skull.

Mr. Langdon liked accuracy. He pointed

out that his friend's head was located several inches above his breastbone.

"Who cares?" Max scowled at the bottle for a moment before refilling his glass. "Is she?" he asked. "Is she preachy as ever?"

"Miss Pelliston is never preachy," was the reproachful reply.

"Not with you, I'll warrant. You never do everything wrong. You talk to her about books and never put her in a temper or tease her just to see her eyes flash and her chin go up and her face turn pink. And her hands." He stared at his own. "Small white hands all balled up into fists. It's completely ridiculous. Why, if she hit you, you'd think maybe a fly had landed on your face."

Jack's countenance grew very grave. "Max," he began. Then he stepped back, startled, as the door flew open and a hideous little goblin burst into the room.

19

Upon closer examination, the goblin turned out to be Jemmy, sporting a bloody nose, a cut lip, and what promised to become an organ of such magnificent colour that "black eye" could scarcely do it justice. At present that eye was swollen shut.

"What the devil happened to you?" Lord Rand asked the apparition. "Trampled by a horse, were you?"

Jemmy burst into rapid speech, or what would have been speech to Mr. Blackwood. As far as Mr. Langdon was concerned, the boy might as well be speaking Chinese.

Lord Rand's perceptions were at present not very quick. Even he needed several minutes to decipher any part of this oration.

"I see," he said finally, as he refilled his glass. "A thief taker grabbed you. You bit him. He hit you. You kicked him where it matters and escaped. You have had an interesting adventure. Now go and wash yourself."

Jemmy turned to Mr. Langdon. "Is he deaf?

Din't I jest say as she went off to the beak's wif him in a hackney and him been hangin' 'round like that every Monday and Wednesday. I was goin' to tell her about it too today, only what happened —"

Here Lord Rand interrupted, mainly because the mention of "Monday and Wednesday" shot a beam of light into his clouded mind. Catherine went to the shop on those days to give Jemmy lessons. Therefore this hysterical speech had something to do with Catherine. Now that he'd identified "she," he demanded to know who "he" was.

Given that Lord Rand was a trifle foxed and Jemmy incoherent, it was some time before the viscount began to grasp the problem.

"Are you telling me Miss Pelliston has gone off in a hackney with Lord Browdie and they're headed for the magistrate's? Why?"

"Because she thought 'at trap took me there. Which he tried, like I said, only —"

"Only you got away. Well, when they get to the magistrate's, they'll discover their mistake, won't they?"

"If 'at's where he was goin'," Jemmy hinted darkly.

"Why do you suppose otherwise?" Mr. Langdon asked.

Jemmy gazed at him in exasperation. "Din't I jest tell you? He's been spyin' on her and askin' fings all week. Besides, 'at big one 'at grabbed me ain't no trap, neither. Almost as big as you are," he told Lord Rand, "only fatter and his nose all mashed in. I knows all on 'em and he ain't one."

"Are you sure? He might be a new officer who mistook you for another boy."

"Not him. He wouldn't be nowhere's near 'em traps and horneys."

This Lord Rand translated for Mr. Langdon as referring to thief takers and constables respectively.

"I seen him once at a gin shop when I went arter me mum. She wanted him to get her a job in 'at house he worked at, but he wouldn't on account he said she was too old and ugly an' 'd fright the customers."

Lord Rand abruptly became sober and asked if Jemmy was referring to a brothel.

"A bawdy house she wanted. 'At's wot she allus said in the winter, as how she wanted a nice warm house and not out in the streets."

"Good God!" Mr. Langdon exclaimed. "He speaks of a whorehouse as though it were the vicarage. How do these children survive?"

"The question at the moment may be Miss Pelliston's survival, Jack. Save your aristocratic dismay for later."

The viscount turned back to Jemmy. "Do

you know the fellow's name? Was it Jos, perhaps? Or Cholly?"

"Cholly," was the prompt answer. "Jolly Cholly she called him. But I tole you about him. It's 'at other one got Miz Kaffy. 'At tall one wif orange hair."

Lord Rand stood up. "If that other one did not take her to the magistrate's, our friend Cholly may be the only one who knows where they did go."

He summoned Mr. Gidgeon and told the butler to send up a bucket of cold water to his chamber and have someone get them a couple of hackneys. Then the viscount strode from the room. Mr. Langdon and Jemmy followed.

Some minutes later, the two watched in amazement as Lord Rand, naked to the waist, bent over his washbasin and poured the cold water over his head. After towelling his head quickly and vigorously, he tore off the rest of his clothes. With Blackwood's assistance, he changed into the attire of his pre-heir days. This business was speedily accomplished, the viscount having no patience with idiotic questions from his audience. When he was ready, he turned to Jack.

"Now," he announced, "you're going to rescue her."

"I?" Jack asked, taken aback. "Well, of course I'll help."

"No, I'm helping. You're going to rescue the damsel in distress — which she'd better be, or we're going to look like a pair of bloody fools."

Mr. Blackwood was dispatched to investigate the two likeliest magistrate's offices — at Great Marlborough Street and at Bow Street. If Browdie and Miss Pelliston were at either of these places, the valet had only to inform them that Jemmy was safe, and to make sure the lady was brought home safely herself. Lord Rand and Mr. Langdon, meanwhile, would seek out Cholly.

Accordingly, Mr. Blackwood set off in one shabby hired coach and the two gentlemen, accompanied by Jemmy — who vociferously objected to being left behind — went off in the other.

The coach windows were so encrusted with soot and grime that Catherine could scarcely make out the passing scene. Her sense of direction being as deplorable now as when she first arrived in London, looking did her precious little good anyhow. Still, she did know that the nearest magistrate was at Great Marlborough Street. She pointed out to Lord Browdie that the carriage seemed to be heading the wrong way.

"Oh, he won't be there. From what I heard, the crime happened in Bow Street territory, and you know how jealous those fellows are. Sounds like Townsend himself picked up the boy," Lord Browdie added, carelessly dropping the name of a famous Bow Street officer.

Catherine was duly impressed, having heard the name before. She did not know that Mr. John Townsend — whose clients included the Bank of England and the Prince Regent — would never trouble himself with such small potatoes as an eight-year-old boy accused of pilfering a pocket watch.

"Not to mention," the baron went on airily, "Conant's a friend of mine, and since he's the chief magistrate, we'll have all this set straight quick enough."

"Is that not the place?" Catherine asked a while later, as the coach turned onto Bow Street. "I'm sure Lord Andover pointed it out when he took me around town."

"Oh, that's the office all right. But they hold the prisoners a bit further on, at the Brown Bear."

"Good heavens — isn't that a public house?"

"It is. Didn't I tell you it wasn't a place for ladies?" Lord Browdie smiled contemptuously. "I expect you've changed your mind about your Christian duty?"

"You might have mentioned we were going to a public house. Obviously, I cannot enter such a place."

"No, of course not. Only brothels, eh, Cathy?"

Miss Pelliston drew herself up. "You will have the courtesy, I hope," she replied with cold dignity, "to refrain from raising that objectionable topic again. It does not become you as a gentleman to mention such matters in a lady's presence."

"Oh, don't get on your high ropes, gal. I was only teasing. And you ain't so missish as all that. Your papa talks plain enough in front of you."

Lord Browdie was highly pleased with himself. He thought he was the cleverest fellow in creation. How easily she'd come! He needn't have wasted so much time planning how to coax her. Not a word about needing her maid by, or demanding the dressmaker come along, or sending for her cousin. He was in such high spirits that he took no offence at her shrewish remarks. She could say what she liked now. She'd learn humility soon enough.

"'Course I don't believe it, m' dear," he went on unctuously. "Fact is, I was a trifle foxed that day. Wanted to apologise, but you're devilish hard to get at lately. All them chaperones and maids, not to mention them beaux of yours. Heard Argoyne offered for you and Andover put him off. Holding out for Rand, were you? Well, it's an ill wind blows nobody good. Might as well be a duchess if you can."

Though this topic was even less agreeable than bawdy houses, Catherine contented herself with a disdainful sniff. She was immediately sorry. The interior of the coach smelled like something had died there days ago. She was not certain whether this fragrance emanated from the vehicle itself or from the gentleman sitting opposite, and was not eager to find out. All she wanted was to get out of this foul, jolting cage.

The hackney finally rattled to a stop. Lord Browdie alighted first and offered his hand to help her. She pretended not to notice and climbed down the steps unassisted. She began to draw a deep breath, then realised the air outside the coach was scarce fresher than that inside. She also noted that they were no longer in Bow Street, and with a vague stirring of alarm asked where they were.

"Just around the corner from the Brown Bear. Since I can't take you into the place with me, I figured you could wait here."

He gestured towards the entrance of a building whose soot-encrusted windows were crammed with a haphazard display of articles that included gentlemen's coats of the previous century, broken swords, rusty toiletries, crumpled bonnets, and other objects too moldering to be easily identified. Three balls hung over the door.

"This is a pawnshop," said Catherine unhappily.

"Well, it ain't a public house and it's the best there is in the neighbourhood," he lied. "Friend of a friend runs it. You'll be safe as houses. Soon as I can get the boy moved to the office, I'll come back and get you."

Miss Pelliston struggled for a moment between Scylla and Charybdis. The hackney had already departed. She could not accompany Lord Browdie to a public house, and certainly not the Brown Bear. She dimly recalled Lord Andover's remarks about the place being no better than a thieves' den, filled with law officers as corrupt as their prisoners.

She could not wait on the street, either. The unsavoury block brought back memories of Granny Grendle's and the foul alleys Lord Rand had carried her through on the way to his lodgings.

She gazed at the pawnshop door and swallowed. "I see there is no choice. I will have to make the best of it. But you do promise to hurry?"

"Of course I'll hurry. Now, now, you'll be fine," he went on in those falsely avuncular tones that made her skin crawl. "Mrs. Hodder has a quiet back room where you can sit and have a cup of tea while you wait. I know it don't look like much, but she's a good old gal. Wouldn't hurt a fly. You'd be surprised how many of the gentry come here — ladies too — like when they had a bad night at the faro tables and don't like to tell their husbands."

So saying, Lord Browdie yanked open a sticky door. Catherine reluctantly entered.

An enormously fat woman sat by a counter, knitting. She gave a curt nod as they entered. Lord Browdie spoke briefly with her in a low voice. She shrugged and made a vague gesture towards the rear of the shop.

The baron led Catherine in this direction and pushed open another sticky door.

Miss Pelliston had had a trying day. She'd been coaxed into the role of bosom-bow by Lord Rand's fiancee, whose height, classical proportions, and serene, fair beauty had made Catherine feel like an ugly little dwarf. That fiancee had taken advantage of Catherine's good nature, engaging her as co-conspirator in a most improper situation. The goddess had compounded the error by dragging out the business for a full half hour, and Catherine had not even had the opportunity to deliver the lecture that lady so richly deserved.

Add to that the incompetence and corruption of a legal system that must persecute innocent boys, Madame's helpless hysteria in the face of this injustice, Lord Browdie's swaggering imbecility, and the provoking unavailability of the one man who could have quickly set matters right, and one had a young lady in a most unladylike state of temper.

From the time she'd entered the dressmaker's shop, Catherine's thinking — what there was of it — had been dictated by blind rage against a world that today utterly refused to behave itself. Being in such a state, it had not occurred to her to do anything but dash recklessly to Jemmy's rescue since no one else was capable of handling the matter intelligently.

As she entered the back room of the shop, Catherine's anger began to recede, and second thoughts crowded into its place. The room was a dark ugly one whose sole window was boarded up. The space contained two rickety chairs, one filthy mattress on an equally filthy floor, and nothing remotely resembling accoutrements for the tea Lord Browdie had promised.

It abruptly occurred to her to wonder how Lord Browdie proposed to have Jemmy removed from the Brown Bear when the baron was unable to identify the boy.

The door slammed shut and Catherine heard a key turn in a lock. A cold chill ran down the back of her neck as she turned to Lord Browdie. His avuncular smile had vanished, replaced by a sneer.

"Now, Miss Hoity-Toity," said he, "we're going to settle this business once and for all."

Mr. Langdon had not much to say for himself during the bumpy ride that seemed to be taking them into the very heart of London's underworld. He knew a good deal about it, having read many works on the subject — among others, the anonymously published *Letters from England,* Mr. Patrick Colquhoun's *Treatise on the Police of the Metropolis,* and the recently published report of the Parliamentary Select Committee that had enquired into the state of London's Watch. He knew, therefore, that London's criminal classes and their habitations flourished much as they had in Sir Henry Fielding's time.

Mr. Langdon had never explored this world firsthand, however, and he was appalled. Around him he saw filth and wretchedness of every description, the population resembling rodents as they darted nervously into alleys and doorways or else stared with undisguised hostility at the vehicle that dared venture into their noisome haven. No wonder Max had not wanted to take his own carriage.

Mr. Langdon was equally shocked by the confident familiarity with which his friend directed the increasingly reluctant coachman. Occasionally Max halted the vehicle, alit, and disappeared into a noxious hole of a gin shop or a black alley that looked like the entrance to hell. Rarely did he stop more than a few minutes — though to Jack every second dragged by like centuries — before emerging with new directions for the driver.

Jack had a pistol, courtesy of the viscount, and was determined to use it if necessary. He would have preferred that he knew how to use it, and cursed himself for wasting his life away in books and never acquiring a productive skill. What earthly good was a bookworm to a young lady in danger?

Now, as the coach halted before a decrepit tavern, Mr. Langdon decided that if he was to be of any use at all, he must be confident. He'd been visiting the boxing saloon religiously for a fortnight and, according to his instructor, was making rapid progress. He told himself he was not completely helpless.

Reassured, he contemplated the damsel in distress. Miss Pelliston was so agreeable. She always had intelligent comments or questions for him, never seemed bored or impatient. In fact, she was the only woman he'd ever met who understood him at all. He was not sure if he understood her — he sensed there was more to her than one saw on social occasions. That "more" occasionally made him uneasy. It was rather like the faint rumblings of a storm many miles away.

All the same, to be understood by a woman was a rarity. He doubted he'd ever find another with whom he felt so comfortable. Their acquaintance was developing into genuine friendship, and what better match than one between friends? A marriage begun in friendship could ripen into deep affection . . . even love.

Naturally he was willing to do or risk whatever he must to rescue her. He was not sure the very proper Miss Pelliston would, as Max had claimed, throw herself into his arms with admiration and gratitude and be swept completely off her feet. If that did happen, though, Jack must offer for her immediately. He who hesitates is lost, as his friend had repeatedly reminded him.

The trouble was, he rather suspected . . . but that was absurd. Max was engaged to Lady Diana Glencove. Those comments about Miss Pelliston and the bitterness Jack had heard must be blamed on the champagne. Max was having typical second thoughts about being leg-shackled and the champagne had made him maudlin. Whatever was troubling Max was Max's problem. One had better concentrate on acting heroic.

Mr. Langdon stopped raking his hair and squared his shoulders instead. He met Jemmy's puzzled gaze and flushed.

The coach door opened and Max climbed inside. "He just went into that coffee shop a couple of doors along."

"Are we going in after him?" Jack asked, fumbling for the pistol.

"Of course not. The place is jammed to the rafters. We can't take on the whole murdering crowd at once. We've got to get him out. There's an alley next to the building. I should like to speak with him there, I think." Max smiled thinly at Jemmy.

"Want me to get him out?" the boy asked eagerly. "I ken do it."

"Good God, no!" Jack cried.

Max ignored his friend. "You'd better do it," he told Jemmy, "or we'll have to wait until he comes out on his own and that could be hours. He went in with a female companion — Bellowser Bess, I think the name is."

"I knows her," said Jemmy. "Her old man got lagged."

"Transported," Max translated for his

friend. "Thus the nickname — 'bellowser' is cant for transportation for life. Add that to your etymologies." He turned back to Jemmy. "Can you do it, then, and not get your head broken? Because as it is Miss Pestilence is going to ring a peal over me about that black eye."

Jemmy threw the viscount an indignant glare. "A baby could do it," he retorted, "in a minute."

In a fraction of that time he was out of the coach. The two men followed. The boy waited until they had turned into the alley before he disappeared into the coffee shop.

True to his word, Jemmy was out again in less than a minute, with Cholly in hot pursuit. Jemmy dashed into the alley. Cholly followed, but as he rounded the corner, he stumbled over a boot. A hand grabbed his shoulder, righting him roughly, and an instant later a fist that closely resembled a millstone drove itself into his face. Reeling from the blow, Granny's employee fell back against the side of the building.

Lord Rand grabbed him by the throat and banged his head against the wall a few times, perhaps to clear Cholly's mind.

"Good Lord, Max," Mr. Langdon gasped. "He won't be any good to us dead."

"He ain't any good to anybody alive that I

can see," Max answered. "Are you, Cholly? No good to anyone."

Cholly's response was unintelligible.

"Get over here, Jack," came the curt order. "Just rest the muzzle of your pistol against his ear."

Mr. Langdon obeyed. He was amazed to discover that his hand did not shake.

"Now, my lad," Max said to Cholly, releasing his grip just enough to allow the man to speak, "maybe you'll tell us exactly what possessed you to kidnap this lad of tender years. Maybe you'll tell us who paid you to do it and why and what else you've been doing lately that you shouldn't. And you'd better say it fast and not think of calling for help because I'd as soon dash your brains out and my friend would like to shoot 'em out and maybe we'll both get our wish if you make us impatient."

20

Catherine stared coldly at her captor. She hoped her heart was not pounding as loudly as she thought it was.

"It is obvious what has happened," she told him. "This is what comes of incessant gluttony and drunkenness. Your dissolute habits have led to mental decay. Don't expect any pity from me. You have brought it all upon yourself."

Lord Browdie was beginning to believe he *would* go mad if he spent another minute with this termagant. He had thought that the bare room and impossibility of escape would awaken her to a sense of her peril, that within five minutes at most the witch would be terrified into submission — but no.

For more than half an hour Catherine Pelliston had stoutly denied ever having been in the brothel. She had plenty else to say besides, enough to make his head throb. If it had not been for those rich acres and the dowry and a gnawing hunger for revenge on Lord

Rand, the baron might have been more sensible and beaten a tactical retreat.

He was not sensible. A fortnight of watching, waiting, and plotting had in fact made Lord Browdie a trifle mad.

He was moody by nature, vengeful when thwarted in any whim. Catherine had thwarted him repeatedly since the day she'd run away and he blamed every unpleasantness that followed, from the humiliating rebuffs of other marriageable females to the tradesmen's bills Lynnette mounted up, on her. Besides, Catherine had played him for a fool — was even now doing so, the lying slut.

"Going to keep it up, are you?" he growled. "Going to keep pretending it wasn't you? Don't think I've got witnesses? Well, I do, and you ain't changed all that much they won't know you close up. Lynnette seen you and Granny and Cholly and Jos."

Catherine stared coldly past him at the wall, which enraged him further.

"You remember Cholly, don't you? Big, handsome fellow. He told me you was pretty entertaining between the covers, for a beginner and one mostly asleep."

The colour drained from Catherine's face and her knees buckled. She had been standing behind one of the chairs. Rather inelegantly she sat down in it.

"Oh, that jogged your memory, I guess. Surprised? Don't see why you should be. That's what they always do with the new ones — give 'em to Cholly or Jos first — so when the gal wakes up, it's too late to be crying about her honour."

The possibility that she'd been deflowered while unconscious had never occurred to Catherine, and the thought was devastating. Still, that could be lies. Lord Browdie did look half-demented. No wonder, she thought sourly. He hadn't had a drink in over an hour at least.

Whatever happened, she must not give him the upper hand. She had betrayed herself for a moment, which was dangerous. Summoning up twenty-one years of rigid training, she stiffened her spine and retorted icily, "You are not only mad, but a swine. I have nothing further to say to you."

He would like to beat her until she screamed for mercy, but he knew from painful experience that women didn't fight fair. They kicked and clawed and yanked your hair and bit, behaving generally in the most unsporting way. Also, Catherine may have inherited her father's temper, and that was an ugly thing unleashed. He'd rather save beating as a last resort. Besides, his throat was parched with all this palavering.

"The trouble with you, my girl, is you ain't thinking straight. I'm going to get us something to drink, so we can sit and be cosy until you get sensible. Just remember that if you're gone too long — like 'til tomorrow morning, maybe — you'll have a lot of explaining to do."

He moved to the door. "Oh, by the way — your hostess is deaf as a post when she's paid to be and screams ain't nothing special around here. I won't be but a minute, but no one'll pay you any mind, m' dear, so make all the noise you like."

True to his promise, he returned in a very few minutes with two bottles of wine and two greasy mugs. When Catherine disdainfully declined the cup offered her, he flung himself into the other chair and attended to quenching his own thirst. A bottle and a half later, he grew imperiously confident. She was only a slip of a girl, after all, easily overpowered if it came to that. Not a bit like the buxom milkmaid he'd tried to rape a few years back.

He pointed to the mattress and jovially informed her that while she was thinking things over she might as well show him what Cholly and Rand found so entertaining. Catherine suppressed a shudder and resolutely refused to understand him.

Lord Browdie rose unsteadily from his chair

and staggered towards her. He was breathing hard and she felt a surge of nausea as the wine-laden fumes rose to her nostrils. Then she saw a hairy hand reaching for her bodice. Shuddering, she knocked it away, and hastily made herself stand to face him.

Her limbs weak with fear, she clutched the chair back for support, but the chair over-balanced and she stumbled with it. As she was righting herself, he grabbed her hair, making her cry out with pain. Fear blazed into rage. How dare he touch her!

Furious, she dug her nails into his hand. He jerked away with an angry yelp.

"You little hellcat!" he screeched. Then he lunged at her.

There was no time to think and nowhere to run. Catherine grabbed the chair and swung it at him. He tried to dodge her, but wasn't fast enough. The chair caught him on the hip before it finally broke against the wall. Lord Browdie stumbled backwards, cursing. More cautious now, he stood a moment, eyeing her with hatred as he gasped for breath.

"That ain't smart, Cathy," he warned, his voice hoarse. "No use fighting me. It'll end the same whether you do or don't, only you'll make me mad and that'll be the worse for you."

Yes, the end would be the same, she knew.

There was no way out of this filthy room, and he meant to rape her. She could not dwell on that, because the thought sickened and weakened her. She focused on him. How long could she fight him? He was bigger, stronger, but she was younger. Who would tire first? The longer she held out, the greater chance that her family — someone — would realise something was amiss and try to find her. But how? When? How long?

Then she saw his body tense. Catherine darted towards the pile of broken wood. Just as he threw himself at her, she snatched up a chair leg and swung it at him. He dodged, then lunged again. She quickly sidestepped him and swung her weapon once more, lower this time, aiming for his knees. Had she aimed higher or lower she'd have only struck padding and done little damage, but she aimed true.

She heard a crack as wood struck bone. Pain shot through her wrists from the force of the blow, making her eyes fill with tears, but she didn't dare let go of the chair leg. In a wet blur she watched Lord Browdie topple to the floor while his howled curses pierced the air.

There was another, more resounding crack. The heavy door shook and shuddered an instant before swinging into the room and crashing against the wall. Lord Rand came crashing in after it, Jack and Jemmy at his heels.

Catherine still held the chair leg. She swung it again reflexively, too blinded with pain and rage to know what she was aiming at. Lord Rand caught her wrists midswing.

"That's enough, Cat," he said. "You can't kill everybody, just because you're a trifle out of sorts."

She stared blankly at him for a moment. Then the chair leg dropped from her suddenly nerveless hands and she threw herself against his hard chest.

"Oh, Max," she cried. "I thought you'd never come."

Lord Rand must have forgotten who was supposed to be the hero in this scene, because he never looked at Mr. Langdon. He never looked at anybody. His arms closed around Miss Pelliston in a crushing embrace, and he buried his face in her hair.

"Oh, Cat," he murmured. "My poor, dear, brave girl." His hands stroked her back, then the back of her neck, while she sobbed against his chest. "It's all right now, sweetheart," he comforted softly. "It's all right, my gallant darling."

He uttered more tender praise and endearments, and even some gentle teasing, as he told her she might have left him something to do besides clean up the mess she'd made. Fortunately, most of this was unintelligible to all but the young lady. That she understood was evident, because the sobbing gradually eased, though her face remained buried in the viscount's coat.

Mr. Langdon politely looked away . . . and caught Lord Browdie attempting to crawl out the door. Jack drew out his pistol and pointed it at the baron's head. Lord Browdie froze.

Jemmy, for once in his life, was mute. Less courteous than Mr. Langdon, he watched the embracing couple with every evidence of satisfaction. He had not been able to contribute much to the rescue beyond tripping up Mr. Langdon when the viscount kicked in the door. Even though Lord Rand had not looked like he meant to wait for his friend, the boy must have recalled Mr. Blackwood's advice regarding the gentry's need for firm guidance.

Catherine, trembling in Max's arms, had evidently forgotten that the man holding her so possessively belonged to someone else because she remained there quite contentedly even after her tears had ceased. When she did finally remember, there was a brief struggle — the viscount's memory proving more sluggish — before she managed to break free.

Lord Rand gazed blankly at her for a moment while his handsome face coloured. Then he cleared his throat and turned to Lord Browdie, who was cowering by the door, al-

ternately moaning and muttering impreca-
tions.

"We seem to have a problem of protocol
here," said the viscount, "and of course I want
to do the proper thing. What would that be,
I wonder? Do I beat you to a bloody pulp?
Shall I give Jack leave to pull the trigger? Or,
since you've lost your way to Bow Street, shall
we simply take you there and let the magistrate
sort out etiquette? Let me see — kidnapping,
violent assault, and attempted rape of a gen-
tlewoman. I wonder if they'll hang you, send
you to the Hulks, or simply transport you for
life."

"Assault?" Browdie screamed indignantly.
"I never touched her. I'll have her up on assault, the murdering jade! And tell some
things about her. I've got witnesses too."

"The man is unhinged," said Mr. Langdon.
"We'd better bring him to a lunatic asylum
instead. He wants treatment."

"Do I? Then fetch a doctor. We'll see how
crazy I am. Maybe that doctor'll want to have
a look at you as well, eh Missy?" He shot
Catherine a murderous look.

Catherine glared right back. "You are a
filthy, lying swine," she snapped. "I wish I
had dashed out your brains."

Mr. Langdon's jaw dropped, though he did
not take his eyes off his captive. Perhaps it

occurred to him that the storm had finally moved in to burst about his ears.

"Harlot!" shouted Browdie. "Slut!"

Mr. Langdon hustled Catherine and Jemmy out into the shop. "This is no spectacle for a lady," he said. Then, his own face reddening, he returned to the back room.

Lord Browdie's compliments had abruptly ceased meanwhile, because in one graceful movement Lord Rand had yanked him up by his coat lapels and knocked his head against the wall.

"You'll keep a civil tongue in your head, Browdie, if you know what's good for you."

When he saw that his interlocutor was more disposed to listen, the viscount added, "There's nothing I'd like better than to kill you. But that just might get me hanged, and you aren't worth swinging for, are you?"

Another crack of skull against plaster was deemed a necessary aid to decision making. This must have helped, because Lord Browdie shook his head.

"I'm so happy we agree," said Lord Rand amiably. "Since you're disposed to be reasonable, let me offer you two courses. The first is that you get on the very next ship leaving England. I can recommend North America from personal experience, but you can go where you like, so long as you never come back — except perhaps in a casket."

"I ain't going nowhere," the baron growled.

"The alternative," the viscount continued, unheeding, "is that I take you to Bow Street and bring the charges I mentioned. You may say what you wish in your behalf — but do rest assured, dear fellow, that if you're indiscreet and a soft-hearted magistrate releases you, I'll find you, wherever you hide, and break every bone in your filthy body. Oh, I should mention there's a fellow named Cholly who'll be looking for you as well. He's disappointed about something. I think it's a broken jaw. Coarse fellow, that Cholly. Doesn't care a bit for gentlemanly codes of honour. Has a way with a broken bottle, I understand."

Being bested in physical combat by a mere slip of a girl cannot be agreeable to a man's *amour propre*. Instigated by a combination of too much wine drunk too fast and humiliated rage, the baron had been incautiously belligerent. Lord Rand's suggestions, along with the occasional physical reminder, had restored Lord Browdie's reasoning powers. Being a coward, he would have run very far away on his own, if Mr. Langdon had not prevented him.

The baron elected exile, though he did so most ungraciously.

"That's settled, then," said the viscount. He

abruptly released his hold on the man, who crumpled to the floor.

"Jack, you'd better take Cat — Miss Pelliston — home to Louisa. I want to take our friend to an acquaintance of mine who'll make sure he keeps his promise."

"Why don't you let me go with him?" Jack offered. "It seems there's something . . . well, maybe you and Miss Pelliston need to talk —"

Lord Rand's face hardened. "No. Take her and the boy back and tell Louisa I'll explain everything later. On no account is she to trouble Catherine. Is that clear? Just tell her to put the girl to bed."

En route to Andover House, Jemmy was deposited at the dressmaker's with adjurations not to reveal unpleasant details to Madame. The lad having a discretion beyond his years, all the *modiste* ever learned was that he had been mistaken for another, but had managed to escape. She believed that Lord Browdie and Catherine had simply been delayed at the magistrate's office by the usual bureaucratic incompetence.

Lord and Lady Andover were told only to wait for Max, who would explain everything. Fortunately, these two had not had time to become unduly alarmed. Catherine customarily lingered two hours or more at the dressmaker's, and their carriage had returned without her scarcely half an hour ago. If they were alarmed now, they were too tactful to show it. They assured Mr. Langdon they would do as he asked. They would wait up for Max, however late he returned.

Spared an interrogation, Catherine escaped to her room. She found a hot bath waiting for her, but there was no ease in it, except perhaps for her aching muscles. Even though she was safe, she could not stop trembling. She would never feel safe or right again, would never feel clean again.

Why had she gone with that horrible man? How could she have been so foolhardy? Though Jack had promised that Lord Browdie would never trouble her again, Catherine knew he would. All the rest of her days Lord Browdie would haunt her because he'd told her about Cholly, told her she was soiled, polluted, foul.

She could never marry. She would never know the quiet joy of being cared for, of having children to care for. Still, since it would never be Lord Rand caring for her or his children she might love, it was just as well there would be no one.

She'd convinced herself that she could be

happy with Jack, or at least content. Now she realised how selfish that was and how unfair to Jack. She'd seen that when she'd drawn away from Max and caught a glimpse of his friend's face, so shocked and — oh, she hoped he wasn't hurt. Jack was so kind and gentle. It wasn't fair that he should be hurt because she was a fool.

Catherine crawled under the bedclothes and buried her face in the pillow, but the tears she expected wouldn't come. Her throat raw, she lay curled up in a tight ball, unable to weep.

"My brave girl," Max had called her — that and so many other tender words — as his strong arms sheltered her. He had been her shelter from the start, hadn't he? She had trusted him instinctively, from the moment she'd first asked his help. She'd continued to trust him, though she hadn't realised it because she'd been too busy finding fault with him.

How could she have believed he was her bad angel, when all he ever drew from her was honesty — the truth of her feelings. In response, she'd insulted him repeatedly. Instead of appreciating Lord Rand's kind, noble heart, she'd fixed instead on trivial misbehaviours, exaggerating them into major character flaws.

How on earth could she have believed he was just like Papa? When had Papa ever been kind or gentle? When had Papa ever tried to comfort or help her or even tease her out of her overnice notions of propriety? When had anyone in her whole life ever made her feel so interesting and feminine and special?

With his teasing and prodding, Viscount Vagabond had uncovered the real Catherine: the short-tempered, passionate, willful, occasionally improper young woman under the stiff schoolmistress's pose. Along the way, he'd revealed himself as well, only she had been too stubbornly blind to see who the real Max was and how much she loved him. Oh, she did love him dearly, passionately, and would always love him . . . hopelessly.

Utterly hopeless. She gasped as despair flooded her heart. The dam gave at last, and she broke into wracking sobs that shook her frame until she wept herself empty. Finally, exhausted, she fell asleep.

Max did not arrive until after midnight. Lord Andover had had an urgent summons from Lord Liverpool meanwhile, and was not yet returned. Thus Max had only his sister to tell his tale to, and because she was his sister, he found himself telling her everything.

She bore the news about the brothel with

not a hint of swooning. Rather, she spoke with admiration of Catherine's courage. "That is one of the things I like so much about her, Max. She is a perfect lady, yet amazingly capable and fearless. Not nearly as fragile as she looks. From the first moment I saw you with her, I rather hoped —"

"I know you're breeding, Louisa, but even in that condition, sentiment doesn't become you," he interrupted hastily. "Anyhow, whatever you hoped, the fact is, I offered twice for her and was rejected in no uncertain terms."

Louisa sighed. "I can think of a dozen reasons for her to refuse when she would rather accept, but you are determined to be thickheaded."

"I'm engaged to be married, Louisa," was the quiet answer. "To Lady Diana Glencove, remember? Maybe you also remember that a gentleman can't jilt a lady. I might as well be thickheaded, don't you think?"

21

For a man whose head is not only thick, but hard, two glasses of brandy cannot be sufficient to induce unconsciousness if he is otherwise inclined. Lord Rand was not so inclined. He did not fall asleep until well after daybreak. Thus he slept soundly until midafternoon, when he was awakened by a pair of rabbits hopping on his chest.

He opened one eye to discover not rabbits, but two small grubby fists. He opened the other eye and discerned that the fists were attached to a pair of short arms, in turn attached to the personage known as Jemmy.

"Get away from me," his lordship grumbled. "What the devil are you about? Curse me if the boy has any manners at all, and respect for his betters is out of the question."

"Get up, will you? Wot are you waiting for?"

"Judgement Day. What in blazes do you want?"

Blackwood appeared at the bedside, having entered the room in his usual noiseless fashion.

He pulled Jemmy away and apologised for the lad's outlandish behaviour. Unfortunately, the boy had dashed up the stairs so quickly that Mr. Blackwood had been unable to catch him in time.

"There is rather odd news, My Lord," he explained.

"She's bolted," Jemmy cried, thrusting himself in front of the valet. "Run off wif a sojer."

Lord Rand jerked himself upright. "What? Cat? When? What soldier? Drat her, why don't that woman stay put?"

He threw back the bedclothes, thereby presenting Jemmy with the interesting spectacle of a naked aristocrat. Duly impressed, Jemmy backed away as the viscount scrambled out of bed and ripped the dressing gown out of his servant's hands.

"I beg your pardon, My Lord. The young lady in question is Lady Diana Glencove."

Lord Rand, who had hastily wrapped the dressing gown around himself, was about to tear it off again, having evidently decided on dressing immediately and eliminating the middleman. He now sat back down upon the bed.

"Lady Diana?" he echoed blankly.

"Your fiancee, My Lord," Blackwood clarified. "I'm afraid the news is all over Town because Lord Glencove's servants have been everywhere looking for her since yesterday afternoon. I heard from his lordship's footman that the family received a message from the young lady this morning. She was married by special license last night, as I understand. Her message said nothing regarding her subsequent itinerary. One imagines that was in order to elude pursuit."

"Well," said Lord Rand.

"Indeed, My Lord, most shocking. Lord Glencove sent the footman round with a message asking you to call upon him at your earliest convenience. I believed it proper that his lordship should break the news to you, but unfortunately, Jemmy has anticipated that."

"Yes," said Lord Rand with a dazed look at Jemmy.

"I heard it at the shop first," the boy said defensively. "They come by asking for her yesterday and today again and today when they come they tole HER and SHE tole Joan and she tole me so I come to tell you."

"I see," said the viscount, still looking blank. "I had better get dressed."

Lord Rand's interview with Lord and Lady Glencove was not the most agreeable of his life. Lady Glencove was beside herself with grief. She raved about annulments and having the fiend horsewhipped, hung, drawn and quartered. Occasionally she remembered to feel sorry for the betrayed fiance and that was even worse.

Lord Glencove, fortunately, was of a more philosophical temperament. He had, not an hour since, received encouraging news about his daughter's new husband. Though the man's immediate family was relatively obscure, the late father had been a man of property, which compensated somewhat for the maternal connection with commerce. The son — Colonel Stockmore — had a respectable income. He also had prospects: that is, he had a very ill, very old eccentric bachelor cousin who happened to be a viscount. From this cousin Colonel Stockmore would inherit a title. A prospective viscount was not a prospective Earl of St. Denys, but a man cannot have everything. Or a woman, either, as Lord Glencove was forced to remind his wife at tediously frequent intervals.

Lord Rand was also philosophical. He bore his disappointment with a most becoming manliness, which provoked Lady Glencove to another plaintive outburst after he was gone.

From the home of the Earl of Glencove, the viscount proceeded to Lord Browdie's love nest. There he purchased a peach muslin gown for five hundred pounds. Being philosophical enough for any two aristocrats, Lynnette bore her own assorted disappointments like the Stoic she was.

Molly related the news of Lady Diana's elopement before Catherine had even opened her eyes, and accompanied the dressing process with recitals about the mysterious ways of Providence, and human beings refusing to understand what was good for them, and the course of true love being a rocky one. The maid concluded with fervent thanks that she herself was content to love from afar, because getting close made folks act so foolish.

Fortunately, Lady Andover had very little to add at breakfast or thereafter.

"I suppose Molly has told you," she said, "with more detail, I am sure, than I could. It is astonishing. I had always thought Diana completely under her mother's thumb. I am relieved she is not. Their temperaments were badly unsuited. She would have bored Max to distraction and he would have taken up a life of crime in consequence."

Catherine mumbled something about being amazed. That was the end of the subject.

Chastened by the revelations of the previous night, Miss Pelliston elected to spend the afternoon in the library reading Foxe's *Actes and Monuments of These Latter Perilous Days.*

Her mind, however, refused to concentrate on the Protestant martyrs of the sixteenth century.

One did not require above-average intelligence to ascertain that Lady Diana's rendezvous with her forbidden love had been devoted primarily to plans for immediate elopement. As participant, however unwitting, Catherine should at least be displeased with herself for not sensing what was afoot and striving to set Lady Diana back upon the course of duty.

Miss Pelliston could not be displeased or even surprised, considering the startling insights she'd had regarding her powers of perception. She could hardly expect to read another lady's mind when her own was such a miserable muddle.

Besides, she defiantly admitted to herself that she was pleased with the news. Even though it changed nothing for her — Lord Rand was still forever beyond her reach — he at least would have a second chance. Perhaps this time he would find a woman who truly loved him. That could not be difficult. Only fools like herself were blind to his perfections.

All she could pray for was an opportunity to apologise for more than a month of ungrateful, childish behaviour. For more than that she could not hope. She was beyond the pale.

This morning, after a long struggle with her conscience, Catherine had decided no useful purpose would be served by confessing her shame. To tell her cousin or Louisa about Cholly would only distress them needlessly. She would plead exhaustion and tell them she wished to go home.

After that, the years seemed to stretch out interminably. Perhaps she would sell Aunt Eustacia's property, invest the money, and live quietly, humbly, alone. She would devote herself to good works among those even more wretched than herself. She would work among the poor. Perhaps she would contract some loathsome disease that would put a period to her vile existence.

Thus she reduced herself to a deeply penitential, utterly tragic state with no assistance from *The Book of Martyrs*. The volume proving useless, she very sensibly closed it and commenced to dolefully studying the carpet.

There was a tap at the door. She looked up to meet Jeffers's dignified gaze.

"Lady Andover's compliments, Miss, and would you please be so kind as to join her in —"

"Oh, do be quiet," Lord Rand snapped,

pushing past the butler. "I ain't sitting in some damned parlor waiting for tea and making small talk with my own sister. Go away, Jeffers."

Jeffers sighed and went.

Lord Rand strode towards her. Under his arm he had a package which he now dropped at Catherine's feet.

"There's your dress," he said. "It cost me five hundred pounds. Then there's the fifty from a month ago. Altogether I've paid five hundred fifty quid for you."

Catherine's heart immediately commenced a steady *chamade*. She stared blindly at the package. Then she slowly dragged her gaze up to the viscount's face. His eyes were the blue of a frosty moonlit night, chilling her. He hated her. She deserved to be hated, she told herself. Even so, temper began to rise within her. He needn't be so callous . . . and mean.

"I can do sums," she said rather unsteadily. "I shall write to Papa for five hundred fifty pounds. Or do you require interest as well?"

"You will write to your papa, young lady, to tell him we're going to be married."

Inelegantly, she gulped. "I beg your pardon?" she said stupidly. She would like to say — and do — a thousand things, and could not think where to begin.

"You're not deaf, Cat, so don't pretend to be. We're going to be married, as we should have done at the start."

The viscount looked hastily away from her face and began pacing the room.

"I don't know who had the training of you," he continued determinedly, "but your morals are shocking. You spent a night in my bed, remember, after a night in a bawdy house. You go about collecting street urchins and letting inebriated vagabonds kiss you, and then you get into brawls in pawnshops. You are probably past all redemption, but I'm going to reform you anyhow. If you behave yourself, perhaps I'll let you reform me on occasion, but I make no promises."

"Oh, Max."

He did not seem to hear the pitiful sound, because he went on heatedly, "There's no point telling me everything that's wrong with me, because I know all that by heart. I'm a bully and a ruffian and a drunkard and a gambler and I act before I think, always. I'm also short-tempered — and yes, mad, bad, and dangerous. Just as you are — which is why we suit so admirably."

"Oh, Max," she said once more, as a tear trickled down her nose.

He stopped pacing to glance at her. "There's

no use crying," he said, his voice less assured now. "You can't manipulate me with tears. I've made up my mind . . ." His voice trailed off. "Drat," he muttered.

He stood uncertain for a moment, clenching his fists. Then he sighed, moved closer, and knelt down before her. "Come, sweetheart, is it so bad? Don't you like me even a little?"

"Oh, Max," she cried. "I love you madly."

In the moment it took him to digest this stupendous news, Lord Rand's face lighted up. It turned, in fact, slightly red about the cheekbones.

"Do you darling?" he asked tenderly, taking her hand. "Do you really? But of course you do — you must — as I love you."

She stopped him with a small, sad gesture. "Still, I can't marry you." Before he could argue, she plunged on, desperate to put this agonising scene to a speedy end. "I can't marry you — I can't marry anyone — because I'm — oh, Max, I'm ruined, truly ruined."

Lord Rand patiently told her that she was hysterical. Citing her shocking travail of the previous day, he generously excused her, in between telling her not to be silly.

Catherine knew she was not being silly — not, at least, about this. She found her handkerchief, wiped her eyes and nose, and confided as calmly as she could what Lord

Browdie had told her about Cholly.

When she'd come to a shuddering end, Lord Rand drew her up from her chair and into his arms. "I'm sorry, sweetheart," he said softly against her curls. "That was a terrible thing for him to tell you, but it's past and done. We're going to be married. Forget Cholly and think about us — about our happiness."

She pulled away slightly to examine his face. "Didn't you hear me, Max? I just told you I'm not — not pure."

"I'm not exactly Sir Galahad myself, sweet."

"That's different. Men are expected — oh, Max, you can't marry me. A gentleman expects his bride to come to him untouched," she patiently reminded, while her heart fluttered madly between hope and despair.

"I'm not like other gentlemen, as you well know." He brought her near again and let his fingers play among the light brown curls. "Nor are you like other ladies. You're Cat, the lady I found in a brothel, the lady who scolds me endlessly, the lady I love madly. Put Cholly out of your mind." He lightly kissed her nose.

"Come, sweetheart," he added when she did not respond. "It can't be so hard. Browdie could have been lying — and if he wasn't, you weren't even conscious at the time. Besides, didn't I break Cholly's nose that night? And yesterday I broke his jaw, I think. If you like, I'll break everything else, but I do think the poor fellow's paid dearly already."

This was reasonable enough, though it was his peculiar sort of reason. Catherine let her anxieties evaporate in the warmth of his love.

"I suppose," she murmured to his lapel, "if I don't believe you, you'll dash my head against the wall until I do."

"I might," he answered. "I'm very stubborn and ill-behaved."

"Yes. No wonder I love you so."

There was only one possible conclusion to this sort of intellectual exchange. Lord Rand tightened his clasp and kissed his darling thoroughly and repeatedly until they were both in a highly agitated state, not at all conducive to abstract reasoning.

Fortunately, Lady Andover put her head in the door at this perilous moment.

"That will be sufficient for the nonce, Max," she said composedly. "You are wrinkling Catherine's dress and Molly will be in fits. Now come out and talk to Edgar like a gentleman."

Not all the viscount's ranting, raving, and threats of violence could hasten the wedding day. Six unbearably slow weeks crept by because Lady Andover insisted that any earlier date would be unseemly as well as inconvenient. This would be the wedding of the year.

If Society was duly impressed with the result, Catherine and Max were not. They were oblivious to all that went on about them. Except for the moment when they were pronounced husband and wife, all that stood out for Max among the blur of chaotic activity was meeting Catherine's formidable papa.

From all he'd heard and all he'd guessed, Lord Rand was expecting Attila the Hun. During the wedding breakfast, the viscount found his eyes drawn repeatedly to a pear-shaped man of middling height who hovered about his baroness like a sycophantic courtier.

Since Lord and Lady Rand would not commence their bridal trip until the following day, they spent their first night as a married couple in his townhouse amid a staff of deliriously happy servants. What the house needed, they'd all agreed long since, was a mistress. The master was universally adored, but he needed a deal of looking after. According to young Jemmy and the all-knowing Blackwood, Miss Pelliston was the only woman capable of managing this fearsome task. His lordship, Mr. Blackwood pointed out, was a handful, but his new wife was more than a match for him, despite her modest physical stature. Even Mr. Hill agreed dolefully that his master might have done worse.

That evening, therefore, Lord Rand and his bride supped quietly at home, surrounded by a beaming staff and a smug Jemmy, who insisted upon waiting at table with the other footmen.

After dessert was served and the room emptied of fawning menials, Lord Rand remembered the papa and teased his bride with charges of calculated overstatement.

"He was meek as a vicar, Cat. I'm sure he never had more than two glasses of champagne the whole time, and he sipped them like a deb at her first party."

"I know," she answered distractedly, her mind on other matters. "I scarcely recognised him myself. My stepmama appears to be an extraordinary woman."

"Must be. Between her and my own Old Man, they've convinced your papa to take his seat in Parliament."

"I can only hope the country will not suffer for it. Still, she has a way about her. She has only to raise an eyebrow at him and he's subdued. I saw how she looked at him when he came up to greet us. He took my hand in the most courtly way and said I was a good girl and made him proud, and kissed me." She touched her cheek. "He has never done that before. I nearly fainted from shock."

Lord Rand casually mentioned that if such a trivial matter shocked her, he must be sure to bring burnt feathers and sal volatile to their bedchamber tonight. He glanced at her untouched dessert and wondered aloud if she was quite finished.

She had no time to answer. Jemmy instantly darted in and snatched up her dish. Likewise he removed the viscount's plate, and with a knowing wink, took himself away.

Mr. Langdon had been awarded the signal honour of standing up for the friend of his college days. Rather like a consolation prize, he thought, as he settled himself into an armchair and opened his book. If the experience had not been altogether consoling, neither had it been a bitter punishment. One could not, should not feel bitter. Not when one saw the clear, bright face of love shining so happily upon its object. He had seen this when his two friends gazed at each other, and somehow that had heartened him.

Besides, as the Bard had said, "Men have died from time to time and worms have eaten them, but not for love." Jack would not die, would not even sicken. Though the blow had staggered him it had not crushed him. He had actually gained a great deal from the experience. The trouble was, among the bits of wisdom he'd acquired was one new sensation: for the first time in his quiet, dreamy life he was lonely.

He closed his book and departed from his club unremarked by the increasingly boisterous crowd gathering as the evening wore on. He stopped briefly at his home, where he collected a few belongings and ordered his horse. As the watchman announced to interested listeners that the sky was clear and the time was eleven o'clock, Mr. Langdon rode off into the night.

Lord Rand drew his bride close to him. "Are you all right, Cat?"

She didn't answer for a moment, being preoccupied, perhaps, with locating a comfortable spot near his shoulder where she could nestle her head.

"Cat?"

"Oh, yes. I'm . . . well, that was rather . . ."

"Shocking?"

She sighed. "I'm afraid not. I ought to have been shocked, but . . . how gentle you are, Max. I shall have to leave off calling you a bully, and your reputation will go all to pieces."

"We'll keep that private, shall we, m'lady?"

She giggled and snuggled nearer.

"I'm glad you're all right, because you are, you know — or were — pure as the driven snow. Browdie lied, sweetheart. There's no question about it. Will you put Cholly out of your mind now?"

"I will endeavour to do so," she whispered, "though I may want help."

"Very well. Just let me know when he pops into your mind. I'll try to think of something to distract you."

"Max?" came a shy voice, a while later.

"Yes, sweet?"

"I wonder if you might think of something . . . *now.*"

THORNDIKE-MAGNA hopes you have enjoyed this Large Print book. All our Large Print titles are designed for easy reading, and all our books are made to last. Other Thorndike Press or Magna Print books are available at your library, through selected bookstores, or directly from the publishers. For more information about current and upcoming titles, please call or mail your name and address to:

THORNDIKE PRESS
P.O. Box 159
Thorndike, Maine 04986
(800) 223-6121
(207) 948-2962 (in Maine and Canada call collect)

or in the United Kingdom:

MAGNA PRINT BOOKS
Long Preston, Near Skipton
North Yorkshire,
England BD23 4ND
(07294) 225

There is no obligation, of course.